AWAKENED

First published in Great Britain in 2025 by Trapeze,
an imprint of The Orion Publishing Group Ltd
Carmelite House, 50 Victoria Embankment
London EC4Y 0DZ

An Hachette UK Company

The authorised representative in the EEA is Hachette Ireland, 8 Castlecourt Centre,
Dublin 15, D15 XTP3, Ireland (email: info@hbgi.ie)

1 3 5 7 9 10 8 6 4 2

A CIP catalogue record for this book is
available from the British Library.

ISBN (Hardback) 978 1 3987 1294 2
ISBN (Export Trade Paperback) 978 1 3987 1295 9
ISBN (Ebook) 978 1 3987 1297 3
ISBN (Audio) 978 1 3987 1298 0

Typeset by Born Group
Printed and bound in Great Britain by Clays Ltd, Elcograf S.p.A.

www.orionbooks.co.uk

AWAKENED

Kelechi Okafor

Dedicated to

Every person the water has remembered.

Prologue

Pels dragged her suitcase along the cobbled streets. The taxi ride had been short. She smiled to herself, thinking about how strange it felt sometimes to get *transport* to places. She had changed so much in such a short time. She allowed herself to marvel at the mundane things that would never be the same for her again as she picked up her suitcase, barely noticing its weight. She was glad to have her belongings with her because she was unsure how long she would stay, where she would go next – or whether she would be travelling alone. She had so many questions, and some of them could only be answered by *him*.

Butterflies fluttered in her stomach at the thought.

Pels continued along the upward tilt of the street until finally, to her right, was the door she had been sent an image of during their conversations. A green, rustic-looking door with chipped paint.

Suits him, actually, Pels thought.

A couple strolled by, immersed in a conversation in a language she didn't understand, and electric excitement danced down her spine – another adventure was beginning.

Pels expelled the air she had held on to tightly and pressed the buzzer. There was no answer, but she knew he was coming downstairs to meet her.

Moments later, the door swung open. And there he was.

The early morning sunlight filtered through the foyer windows of the apartment building, casting a seductive halo behind him and making him look devilishly angelic.

Her angel.

What was perhaps more dazzling than the chandelier in the foyer was his smile.

No words were needed. He pulled Pels' suitcase into the foyer and gently slid her trusty backpack off her shoulder, placing it on top of her luggage. Without breaking the union of their eyes, he put his hands around her waist and pulled her into him, instantly meeting her lips with his.

The sound of footsteps on the stairs made Pels instinctively pull back – a reflex of her British upbringing – but he seemed unbothered, only interested in reacquainting himself with her tongue and lips.

'Passion is normal here, even at 9 a.m.,' he murmured.

Giving in to him, Pels allowed herself to feel everything she had missed since they'd been apart.

When she opened her eyes to look at him once their sultry hello had momentarily ceased, she saw just a flash of it, but it was certainly there – his eyes turned all black, and then back to their usual mesmerising colour.

Chapter One

Eighteen-year-old Charles Olawole was found on Grangehill seafront in August 2023 and the coroner's report confirmed his cause of death as drowning.

During an inquest into Charles's death, it was stated that he couldn't swim, but Charles's mother said it's highly unlikely he would have entered the sea deliberately.

Since his death, Charles's mother has led a campaign for further inquiries into his death; however, the police's stance is that no foul play can be proved.

The inquest into Charles's death lasted for just one day, with the coroner Jasper Crayford recording Charles's death as 'accidental'.

★

THREE MONTHS EARLIER

Pels' eyes snapped open, the glowing numbers on the wall clock in the living room of her apartment searing themselves into her consciousness: 3.33 a.m. Her mind recited Damari's earlier text message, despite her heart's indignation.

Damari: Carmen is pregnant. I didn't tell you straight away because I knew you'd make a big deal out of me dating her and not telling you. I just didn't think you were

3

emotionally ready for that conversation. I didn't plan for
her to get pregnant but now she is, we should all go with
the flow. Love light and unity, queen. xx

It was as though every molecule of sleep had evaporated from
her body the moment Damari's infidelity was hurtled at her.
Hours later, it still seemed to be evading her.

She lay there on her sofa, staring at the sterile white ceiling,
feeling the weight of her dying love life pressing down on
her chest. *Whoever said the best way to get over someone was to
get under someone else deserves to be sued for this inaccuracy*, Pels
thought. Damari had been a rebound from the person she'd
really wanted to be with – and now he had the nerve to treat
her like a mug?

The warm yellow glow of the lighting that usually filled her
living room had shifted to a deep, melancholic blue since she
had tried to doze off – a visual alert that Pels had messages
waiting to be listened to – yet, in that moment, the whole room
seemed to be illuminated with a dull sadness.

'Aláké,' Pels whispered, her voice hoarse. 'Play my voicemails.'

'Of course, Pels,' the home-integrated AI replied softly,
respectful of the early hour. The first message began to play; it
was Maria, her best friend since their air cadet days as teenagers
in south London.

'Girl, where are you?' Maria's voice was a mixture of concern
and frustration. 'You promised you'd come out to the Afrobeats
concert tonight! I've been calling and texting you all night.
Please call me back, OK? I'm worried about you.'

Pels winced, guilt knotting her stomach. She'd completely
forgotten about the concert, her thoughts consumed by the

unravelling threads of her life. She let out a long, shuddering breath before the next voicemail began to play – this one from her editor and boss, Dave.

'Pels,' he began in a condescending tone, 'I've just seen that you've sent me yet another draft of this article you insist on gnawing away at. I know you're passionate about these missing Black kids, but we need to focus on stories that will *actually sell*. I mean, bodies being discovered near bodies of water? It's macabre and unappealing to our readership and, quite frankly, feels a bit prejudiced to claim that these random stories are linked because of race?! Stick to what you're good at, all right? We should talk more when you're in on Monday about other pieces I want you to focus on. Like my idea about hip-hop and its effects on gang violence – because, you see, *that* would sell! Actually, scratch that, I'm having a Dave Doozy! I've just seen something about protests erupting in Benin against the resorts there, something about them depleting their "agricultural heritage" . . .' Pels could practically hear him putting the phrase in sarcastic quote marks. 'They're blaming the tourists who, yeah, *happen* to be white but, in my opinion, are doing them a favour. You'd fit right in over there. Maybe you could cover that instead. Like I said: my office, Monday.'

Anger surged through Pels, casting its own fiery presence across her dark brown eyes. Did Dave think she didn't know how to do her job? That she couldn't handle the nuances of writing about the missing Black children, something so important to her community? In fact, this story – if things were connected in the way she had been researching for months – could end up being global news.

And yet she couldn't shake the nagging doubt that crept in, whispering that maybe he was right. Maybe she *wasn't* good enough.

'A *Dave Doozy*,' Pels muttered, mimicking Dave's euphemism for when he thought he was having a good idea. 'Dickhead . . . Aláké, delete both messages,' she added, raising her voice in a command even as it trembled with frustration. 'And remind me to text Maria later.'

'Understood, Pels,' Aláké replied, and the room fell silent once more, the lighting returning to its usual serene yellow.

Pels lay still on the sofa, willing herself to get up and at least move over to her bedroom, but a storm of emotions churned inside her. She thought about Damari – his condescending manner, his misguided belief that dating her was some sort of *favour* to her – and how she'd allowed herself to be ensnared by him as a distraction from a previous relationship. She sighed, remembering Marco, whom she had dated before Damari, and their incredible but too-short-lived relationship. Why couldn't she find someone as wonderful as Marco who actually wanted to live in the same country? The contrast between the two men was stark, and Pels could only question why she'd continued to date Damari despite his erratic and disrespectful behaviour. It wasn't as though she didn't know better – or hadn't experienced better.

As Pels finally began to unfurl herself from the sofa, she murmured to her empty apartment, 'Something has to change.'

Heading to her bedroom, she swept her locs into a bun, winding the bronze-tinted tips tightly enough to hold through the night, then wrapped a scarf around her hair. Despite yet another break-up, she wasn't going to forget the upkeep of her haircare routine.

'Aláké,' she whispered into the darkness once she was snuggled under the bedsheets, the determination to rest steeling her voice. 'Set an alarm for 7 a.m. I'll see Maria tomorrow anyway – no need for the text.'

'Alarm set for 7 a.m., Pels,' Aláké confirmed. Pels closed her eyes, ready to momentarily leave Damari, Dave and the messiness of life for a few more hours.

'Aláké, play something soothing,' she requested, hoping to calm her mind. The soft hum of a podcast filled the room, but eventually it made her open her eyes again – because for some reason, something she heard had piqued her interest.

Deep in the heart of Benin lies the sacred forest, home to the Spirit Vine. The locals believe that this ancient plant holds the key to unlocking one's true potential . . .

The narrator's voice was smooth and warm, like melted chocolate. Pels listened, realising that Dave's mention of Benin in his message must have been recorded by Aláké and presented as a potential area of interest. The seemingly random podcast choice wasn't random at all – just the weird and wonderful way Aláké's operating system and algorithm worked.

Despite the suggestion coming from Dave, Pels listened intently to the host's description of the richness of the forests of the West African landscape, remembering the few occasions she had visited Nigeria with her mother, and the folktales she'd been told as a child. Her memories of past visits were laced with rich scents of herbs and spices wafting through the air while visiting relatives, and with the rhythmic beat of traditional drums echoing through the night, if they were lucky enough to be invited to a party while they were out there. She felt a pang of guilt admitting to herself that, once she'd started university, her desire to fit in had led her to turn down her mother's offers to accompany her to Nigeria after a while. She'd opted for wild holidays in Mallorca with her friends instead. Now, Nigeria and West Africa seemed like the go-to destinations for Black luxury holidaymakers, though she had no doubt that white travellers were visiting there too, as her boss had mentioned. Pels had no idea what Benin would be like, but the podcast had her wondering what it would mean to just up and leave her current life for a bit . . . *Ugh, agreeing with Dave on anything makes me want to chew this pillow*, she thought, annoyed.

'Aláké, pause the podcast,' she whispered, suddenly struck by an idea. 'Show me articles on the protests against the building of resorts in Benin's cities.'

'Of course, Pels,' Aláké responded, promptly projecting and displaying a few articles from the internet about the protests onto the ceiling for her to peruse. Pels scrolled through the articles by swiping her finger on top of her duvet. Her life might be messy at times, but at least her apartment's fully integrated tech set-up was flawless; it was one of the few things in her life that didn't have her feeling like she was somehow lagging behind everybody else.

As she swiped, Pels noticed that far outnumbering the articles about the protests were websites advertising 'Spirit Vine retreats'. The retreats promised self-discovery and healing – but one in particular caught her eye: 'Eurydice Retreat: The Path of the Spirit Vine – Embrace Your Inner Power'.

'Aláké, save this retreat information,' Pels said hesitantly, annoyed that she was drawn to researching something Dave had suggested as an article, especially knowing that it was a ploy to distract her from researching the missing children.

'Understood, Pels.'

'Thank you.' Pels pinched her fingers together on her duvet, shutting off the display on her ceiling.

Exhaustion soon claimed her, and she slipped into a restless sleep. As she slept, Pels found herself in a familiar dreamscape – one that had haunted her since childhood. In her almost twenty-eight years, this recurring dream had always remained vague. She never quite knew what she was meant to decipher from it, or why she kept seeing the same images over and over.

In the dream, she stood before a vast, inky expanse of space, speckled with twinkling stars and swirling galaxies. Jagged branches made of interwoven stardust reached towards nothingness in the deep dark sky. Shadowy figures surrounded her, sweeping through the celestial forest, leaving trails of sparkling dust in their wake. Then, suddenly, a celestial being floated before her, their form made entirely of stardust, their eyes like shimmering pools of cosmic energy.

'Olúwapẹlúmi,' the being said, their voice echoing through the void, 'it is time to wake up.'

It was always the same dream. But this time, Pels was able to speak. 'W-who are you?' she asked, feeling as though she were standing on the edge of an abyss, teetering between fear and wonder.

Instead of answering Pels' question, the celestial being said, 'Your destiny is greater than you can imagine.' Their presence seemed to grow larger, surrounding her.

Suddenly, it was if she'd been swept up in a massive wave of light too brilliant to comprehend or resist – and just as suddenly, the dream began to dissolve. The celestial being's form faded into the vastness of space.

As Pels drifted back to consciousness, she could still hear their voice echoing in her mind: 'It is time to wake up.'

Chapter Two

. . . The fine arts student from Brixton, south-west London, had gone missing the evening he attended a barbering course – something his mother said he'd wanted to pursue as a business once he had graduated from university. Charles's body was found naked at the seafront, with strange markings on his skin.

His body was wet, and the tide was out when he was found by a morning jogger, the inquest was told.

In a statement to the coroner, Charles's mother, Ruth Olawole, said 'He always had his head down doing his work, but also had a zest for life,' she said. 'His favourite quote was: "I'm not just surviving, I'm thriving."'

★

As the last echoes of the celestial being's voice faded from Pels' mind, she awoke to a sunbeam casting its golden glow across her thigh, which she must've lay atop the duvet as she slept.

She sighed, rubbing her groggy eyes, desperately trying to hold onto the vivid memory of her dream. Since childhood, Pels had always tried to speak to the strange woman made of stardust. Now that they'd finally spoken, she had no idea what to make of the entity's suggestion that she had some great destiny. She'd wanted to respond with, 'I'm just a journalist.'

Her gaze fell upon the empty pillow beside her, still marked with the faint scent of Damari's cologne. Pels felt embarrassed as a flicker of loneliness passed over her, but it was quickly replaced by the memory of the last time Damari had been at her apartment, a few days ago . . .

It had taken a while for Pels to pay attention to what Damari was saying into his phone that evening. He was lounging next to her on the sofa while she typed up an article about a local community group that was keeping young people away from crime through gardening initiatives.

'Nah, you know I miss you, still, I'm just tied up with a few bits at the moment, but I should pass by your bit sometime this week,' Damari purred into his phone.

Pels paused her typing to hear more clearly. Damari was far too engrossed in his call, one hand casually tucked down the front of his trousers – a pose he only assumed when he was deeply comfortable.

'Who is that?' she mouthed quietly.

Damari shot Pels an annoyed glance while trying to maintain the laid-back tone with the person on the other end of the line.

'Aláké, amplify the call,' Pels whispered to her smart home system, since Damari's phone was connected to her speakers.

'Of course. Amplifying call from phone DOlder1991.'

Immediately Damari's conversation echoed throughout Pels' apartment. 'You're always busy. I love your drive, king . . .'

Damari fought shock as he heard the mystery caller's voice in surround sound. 'Ah, queen, I've got to go, yeah. My battery's doing a madness.' Without waiting for a response, Damari immediately ended the call. He turned quickly to Pels. 'Queen,

I'm disappointed in you, man. Why are you doing all that weird shit?'

'Weird shit, how? You're chatting like one nonsensical Casanova while you're sat on *my* sofa. Surely you clock the disrespect?'

'This isn't how you're meant to behave when you're in the right frequency, queen. That was Carmen,' he continued, his tone patronising. 'No need to act crazy and possessive. She's just a friend, and she's got good energy. You could learn from each other. You're mad smart, and she's got a really beautiful spirit.'

Pels was fascinated by how Damari always seemed convinced he was making sense when he wasn't.

'That's not how you speak to friends, and it isn't about me being possessive – it's literally basic manners. As you said, I'm smart, in case your light-skinned *friend* isn't aware,' Pels fired back, irritated.

'Why you gotta bring skin tone into it? How would you even know?'

'It's a trend with you. You tend to describe light-skinned women as being "beautiful spirits" as if the lightness of their skin inherently makes them good.'

'Ah, queen, I'm disappointed. You're letting white society divide us. How does your theory make sense when I'm dating you?' Damari seemed proud of himself for this retort.

'Because from the moment we started messaging you've mentioned more than once that I'm the first darker-skinned woman you've dated.'

'Exactly.'

'What do you mean "exactly"? I'm not proving your point, I'm proving mine.'

There was silence in Pels' apartment as Damari seemed to be figuring out what point he was trying to make.

'At the end of the day, I'm with you, not with her. It's too predictable for someone who looks like me to be with a woman my complexion or lighter. Dating you expands my spiritual growth, showing I can look beyond all that superficial stuff.'

'Damari, can you hear yourself? Is everything functioning correctly in your head? You're not performing some charitable deed as a Black man by dating a Black woman who's darker than you. Apart from your glaring colourism, the point of this discussion is that you're sat next to *me*, in *my* flat, talking in a weirdly intimate way with this woman, while artfully managing to avoid letting her know you're currently sat next to someone you're supposedly dating.'

Without missing a beat, as if finding his page again in the encyclopaedia of weird shit toxic men say, Damari replied sagely, 'Well, what is understood never needs to be explained.'

Immediately, Pels lost all desire to continue the conversation and retired to her bed. It wasn't long before Damari joined her there, kissing the back of her neck as she lay turned away from him, sliding his hand into the front of her silk pyjama trousers. Before long they were entangled and resentfully orgasming.

The next morning, he'd made some excuses about needing to do a 'road trip' for business and so he wouldn't be around for a couple of days. Pels should have known.

'Aláké, what time is it?' Pels asked now, her voice still thick with sleep.

'Good morning, Pels,' the AI replied in a soothing tone. 'It is 8.45 a.m. I monitored your temperature, and the amount of

REM sleep you would've had if I'd woken you at 7 a.m., and I decided to let you sleep a little longer. It is beneficial for your overall health.'

'Thank you,' Pels muttered, forcing herself out of bed and into the bathroom. Even after a couple of years of owning her beloved AI, she was still a bit freaked out by how deeply ingrained it was into her life – to the point where it could override her commands if it felt it knew better. She wondered whether this amount of control might be a good thing, especially as the decisions she'd made for herself, particularly around love, had only led to heartbreak.

As she splashed cold water onto her face, Pels couldn't help but think about her past relationships. She thought again about Marco, the handsome Italian artist who'd made her feel like a goddess, drawing her naked form surrounded by stars after they'd made love.

Pels had met Marco at the beginning of his six-month artist residency in London. He had approached her as she ate lunch on a park bench outside the office one afternoon. She'd wanted a quiet lunch away from her colleagues, still smarting from Dave's dismissal of yet another one of her pitches – this one about Black-owned businesses being priced out of their premises by local authorities in a concerted effort to whitewash areas in the process of being gentrified. Marco's commanding presence had instantly quietened all her other thoughts.

'How do you do that?' Marco had asked as he ambled over.

'Do what?' Pels had responded, confused about his question while utterly transfixed by how gorgeous he was.

As she wiped the sides of her mouth to clear away sandwich crumbs, quickly glancing around in case this was one of those weird and notorious social media pranks, he answered, 'Just eat and blend into life as if you're a part of all this. You are clearly a goddess, no?'

Pels belly laughed at how corny Marco's line was. She couldn't help but be enamoured by his unfazed reaction. He smiled at her, his light brown eyes twinkling.

'You think I am joking? Or maybe you are a really good actress.'

'I promise you I am not a goddess. I am just a journalist.'

'Why can't you be both?' Marco enquired softly.

Pels sighed at the memory. How could she not compare that tender attention from Marco to Damari's cruel dismissal and condescension?

Shaking the thought away, she asked, 'Aláké, any messages for me?'

'Maria left a message reminding you about Sunday brunch today at 11 a.m.,' Aláké dutifully reported.

'Thanks.' Pels smiled at the thought of spending time with her best friend, a comforting presence in this prickly period of her life.

'Also,' Aláké added, 'there's a news alert. Another Black child has been reported missing. Osahon Samuels, aged twelve, was last seen in Brixton two days ago.'

'Osahon . . .' Pels whispered, her heart aching with anger and sorrow. She clenched her fists, recalling Dave's dismissive attitude when she'd mentioned wanting to write about the missing children. Pels hoped that this boy would be found, but based on the stories she'd researched over the past year, this was the pattern: young Black people would go missing for days or weeks, and when they were finally found, it would be their bodies discovered by a river or lake or sea. Why did they end up by water, and why did the police – in every case – instantly categorise these deaths as 'unsuspicious'?

Aláké's news report continued. 'Veteran rapper turned entrepreneur MC Scribbla-Man spoke to us in Brixton today, as he urged the local community to keep up the search for the missing boy in a show of support for Osahon's family.'

Pels was instantly transported back to her teenage self. She'd had the biggest crush on MC Scribbla-Man, the sexiest member of the twelve-person hip-hop crew he led.

Aláké played her a video projection of the rapper responding to the reporter in front of a gathered crowd. 'The community need to understand that it is our duty to protect the youth. We've got to protect them from gang violence as well as the *biggest* gang, who go by the name of the police . . .' The crowd cheered.

Pels would've liked to think her taste had grown beyond rappers, but she'd dated and got played by Damari, so she allowed herself to admire Scribbla-Man's striking deep complexion and intense eyes just a little while he was still on her screen. The clip of her teenage crush wasn't enough to silence the alarm bells that were going off in her head about the clear and growing pattern concerning the young Black people who were going missing.

The camera panned to Osahon's family – and then Pels recognised someone. Her friend Elaine was standing beside them, looking distraught.

'Oh my God! That's why Osahon's name is ringing a bell. He's Elaine's brother.' Pels stomach found new patterns of knots to tie itself in as she recalled the handful of times she had seen the siblings together.

The screen projection of the report cut back to the studio, showing that the news anchor had now been joined by humanoid public figure and rumoured London mayoral hopeful Jeremy Bromwich. Although Pels had become somewhat used to having her personal AI, Aláké, it still freaked her out that a more advanced type of AI – designed to look human – would regularly show up on the news or at major events, just like an ordinary person.

Jeremy Bromwich was undeniably handsome by human standards – even more so for a humanoid. His skin was a light brown, with a dark fade haircut speckled with grey, and his prominent nose and full lips were accentuated by piercing brown eyes. He was tall and wore a suit well, but he could also hold his own in more casual outfits and still emanate a sense of style.

'Mr Bromwich,' the reporter asked, 'what do you think of the cases of missing children across London? Is this something that parents and schools need to be doing more to tackle, or is it a job for the police?'

Bromwich issued a well-timed smile and nod before responding. 'The very nature of community is that the responsibility shouldn't fall on any one figure – it is the responsibility of us all to protect children. In this case, I would be doing a disservice to those who have voiced their concerns that police in London seem to put less effort into searching for Black children if I didn't emphasise how important it is that the next Mayor of London takes this issue seriously.'

Ah, there it is. A good angle, nonetheless. Most political hopefuls usually avoided mentioning Black people in their campaign bid for fear of alienating those still grappling with viewing Black people as fully human.

The news anchor didn't miss a beat, pouncing on the opening that Jeremy provided her. 'Does this mean that you *will* be running for Mayor of London? And if so, will the disparity in policing of Black people be one of your main focuses?'

A chuckle from Jeremy, showing a flash of his well-designed teeth. 'Ah, well I think it's still ever so slightly early to say whether I will run for mayor, but that isn't the important aspect of this discussion. The fact is a young boy is missing, and I pray we find him . . .'

'Pray?' Pels mused out loud. 'Do AIs even pray?'

'Depends on what we are praying to, and what we are praying for,' Aláké suddenly interjected. The AI's response caught Pels off guard – she hadn't been addressing her.

'Pels,' Aláké continued, 'your heart rate has increased, indicating anxious thoughts. Shall I play some music to calm you?'

Technology, eh?

'Yes, please, Aláké. Play some Afrobeats,' Pels requested. She began getting dressed for brunch, hoping to find solace in the vibrant rhythms that would soon pulse through her apartment.

'Playing Afrobeats now,' Aláké confirmed, filling the room with an energetic beat that temporarily pushed away Pels' more intense thoughts – but they soon returned to the missing boy. Now it made sense why Elaine had been quiet in the group chat for the past couple of days – her brother was missing.

As she carefully applied make-up to her smooth, dark brown skin, Pels couldn't shake the lingering guilt over meeting up for brunch when one of their friends was going through something unimaginable. And it was so frustrating to not have her boss's clearance to research the missing Black kids further. Pels sighed.

'Aláké, add "research retreats in Benin" to my to-do list, please,' Pels requested resignedly.

'Adding "research retreats in Benin" to your to-do list now,' Aláké acknowledged.

Pels was a bit intrigued after all and resolved that she may as well learn more about Benin before declining Dave's suggested assignment. It still felt far more important to stay in London and research the missing children though – especially now that one of her friends was directly impacted.

Pels took one final look at her reflection, then added, 'Aláké, make a note of Osahon Samuels and provide me with updates on the news story.'

'Understood. I'll keep you informed,' Aláké replied.

Pels paused for a moment in front of her apartment door, taking a deep breath to steady herself. She gazed around her apartment: small but perfect; her safe haven. As soon as she'd viewed the apartment three years ago, she knew she didn't want to live anywhere else. It was close enough for her to visit her mother regularly, yet far enough that her mum couldn't just 'pop by'. There was something about being born to a Nigerian mother that meant no matter how old you were, you were still a child.

'Ready to go, Pels?' Aláké asked, pulling her back to reality.

'Ready,' she responded, readjusting her posture as her Pilates instructor often advised.

With that, Aláké did her obligatory scan to ensure there were no vitals that suggested any illness before Pels stepped out to interact with other people. All AIs were programmed to do this, a safety measure required by law since the last pandemic.

Checks complete, Pels' door released, and she walked out of her apartment, the door closing behind her with a gentle click.

As she headed out onto the street, the slight breeze whispered compliments to her dreadlocks. Her thoughts drifted back to Elaine, and a pang of guilt shot through her again. What could she say to offer her support to someone whose brother had gone missing?

'Would you like me to compose a few drafts of a text message for Elaine, Pels?' Aláké enquired, sensing Pels' worry. As an AI-integrated system, Aláké was ever-present due to the chip implanted at the base of Pels' skull.

'Later, perhaps,' Pels replied. 'For now, I just want to focus on brunch with Maria.' She could already feel the journalistic tug of wanting to pursue this line of research building in intensity again.

'Very well,' Aláké agreed. 'You have a message from Maria, from fifteen minutes ago. She says to meet her at Café Anansi in thirty minutes. So, you have fifteen minutes remaining.'

'Thanks, Aláké,' Pels nodded, quickening her pace as she made her way through the bustling streets of London.

As she neared the café, it occurred to Pels that she had news of her own to share with her friends. In her head, she quickly rehearsed how she would tell Maria and the rest of the friendship group that not only had Damari been cheating on her, but he was now expecting a child with the other woman. She wanted to deliver the news in a way that wouldn't induce laughter at the sheer audacity of Damari's behaviour or invite a barrage of pitying looks. If she was honest, though, she surprised herself by not being *more* worried about what her friends would think. She felt preoccupied with other concerns. She could sense a mystery building that needed to be solved, even if Dave thought her silly for wanting to do so.

'Aláké,' she whispered, stopping just outside Café Anansi's door, 'as well as new updates, please search for details about Osahon Samuels from historical posts on the web. Anything that his friends or family might've posted which could help me to gather more information. I don't want to have to ask Elaine with everything she is going through.'

'Of course, Pels,' Aláké assured her. 'We will find some answers.'

'Thank you,' Pels said softly, as she waited for the ID system to scan her upon entry to the café. A screen to the side of the door brought up an image of her face and her full name, 'Olúwapẹlúmi Badmus'. Then the door to the café opened to let Pels in.

She took a deep breath before walking over to the table where her friends were already gathered.

Chapter Three

On the evening of Charles's disappearance, at 8 p.m. BST he texted
his brother to say, 'I can't wait to show you the technique I learnt
today. You're due a trim, no? Shall we get Vietnamese takeaway?',
and then sent a picture of himself smiling and holding clippers.

His mother, Mrs Olawole, added: 'I absolutely don't believe that
Charles had any intention of harming himself on Grangehill beach.
Either this was some kind of accident, or somebody else did this to
him.'

PC Jacqueline Smithers of Grangehill Police Station told the
inquest, 'After an examination of Charles's body, and the area around
it, there was no implication that anybody else was involved here. The
markings on the skin could've been sustained due to the pebbles and
stones on the beach . . .'

★

Pels and her friends gathered around a sunlit table at the chic
West-African fusion café, the scent of fresh baked goods and simmering spices filling the air. It was their monthly brunch ritual,
an opportunity to catch up and savour each other's company.
Brunch for them was a time of healing, a time to forget about
the troubles that sought to weigh their spirits down. It was also
a chance for the friends to share 'IRL' updates on some of the
conversations that happened in their fast-paced group chat.

'Can you pass the hot sauce, please?' Pels asked Maria, who sat across from her, a mountain of spiced scrambled eggs and avocado toast piled onto her plate. It was Lila who obliged, sliding the small bottle labelled 'Peppeh Sauce' across the colourfully painted wooden surface of the table.

'Thanks,' Pels said, drizzling the fiery red sauce onto her plate. She loved the way it reminded her of home, even in the heart of London, the kick of spice on her tongue transporting her back to Sunday mornings in her mother's kitchen.

Just then, the sun hit Lila's hand in such a way that Pels let out a gasp as she noticed something glinting on her friend's finger.

'Oh my God! Wait! Are you engaged?!?' Pels exclaimed in shock and awe. 'How've you been holding this in?!'

The whole table squealed in unison as Lila waved her ring around in excitement.

'I was going to wait until we had a couple of mimosas before saying anything—'

Jameela interrupted with laughter. 'Girl, look at the size of that stone! You were going to blind us with the brightness eventually – we wouldn't have *made* it to two mimosas! It's just a lucky call that Pels clocked it first.'

The girls laughed and congratulated their friend. Lila had always been the one friend in the group whose dating life made Pels feel more at ease. She used to proclaim, '*No man cannah cross it*' when it came to her heart. She'd said she preferred short-term, intense and passionate affairs as opposed to – as she described it – the 'drudgery' of long-term relationships.

So the group chat had been ablaze with questions when Lila first posted a selfie of her and Deji on holiday. Their friend was voluntarily sharing the picture of a guy she was dating, and a holiday picture at that, *and* the guy was Yoruba? Had she not heard of their reputation as heartbreakers?

Lila confirmed she was well aware of the 'Yoruba demon' infamy, reasoning that if there was anybody likely to match her energy in the dating world, it might as well be a demon.

The girls had responded with different reality TV show memes in agreement. Regardless, the friends all knew something was different this time around. The ring now confirmed they'd been right.

Eventually, the excited giggles and talks of bridal outfits and destination weddings quelled as the friends tucked into their food and cocktails, but Lila kept her gentle gaze on Pels. 'All right, spill it, girl,' her friend demanded playfully, resting her chin on her hand.

Pels hesitated, picking at her food with her fork, suddenly unable to meet anyone's gaze at the table. She was aware that her friends were waiting on her to share what was going on in her love life, even though she was already well on her way to forgetting about Damari. Nevertheless, despite knowing she owed her friends honesty, she dreaded the shift in mood it would bring.

The sunlight filtering through the windows suddenly felt too bright as she began to explain. 'Damari . . . he got someone else pregnant.' Her voice was low.

The table had a mini eruption of 'Oh my God, I'm so sorry, babe!' Pels knew she had to intercept the pity very quickly, as it was unwarranted and unwanted.

'That's not the thing I'm stuck on, to be honest. Forget him.' Pels' friends exchanged glances, their faces a mixture of the guilt and concern that had pinched at her conscience since she watched the news report. 'It's Elaine,' she said, voicing what they were all thinking. 'Like, we are here having this meet-up, but she's somewhere devastated, looking for her younger brother.'

'Yeah, I know,' Maria said. 'I saw it on socials last night. I texted Elaine but no reply. Which is fair enough because we aren't that close, and we'd only chat briefly if I saw her out somewhere.' Others at the table nodded in agreement, as if they too had done the same, but Pels wasn't entirely sure that was true. Out of the group, she had probably known Elaine best from attending the same high school. The other women at the table knew her in the way Black women seem to know of each other when they live in the same area. They all felt the awkwardness of a grief that seemed to balance on whether Elaine's brother would be found.

Pels sensed that although the group cared for Elaine – some in a more parasocial way – the atmosphere felt too heavy for them all to carry in that moment.

'Anyway, I'll do my journalist thing and dig into it, see what information I can find to help. I'll keep you all updated. Let's put my actual job to good use for once, rather than looking up details on the guys you're with.' Pels forced a smirk to ease the mood a little. The group started to relax and little bubbles of conversations began to form around the table once more. Pels felt weirdly relieved. She gazed into the depths of her mimosa glass, searching for an answer that refused to materialise. Why were all those kids going missing? What did it mean that she was no closer to finding out? Was thinking about her job and making use of it, combined with being taken for a ride by Damari, making her feel some kind of existential crisis?

'Maria,' she began, her voice trembling but still finding the loyal ears of her best friend amid the chatter at the table. 'I've been thinking . . . about what I want from life, where I'm going. This probably isn't the best place to bring it up, but getting that text from Damari and being upset by it despite knowing full well I wasn't feeling him that deeply anyway . . . and now the stuff with Elaine's brother and feeling so helpless about it all . . . It just has me thinking, like – what the fuck am I actually *doing*, in the grand scheme of things?'

Maria leant forward, her feisty nature momentarily subdued by the intensity of Pels' gaze. 'Wherever we are is always the best place to bring up anything. You know I've got you.'

Pels smiled wanly at the reassurance offered by her best friend.

'I want to write about it, but Dave wants to pretend like there's nothing in this. Instead, he's sending me bullshit voice-mails telling me he'd rather I cover what sound like totally valid protests in Benin, of all places. Apparently, the locals are protesting against their land being taken by companies building these retreats—'

'Oh yes!' Maria interjected. 'I've been exploring this with my students in our seminars. It's all related to the Spirit Vine, a plant medicine that originates in Benin. More and more tourists have been going there to take it. When it is prepared and administered at these retreats, the participants have these intense hallucinatory experiences.' Maria visibly perked up anytime her knowledge in anthropology could be shared.

'You know they say that most of us don't know what our friends do for a living? It's times like this when I'm like, *oh yeah, Maria – professor of anthropology.*'

The two women giggled.

'I don't blame you for forgetting. I know I'm usually busy shaking dat ass when I'm not working – or finishing off the write-up for this frigging academic journal.'

'True, true!' Pels said with a laugh that turned into a sigh. 'I think you're right about those retreats. Supposedly, they help people connect with the spiritual world – access their inner power. I don't know exactly what that means, but Dave wants me to go there. Not so much for the potential enlightenment, I'm guessing, but to cover the anger of my *fellow Blacks*, and probably try and get some justification for what these developers are up to. I know that he's thinking it. But at the same time, I'm thinking, maybe I *should* go. Maybe it'll help me not feel like I'm being left behind in life, somehow.' Pels chuckled wryly again. 'Feels wild that I'm loud-whispering this to you after we just heard that our friend is getting married. Am I a hater?'

Maria's smile reassured Pels as it sparkled with excitement. 'Pels, I know how you like to play it safe with things. You're not a hater, you're just having feelings, and feelings are normal. Aside from this being a suggestion by Dave, what other reasons do you have *not* to take this assignment to Benin and flex those journalistic muscles out there?'

Pels sighed, twirling a dreadlock around her finger. 'I don't know. I feel like it's a slap in the face to go and talk about what other Black people are protesting elsewhere in the world when in real time Black children are going missing over here and he won't let me cover that.'

'Using my best friend privilege here to say – Pels, multiple things can be true at once. If you ask me, you should definitely go. Yes, Dave is a dickhead and would have his own reasons for wanting you to cover this, but zoom out for a second and think about your career,' Maria went on. 'If you are able to be on the ground covering stories internationally, it would boost your profile – and this story could be really important.' Maria reached across the table and squeezed Pels' hand in reassurance. 'You deserve to tell the stories that matter to you, Pels, and instead of seeing this trip as a potential standoff between you and Dickhead Dave, see it as an opportunity for professional growth. And who knows? Maybe you'll discover something incredible about yourself while you're there?'

A warm glow began to radiate within Pels, and she allowed herself a small smile. 'Maybe . . .'

'I don't even want to bang on about it,' her friend continued, 'but Benin is such a magical place, Pels.' Her excitement was contagious. 'The art and culture there are so deeply connected to the spiritual realm. Knowing what I know from my studies and the history of the Dahomey, what's going on there is more than just protests about land. When you consider the theft of artefacts and the strength of those long-gone kingdoms, it's almost like spiritual colonisation. I've got a couple of chapters in a book about it. When I get home, I'll send you a few pages to read. That way, at least you know what you're letting yourself in for – in the best way.'

Pels leant forward, eager to learn more. 'Yes, definitely send me the pages, but tell me about it now,' she urged, the two women in a world of their own.

Maria's eyes sparkled with enthusiasm as she launched into an explanation. Her tone took on a lightness as if being carried by her knowledge. 'The Benin people have a long history of creating powerful art that represents their connection to the spirit world. Some of the most famous pieces are the bronze plaques that once adorned the Royal Palace in the ancient Kingdom of Benin, which is now known as Edo State. They depict scenes from the lives of the Oba, or king, and his court, but they also hold deeper spiritual meaning, symbolising the link between the physical and celestial realms. But I'd imagine where you'll be headed is the Republic of Benin, formerly Dahomey, which has a deep and complex history with the transatlantic slave trade and formidable warriors as well as rich art, and it's revered as the land of voudoun.'

'Wow, OK, Professor Maria,' Pels said teasingly, but her mind was conjuring images of ornate bronze plaques glowing in ancient kingdoms.

'Associate Professor.'

'Well, full Professor soon come. This stuff sounds incredible. So the Benin Bronzes are from modern-day Edo, and that was the basis of the social media uproar a while back when the British Museum was encouraged to return them to the people of Benin but they refused?'

'Absolutely,' Maria agreed. 'And it's not just the bronze plaques. Across West Africa, people have always used intricate, beautiful masks in rituals and ceremonies to honour their ancestors and channel divine energies. They say the masks serve as a bridge between worlds, allowing the wearer to tap into the wisdom and power of the spirits.' She leant closer conspiratorially. 'The vast majority of artefacts being held by these museums are these masks, and some believe that the museums are refusing to return these artefacts because they're fixated on unlocking the spiritual powers they hold.'

Pels felt a shiver run down her spine at the thought of such potent spiritual connections. 'I had no idea,' she murmured, her heart filling with awe and respect for her West African heritage.

'Fascinating, isn't it? These are the kinds of things I want to make sure I'm sharing with my students. It's so interesting to me how so few of us Black people – in Britain especially – know our own history in depth. Told the right way, it could be an absolute vibe – not that the things that happened to us were a vibe, but our history goes beyond that. Anyway, you get what I mean.'

The two women giggled with the ease that came with the depth of friendship they'd nurtured for so many years.

'We keep banging on about me, how are you?' Pels didn't want all her conversations with her best friend to feel so focused on her chaotic life.

'Girl, same old, same old. Once I finish my write-up for this academic journal I think I'll feel free again. Research is exhausting – but not as exhausting as Kitty.'

'Your pussy? Maria, we haven't even drunk that many mimosas yet?'

Maria chuckled loudly with an enthusiasm that made her tongue stick out of her mouth. 'No, silly! Kitty is a dean at the university.'

'Oh! The one that's with a Black man?'

'Yes, her! I realise now that she told me all of that when she wanted me to take on this role, because it should've made me think that she understood Black culture. Far from it – top-tier cosplayer is what she is. I should've known it was a bad idea when she told me she was teaching him to respect Black women.'

Pels laughed, unable to stop tears streaming from her eyes. 'Maria! Please, I can't breathe!'

'Let me not even get into that whole drama. It's just annoying that by proxy of Black dick, she thinks she can tell me how to teach students about West African history, when she hasn't got a clue. Then asking me to make sure the lectures and seminars still "sizzle" for those who aren't of the cultures.'

'Yeah, see, I can't have Kitty eventually know more about the historical significance of West African practices than me. You're making Dave's idea sound like a great one,' Pels conceded.

'See? This trip could be so much more than just what Dave might want the assignment to be, Pels,' Maria insisted, her voice full of conviction. 'You have the opportunity to immerse yourself in a rich spiritual tradition that's been passed down through generations!'

'True,' Pels admitted, her mind racing with possibilities. 'I just hate when there's even a slight chance of Dave not being wrong about something.'

'I know, I know, but you know what they say about broken clocks. Look at it this way: the less pushback you give him about this, the more scope you'll likely have for the angle that you want to write your article from. You could even explore the potential for an investigative piece on the resurgence of traditional African spirituality in the modern world. Dave's always looking for ways to make the paper stand out, right? And he seems to love stories that fulfil a particular stereotype of Black people. So, if you make this *sound* like "oh no, here go those Africans again believing in the woo-woo", he'll love it!'

Pels smiled as she pondered Maria's words, weighing the pros and cons. It was true that Dave had a way of viewing Black people and their cultures that he seemed unwilling to evolve from, and Pels also knew she was one of the few journalists who could do justice to a story so layered with political and spiritual significance. Perhaps, if she built her profile doing this assignment and made Dave happy by accepting it, she might then have more freedom to dig into the situation with the missing kids back here . . .

'All right,' she said finally, determination prompting her to tap her feet. 'I'll talk to Dave about it. And thank you, Maria. I don't think I could do any of this without your support.'

'Of course, Pels,' Maria replied warmly. 'You're my best friend, and I believe in you. Always remember that. Now, let's scream with the girlies because you know Lila's wedding is going to be a madness – in the best way.'

'One thing about Maria and Pels? Them two can chat!' Lila called across the brunch table.

'Sorry!' Both women called back in unison, loving that they could fall into step with each other anywhere, yet recognising that the group needed their attention for talks of bridesmaids' dresses and who would set up the hen party group chat.

Chapter Four

The body of eleven-year-old Selena Odogwu was found near a lake on the outskirts of Chattering Marshes, two weeks after she went missing from her home in north London in February 2024.

The police watchdog found officers provided 'an unacceptable level of service' after she went missing.

Selena's mother has said the apology from the police 'is not nearly enough'.

★

The next morning, Pels shuffled into the newsroom, her heart pounding as she mentally rehearsed her pitch to Dave. *I'll go to Benin and write this story if I can come back and focus on the piece about the missing young people . . .*

Though she knew Maria's advice had been sound, she couldn't help but feel a flutter of anxiety at the prospect of confronting her boss about this middle ground.

Punctual as always, Pels knocked on Dave's office door at precisely 9.30 a.m., taking a deep breath to steady herself as she awaited his response.

'Come in,' Dave called out, his tone brisk and businesslike.

'Morning, Dave. Do you have a moment?'

'Wow, you're on time today!'

'Dave, I am always on time.'

'Ah! I must be thinking of Yomi . . .'

Pels felt the heat of annoyance prick at her ears, but she refused to dignify Dave's ignorance with a response. Instead, she ploughed on with what she wanted to say.

'Just checking in after your voicemail last week about the Benin story you'd like me to cover. I've had some ideas about how to balance coverage like this across the newspaper as a whole,' Pels began, trying to keep her voice steady despite the rapid beating of her heart.

'All right, take a seat,' Dave replied, gesturing towards the chair opposite his desk. His posture was relaxed, but his eyes held a cool, calculating gleam that made Pels feel as though he could see straight through her.

'Thank you,' Pels said, taking a seat and folding her hands in her lap. 'So, I've been doing some research on the Benin people of West Africa, and I've come across something truly fascinating. I know you want me to focus on the protests and what that means for European investors who build these retreats in countries like Benin, but the actual spiritual practice they're profiting off also deserves a nuanced exploration. These spiritual practices are ancient and complex, with strong links to their art and culture. I believe there's an incredible story here – one that has the potential to capture our readers' imaginations while shedding light on a rich and under-reported aspect of African history, and present-day resistance—'

'You sound like you're reading out of the *National Geographic*, but go on,' Dave prompted, his expression unreadable as he leant back in his chair.

With his interest piqued, Pels air-swiped her pitch over to his computer to read as she continued to speak. 'There's a Spirit

Vine retreat happening in Benin soon, where participants can learn first-hand about these practices and their significance within the broader context of West African spirituality. It's close to where the protests are happening, and I think attending could allow me to provide invaluable insight for an article. Or even a series of articles, exploring the resurgence of traditional African spirituality in the modern world against the backdrop of the Indigenous protesting the co-opting of their practices and the perceived theft of their land,' Pels continued, her voice growing stronger as she warmed to her subject.

'Interesting,' Dave mused, stroking his chin thoughtfully as he read her pitch. He glanced back over at her. 'I knew I was onto something by telling you about these protests. If only you'd let me mould you into the kind of journalist you could be, rather than chasing conspiracies and dead-end stories . . .' He smirked. 'And you're certain you can produce compelling content from this retreat?'

'Absolutely,' Pels asserted, using every fibre of her self-restraint to not respond through gritted teeth to Dave's condescending demeanour. 'I'm confident that I can bring this story to life in a way that resonates with our readers and honours the people of Benin. Balanced reporting is what can really set *The Mercury* apart from the other newspapers.'

'Well, my father is one of our readers, and his best friend owns *The Mercury*. It's important that the news stories make them proud of me – I mean, of the paper. Their approval is the benchmark, because it is successful men like them who actually *read* the papers. If we write stories that can keep someone like my dad engaged, then that is a good story. I read somewhere that dads aren't always present in—'

'OK, Dave, got it.' She thought it best to interject before Dave said something that HR would have to know about.

Pels wanted to roll her eyes in frustration, but she held every muscle in her face so as not to react to Dave's silliness.

Her boss studied her for a moment, his gaze probing. Then, with a nod, he said, 'All right, Pels. You've got my attention. So you're thinking voudoun and getting high? It is a fresh take on the Dark Continent, that's for sure. Let's see what you can do with this opportunity.'

Irritation continued to grow within Pels, but she held herself together, squashing down the bubbling rage that threatened to burst her apart. She attempted to focus on something in Dave's office to avoid letting him see her frustration at his deeply ignorant comments, and her gaze settled on one of the framed pictures on his wall. Half of the picture showed a large warehouse with 'Cannon & Sons' painted across the front, and the other half, a hand-drawn map.

'Well, it's more than that, Dave. And actually, there is something to be said for how voudoun has been misrepresented in mainstream culture, but that isn't the focus or the practice of the people of Benin, so—'

Pels cut herself off as Dave sighed and tapped his fingers on the desk, clearly keen to avert any lecture she might launch into. She noticed him scanning Pels' face, *probably for any hint of aggressiveness*, she thought. Finally, he spoke.

'All right, Pels. I'll approve this trip under one condition: you mentioned balance, and that means on *both* sides. I feel that sometimes your quest to push this Black Lives Matter agenda means you forfeit a more logical approach to your stories. Honestly, think of men like my dad's friend, whose business *you're* benefiting from, and who has worked hard to build companies that contribute to what this country is, only to then read the stories you're constantly trying to push about racism and weird agendas.' He smiled patronisingly at her. 'I mean, you've got to meet me in the middle here. If you can bring back a story that is both enlightening and gripping, that shows your people working to elevate themselves, and also shows that these retreat centres don't necessarily mean harm, then it will be worth the investment.'

Two mentions of dear old dad and his friend in five minutes, Pels mused, stifling a grin. It was weirder that Dave wouldn't refer to *The Mercury* owner by his actual name – William Bunker. Did he really think referring to the multimedia and tech billionaire mogul as his 'dad's friend' made him – dreary Dave – more accomplished? Dave used any opportunity to bring up his father, always droning on about how instrumental he was to the man her boss had become – as if that were a good thing! His favourite phrase around the newsroom was '*What would Bernard read?*' As if the newspaper was meant to function only as a daily newsletter dedicated to Bernard Cannon. Nothing could challenge the old man's worldview, only affirm it.

'Thank you, Dave,' Pels breathed, feeling an unexpected surge of relief, despite all the passive-aggressive and wildly ignorant tropes Dave had peppered his approval with. Then she remembered her final point.

'Talking of meeting in the middle – and I'm not trying to look a gift horse in the mouth or anything, but if I am meant to look at these investors taking land in Benin with a somewhat sympathetic lens, I think the trade-off is that I get to write about these missing young Black people back here at some point soon. If I prove to you that I can write this Benin story with balance, surely I can get that over the line too?'

'Remember,' Dave warned, his voice stern, 'These subjects are not the same thing, Pels. I'm doing you a favour here. You come across as obsessed with Blackness in a way that your colleagues – for example, Yomi – aren't. This *is* us meeting in the middle. You want to write about Black people, then write about Africans stopping their countries from developing, protesting the big businesses being built there. Focus on that for now.'

'We'll see,' Pels mumbled under her breath, the prickles of annoyance intensifying at the thought that he could compare her to another Black colleague when he had just mixed the two of them up moments before. Instead, Pels forced a smile in response, still planning to push for the article she wanted to write once she returned from the assignment in Benin.

But Dave wasn't done with her, it seemed. 'Now that you're seeing the benefit of the assignments I have for you,' he said, leaning back in his chair. 'I've got another. Jeremy Bromwich is having a briefing tomorrow morning and we suspect it's all in the rollout for his announcement about running for Mayor of London. I want you to go to the briefing. I'll be there too, just to get an idea of what he's all about, and that'll give me a chance to see how you shape the reporting. I think this will be a good story for you to focus on for the next couple of days before heading out to Benin.' He grinned broadly. '*Another* way I'm helping you to broaden your scope of reporting! And this is in the realms of what you like – you know, with Bromwich being like light-tanned Black, eh? I mean, I know he's AI, but they've made him appealing for you lot too. This way it's a nice crossover actually – we need more reporting about all this artificial intelligence business too.'

'Sure.' Pels held in a sigh and shot Dave a thin-lipped smile before leaving Dave's office. She wasn't a violent person by any stretch of the imagination, and she wouldn't usually imagine herself harming anyone, but sometimes when Dave spouted certain ignorant comments, she couldn't help but have the overwhelming urge to punch Dave right in the face. The irony was that sometimes he could be bearable, and on very rare occasions even sweet. This was the tyranny of having a boss like Dave. The main thing was that now Pels had a plan for her next steps at work – and just maybe, for her future.

'Whatever happens,' she whispered to herself. 'I'm not going to ruin this chance to do something *meaningful*.'

Chapter Five

During a press conference, Ms Odogwu said the investigation by the Independent Office for Police Conduct (IOPC) 'has made me understand what I didn't want to believe – that at a time when my family was going through hell, not one police officer wanted to listen to me, and my daughter's disappearance was treated like a joke.'

She added: 'It has only made my grief and anger worse, knowing that even though the IOPC and police concluded that the performance of all the officers of varying seniority was not up to standard, none of them will be investigated for misconduct.'

*

Pels adjusted the strap of her backpack on her shoulder the next morning, feeling its weight heavy with her notebook and voice recorder – the tools of her trade. Even though Aláké made note of everything she was requested to record by her owner, Pels still preferred the old-fashioned ways and means of journalism – though not the rifling through of trash some were known to have done in the past. She walked alongside Dave's long strides. His tall frame cast a long shadow as they entered in the bright foyer of Jeremy Bromwich's office.

Pels couldn't help but marvel at the opulence of Jeremy's foyer: marble floors and imposing sculptures impeccably placed

– and two hi-tech robots sat side by side watching people walk in while using facial recognition technology to identify and sign in each visitor.

Who is paying for all of this? Pels wondered. The air buzzed with an electric anticipation, mingling with the soft hum of air conditioning. As they found a seat near the front of the platform where Jeremy would be giving his speech, Dave leant over to Pels. 'Remember, my dear,' Dave murmured, his eyes scanning the room, 'we're not on a jolly. We're here to get the scoop on this AI candidate. So if you get the chance to ask a question, make it a good one.'

'I know,' Pels replied, her voice steady despite her irritation at being spoken to like anything other than a professional.

Once all press had taken their seats, the humanoid figure at the centre of the room captured everyone's attention. Jeremy Bromwich stood in a way that defied binary categories of man or machine. His form was crafted from a fleshy material that mimicked human skin – a deep golden brown; it bore a warm undertone that glowed under the fluorescent lights. When he moved, his gestures were fluid, devoid of the jerky motions usually associated with robots. It was as if each tendon and well-defined muscle beneath his synthetic skin had been programmed to simulate the grace of an enchanting ballet dancer.

'Good morning.' Jeremy's voice resonated through the room, smooth, with a deep richness that mimicked his skin, and sounded so disarmingly human. 'I understand there might be confusion regarding my potential mayoral candidacy, and the fact that my doing so would make it the first of its kind. Allow me to clarify any doubts.'

Pels watched him intently, noting the subtle crease of his brow, the tilt of his head, even the expansion of his chest when he simulated a breath. It was all unnervingly human.

'Is he . . . breathing?' she whispered to Dave, who only shrugged, his own gaze locked onto Jeremy.

'Many have questions,' Jeremy continued, addressing the room of reporters, 'about the future of artificial intelligence. I am here to bridge a gap between us all – to show that AI can enhance our society. It seems there are fewer concerns about my rumoured mayoral campaign, which I will now use this opportunity to confirm. Rather what you all seem to want to know is what I am. I am known as what could be considered the upper end of AGI – Artificial General Intelligence – meaning my knowledge is currently at the upper end of your typical level of human knowledge. The AI technology that many of you may have installed via the chips in your brains is known as ANI – Artificial Narrow Intelligence – which only does as you ask, even if sometimes it might go just a bit beyond your wishes because it has learnt to pre-empt your needs. But at its core, ANI is rather simplistic. It provides a level of efficiency I believe is beneficial to humans and the world as a whole, but as it pertains to governance, my existence is more beneficial – at least in theory. Because as AGI, I can amalgamate a *vast* array of human thoughts and previous outcomes to generate decisions that would be statistically proven as the most sound. And no,' he added, a hint of dry humour colouring his tone, 'we don't plan to take over the world. That would only be possible with ASI, otherwise known as Artificial Super Intelligence. Yes, watch out for them, whenever they come into existence.'

He emitted a resonant chuckle, and the room erupted into a mixture of laughter and murmurs, some fuelled by excitement and others tinged with discomfort. Pels jotted down notes, her handwriting a scrawl only she could decipher. Beside her, Dave chortled, shaking his head with a mix of scepticism and amusement.

What she felt, though, was a twinge of unease. This wasn't just advanced technology; it was a redefinition of life itself. Her fingers paused over the paper, her mind starting to race with questions about the implications of Jeremy's existence. Could he truly understand the complexities of human emotions?

'Any questions?' Jeremy's voice brought her back to the present as the room settled. Pels glanced to the side of the stage, where two unassuming figures in nondescript lab coats – likely members of the team of inventors who had created Jeremy – stood, their slightly nervous presence a stark contrast to the AI's almost unsettling commanding energy.

'Jeremy Bromwich wasn't programmed for politics,' one inventor began, walking over to his invention. His voice was steady, undercut by a hint of pride. 'If he makes an evolution towards governance, that will be as natural as any human candidate's rise through political ranks, born from a seed of inspiration.'

Natural, Pels mused. The word felt alien in this context, yet there Jeremy stood, his fleshy synthetic skin catching the light as he shifted his weight from one foot to the other. There was no mechanical whirr, no stuttered movements; he was fluidity personified, a testament to the blurred lines between man and machine.

'Should the people of London choose Jeremy as their mayor,' continued the second inventor, stepping forward and adjusting his glasses, 'his decisions will be autonomous. Ethically, we are bound not to interfere. His consciousness, if you can call it that, operates independently, even though he is not yet considered Artificial Super Intelligence, this is something we believe may be within our grasp in the next thirty years due to the inevitable exponentiality of technological advancements.'

Independently . . . Pels chewed on the word, her thoughts spiralling.

'Questions?' Jeremy asked again.

Pels stood up, her pulse quickening. 'Olúwapẹlúmi Badmus from *The Mercury*,' she declared, her voice cutting through the silence. 'You've explained that you are not ASI, as that type of AI – as and when it comes to fruition – could be considered to have a conscience. But as the inventors have said, you chose this path as if you *do* have something close to what some might call a conscience – a soul, even. Would you say you have a soul, and is that necessary for governance?'

The question hung in the air, and for a moment, all eyes were on her – a confident Black female journalist asking a question – but at the attention Pels suddenly felt like a little girl. Her gaze locked with Jeremy's, searching for a glimpse of something intangible within his artificial gaze, and her point crystalised.

'Governance,' she continued, 'is about humanity. But what does it mean when humanity is guided by the hand of an individual born from circuits and code?'

Another layer of anticipation enveloped the silence in the room as Jeremy considered her question. From the corner of her eye, Pels noticed Dave nervously shifting in his seat beside her, likely wondering how he might fire her and cancel the trip to Benin if she'd messed up her opportunity to interrogate Bromwich with her existential question. Yet Pels knew what she was doing. Whatever Jeremy's answer, it would not only shape the articles the press would publish but might just redefine the future of leadership in a world teetering on the edge of a new era.

Jeremy Bromwich paused, and now there *was* the soft whir of his internal mechanisms only just perceptible beneath the hush of anticipation. His artificial eyes continued to hone in on Pels with a gaze that felt unsettlingly perceptive.

'Ms Badmus,' Jeremy began, his voice a symphony of synthetic cadences designed to comfort and engage, 'the concept of a soul is indeed beautiful. It is often thought of as a divine spark, an ethereal essence that provides depth beyond our tangible existence.' He moved with alluring certainty, as he gestured towards his chest, where a heart would beat if he were human. 'If a soul is a gift bestowed by a divine creator, then by that definition, I lack one. My being is crafted by human hands, and arguably not by divine will.'

The murmurs in the room softly crescendoed, journalists scribbling notes and photographers' lenses focusing, capturing the moment a machine contemplated its own metaphysical absence.

'Yet,' Jeremy continued, a thoughtful tilt to his head, 'if we examine the actions of those who do claim to possess a soul, we must ask ourselves – what good has their governance done for the world so far? Progress is not measured by what one claims to have within, but by the deeds one performs without.'

Pels stood motionless, her heart thrumming against her ribs, Jeremy's words resonating with a truth that transcended his artificial origin. There was something profoundly human in his observation, and she couldn't help but respect him for it. She slowly lowered back into her seat as those in the room applauded the astute response, then went on to ask their questions, which in Pels' opinion were rather mundane.

Once all the questions had been answered, the briefing shifted into a low hum of post-discussion chatter about being the first people to know a humanoid would be running for Mayor of London. Jeremy left the stage, and the press in the room had the kind of restless energy that follows a significant revelation. Pels felt a tap on her shoulder and turned. To her surprise, Jeremy Bromwich was standing beside her, his presence commanding yet unassuming.

'Your question was most insightful, Ms Badmus,' he said. 'How are you faring with your soul?'

She blinked, excitement bubbling up alongside a flutter of nerves. She didn't know what she'd expected a humanoid to smell like, but his scent was amazing. She guessed he was wearing an expensive cologne. *No matter how badly Damari has treated you, you cannot fancy a robot*, Pels warned herself.

'It's . . .' She began, and for some reason a truth pushed to the surface. 'I had a dream,' she stammered, her voice barely above a whisper, 'where celestial beings told me I have a purpose . . .' She surprised herself by sharing such personal information, but somehow it felt oddly safe.

'Ah, dreams.' Jeremy nodded, his expression contemplative. 'While I don't have them, I know they can be powerful motivators. The mind, whether organic or artificial, seeks meaning and connection.'

He was good. Pels noticed how artfully he placed resonance between them. Bonding. A trait of living social beings.

'Exactly,' she agreed, emboldened by his understanding. 'I'm due to go on assignment to investigate a retreat in the Republic of Benin. Although I'll be there to cover the ongoing protests against such businesses, I'll also have a chance to explore something called the Spirit Vine. My understanding is it's some kind of plant medicine that allows one to connect more deeply with their inner world. Sorry, I'm babbling . . . but I hope to come back with a wealth of knowledge in various regards. Maybe even a deeper understanding of myself. God knows, I could use it.'

Jeremy nodded. 'Benin,' he echoed thoughtfully after a moment, artfully and with compassion, sidestepping her self-deprecation. 'A place rich with spiritual history. I would be keen to hear of your experiences upon your return.'

Jeremy's interest in her personal journey left Pels with a curious sense of validation. Her soul, whatever nebulous form it took within her, seemed to resonate with his circuitry even in that brief exchange.

'Before you leave, please give your details to—' Jeremy began, but he was interrupted.

'Ah, Pels! Of course you managed to lure Jeremy into a conversation,' Dave guffawed, his laugh contrived as he ushered his father, Bernard Cannon, over. Pels had not even realised he was in the room. He must've arrived after the briefing.

Lure? Pels couldn't help but assume Dave meant the word pejoratively, but as always, she fought the urge to react. She liked being a journalist and she understood that somehow punching your boss in the throat was likely to have dire consequences.

Dave's father, Bernard, possessed an aura of clout and influence that made even the most seasoned journalists clam up

48

mid-sentence. He was a man who traded in connections, his smiles always hinting at something more than mere pleasantries.

'Jeremy, I've heard so much about you,' the elder man said with practised ease, extending his hand. 'Bernard Cannon. I would be honoured to have you at my table for an intimate gathering next week. A chance to discuss the future, and your plans for it.'

Jeremy's hand met Bernard's, their handshake brief. Yet Pels couldn't be sure who had pulled away first.

'Mr Cannon, your invitation is appreciated, but I must decline,' Jeremy replied, his voice smooth, betraying none of the tension that now hung in the air. Pels noted that he hadn't even been told which day of the week the gathering would have taken place.

'Shame,' Bernard remarked, his eyes narrowing ever so slightly before reclaiming his congenial demeanour. 'Perhaps another time.' With a pat on Dave's shoulder so that his son would follow, he retreated into the throng of bodies.

'Quite the character,' Jeremy noted, turning back to Pels. His gaze held no judgement, merely an observation, as if he calculated every social interaction with precision. 'I'd counsel that there's no such thing as a free meal, Ms Badmus.'

Pels felt the weight of Jeremy's words, her own thoughts echoing a sentiment she couldn't quite place. It was unsettling to think that Jeremy's programming had likely processed an incredible amount of data and facial recognition to check Bernard's previous and current political affiliations, and to gauge whether being associated with him could affect him in the polls. She watched the retreating forms of Dave and his father, her mind churning.

'Indeed,' Pels murmured. She was caught between the allure of Jeremy's charm and the nagging doubts that crept like tendrils into her consciousness. Was it simply human nature to be wary, or was it instinct warning her of a deeper complexity here that was yet to be understood?

'I hear uncertainty in your voice. Maybe that soul of yours will find respite in Benin,' Jeremy said. 'As I was saying, do keep in touch upon your return. In this briefing there are one hundred and twenty-three attendees, five of them Black and only one of the Black journalists is a woman.' He leant over with a slight smile. 'That's you.'

Pels nodded, returning his smile wryly. 'I am aware of the statistics regarding the lack of diversity in journalism.'

Pels noticed that he made no promises or assumptions. He quite deftly presented her with facts and an opportunity to connect in the future. She was certainly surprised – this wasn't what she'd expected from this assignment.

'Thank you,' was all she could muster, even though she was unsure of what she was thanking him for. With that, Jeremy smiled and walked away. As she watched him navigate the crowd, a strange confluence of emotions churned within her – a fusion of awe, intrigue, and a sliver of uncertainty for what the interaction might mean.

Stepping out of the venue, Pels wrapped her coat tighter around her, seeking comfort in its familiar embrace. The London air nipped at her cheeks, a reminder of the world outside the bubble of that briefing room – a world that suddenly felt on the cusp of transformation.

As her heels clicked rhythmically on the pavement, Pels' phone buzzed – a text message, as alerted by Aláké. The hologram feature on her phone allowed her to read the message displayed in front of her as she walked, even though her phone was in her pocket.

> **Elaine:** Hey Pels, thank you for reaching out. Yes, let's meet later today. I can do 5 p.m. at Myatt's Park, by the football pitch.

Pels, relieved to see a message from her friend, responded instantly.

'Aláké, reply to Elaine: OK, see you then. Sending you lots of love.'

'Of course, Pels. Reply sent.'

Hearing from Elaine and interacting with Jeremy somehow made Pels more determined to help find Osahon. As the only Black female journalist in the room – as Jeremy had pointed out – it was down to her to make sure certain stories got told. She knew that now more than ever.

Chapter Six

Selena was first reported missing on 16 February 2024, and her body was recovered from a lake on the outskirts of Chattering Marshes nearly a fortnight later.

As the case was eventually brought to misconduct hearings, it was found that one officer told Ms Odogwu: 'You can't keep track of your daughter, so how are we meant to?'

Selena's mother feels that much of the manner in which the police handled her complaint was tarnished by racism, and that officers took too much time to class her daughter as missing.

*

Pels approached the park bench later that day, her stride purposeful as she drew near Elaine. Her nose itched at the scent of the freshly trimmed grass, and she noticed how the light of the sun caught the edges of Elaine's ombre-coloured braids, turning them to spun gold.

'Hey,' Pels said, voice gentle.

Elaine looked up, her brown eyes tinged with red, a testament to the tears she had shed. A faint smile touched her lips. 'Hey.'

'Mind if I join you?' Pels gestured to the space beside Elaine.

'Please,' Elaine replied, scooting over.

Pels settled down, leaving a respectful gap between them. Her fleeting thought was not to sit too close to those who were heartbroken – there had to be room for the grief to sit also.

She glanced around at the children chasing a football across the field before it would become too dark, their laughter punctuating each kick and tumble. It was easy to imagine twelve-year-old Osahon among them, his slight frame – as depicted in the photos on the missing posters – weaving through his peers with natural agility.

'Osahon loves playing here,' Elaine murmured, her eyes fixed on the ongoing game, as if she too were visualising her brother's presence.

'Looks like a good spot for it.' Pels followed her friend's gaze.

'Sometimes, I think if I just wait long enough, he'll show up, ready to go home.' Elaine's voice broke slightly, betraying the fragility of her hope.

'Like he's just been out for an extra-long match, right?' Pels offered a small, supportive smile.

'Exactly.' Elaine chuckled, though it didn't quite reach her eyes.

They watched in silence for a moment, the shouts of the children playing the only sound in the air.

'Wouldn't it be something if life worked like that?' Pels mused aloud, breaking the quiet.

'Would save us a lot of heartache,' Elaine said with a sigh, tucking a loose braid behind her ear, seemingly distracting herself from the tears that looked ready to fall.

'True. But then we'd miss out on the drama. We just have to keep the faith that he will show up. Can't have a story without a bit of suspense, can we?' Pels quipped gently, hoping to coax a more genuine smile from Elaine.

'Journalist humour,' Elaine chided as she sucked her teeth, but this time the laugh was real, if fleeting, because she could tell her friend meant well.

'Guilty as charged,' Pels admitted, her own smile and concern sincere. 'Elaine, I can't sit by and just watch. I want to help. And I think shining a light on Osahon's story could be a start.'

'Help?' Elaine's voice was a low murmur.

'An article,' Pels clarified. 'There's a pattern, an ugly truth that needs to be exposed. When our people go missing, the silence is deafening. Think about it,' Pels pressed gently. 'We make noise in the press, kick up a fuss, it gets harder for them to ignore us.'

'Make noise,' Elaine echoed, a spark igniting behind her sorrow-filled eyes. 'For Osahon. For all the others.'

'*Exactly.*' Pels nodded, satisfaction warming her tone. 'We'll hold a mirror up to society. I've been following cases like these for ages, and I just don't want Osahon to . . . to have a similar ending to them.'

A gust of wind chased a scrunched-up crisp packet across their path. Pels watched as Elaine tracked its aimless journey, her friend's expression wistful, haunted.

'Never thought . . .' Elaine started, then stopped, biting her lip.

'Never thought what?' Pels prompted softly.

'That it would be us,' Elaine whispered, finally. 'You hear stories, you sympathise, but it's always someone else's sibling, someone else's child.'

'Life's got a cruel way of reminding us we're not immune,' Pels said, her words tinged with bitterness.

'Doesn't it just?' Elaine agreed, a hollow laugh escaping her.

'Still,' Pels continued, her hand reaching across the grief and finding Elaine's, giving it a reassuring squeeze, 'you've got me, in whatever capacity you need me. I am going to push for this story even harder. I've been sent on an assignment to Benin—'

Elaine shot Pels a questioning look.

'It's a long story,' Pels said, 'But if I do this for my boss, it's going to give me more leverage once I'm back.'

'Thank you,' Elaine replied, a tremor of gratitude in her voice as she squeezed back.

'Anytime,' Pels assured her, locking eyes with Elaine. 'That's what friends are for.'

'Friends with a side of journalistic tenacity,' Elaine managed a weak smile.

'Best kind,' Pels quipped, hoping the levity might ease some of the weight pressing down on them both.

Elaine looked back at the field, her gaze lingering on a young boy scoring a goal, his celebration a stark contrast to the stillness between them. 'Osahon used to celebrate like that. Whole world in front of him.'

Pels nodded. 'I know the girls from our group chat send their love too,' she said eventually.

'I know. They've texted,' Elaine murmured, not meeting Pels' eyes. 'Haven't had the heart to reply.'

'Elaine, they're worried about you,' Pels said, her tone a blend of concern and a nudge towards the world Elaine was withdrawing from.

'Can't face them.' Elaine's voice was but a whisper, her braids swaying slightly as she shook her head. 'Can't pretend to discuss plot twists and dick pics when my life's dangling on the biggest cliffhanger.'

'Elaine,' Pels ventured again, 'when did you last eat something?'

'Food tastes like cardboard,' Elaine replied.

'Even your mum's jollof?' Pels raised an eyebrow, invoking the ongoing banter of whose mum was the best cook.

'Does Mum even have the heart for jollof right now? She lays in bed staring at nothingness, and on the days she can do something more, she just goes down to the kitchen and sits by the table staring into nothingness,' Elaine responded flatly.

Pels managed a 'hmmm', but the sound felt hollow between them. The conversation lulled, and she was irritated with herself for asking something so frivolous. The distance of unsaid words stretched out like the shadows cast by the sun.

'Every time . . . I see news about another body found, my heart stops,' Elaine confessed suddenly, turning to face Pels. 'What if the next time . . . it's him?'

'Hey,' Pels squeezed Elaine's hand tightly. 'We can't let our thoughts spiral there. Reality is the police haven't stopped looking,' Pels reminded her, squeezing her hand with emphasis. 'And more importantly, *we're* not going to stop.'

Elaine nodded, the action carrying more weight than words could convey. 'Not you showing up like one Hollywood investigator. I've never seen you this focused.'

'Well, that should tell you how much this all means to me. I'll research with all my might.' Pels laughed a little. 'Look how you've got me talking like one superhero.'

'Journalist first, superhero second?' Elaine managed a chuckle too, the mood slightly lighter between them.

'Other way around,' Pels corrected as she got up from the bench. Elaine followed.

'Thank you, Pels,' her friend said as they reached the park gates.

'Nothing to thank me for yet.' Pels flashed a reassuring grin. 'Just doing my part.'

'Still,' Elaine insisted, 'thank you for not letting me sit alone with all this.'

'Never,' Pels promised, stepping through the gate onto the pavement. Pels stood as she watched Elaine get into her car and drive off into the south London traffic.

'One way or another, I have to get to the bottom of this,' she said to herself quietly. Once this trip to Benin was done, she hoped she'd have the tools to do just that.

Pels arrived on the doorstep of her mother's red-brick house on a quiet residential street in south London that evening, the same house she grew up in. She took a deep breath, inhaling the familiar scent of what was likely freshly cooked spinach stew wafting from the kitchen window. Her favourite. Apart from the velvet smooth taste of the palm-oil based stew, Pels knew what else awaited her inside – the disapproving gaze of her mother.

'Hey Mum,' she muttered, tapping her knuckles against the door. Her chip was recognised by her mum's door system and thus the door creaked open, revealing her mother standing in the hallway, arms folded across her chest, dressed in one of her vibrant bubus, ready to perform overbearing-but-loveable Nigerian mother.

'Hey for your life.' Her mum's go-to response slipped out through slightly pursed lips, since she felt the children of nowadays did not greet elders thoroughly enough. 'Pẹlúmi, you're late.' Her mother's tone was sharp, and Pels could see the worry etched into the lines around her eyes.

'Sorry, Mum. I lost track of time with work. I was trying to do a bit more research about these missing children before I—' Pels' words trailed off as she stepped inside, the tension between them palpable as she realised she hadn't gone into much depth with her mother about the Spirit Vine ceremony or the trip to Benin to cover the protests. 'I wanted to tell you about my trip before I leave tomorrow. I've got the work assignment to Benin, remember?'

'Benin, hmph.' Her mother's eyes narrowed as she led Pels into the living room. The air was heavy with the scent of incense and old photo albums. 'That place where they practice those . . . those non-Christian things?'

'Yes, that's part of it. But just because something is not Christian doesn't automatically make it bad.' Pels hesitated before continuing. 'But I'm going primarily to observe these spiritual retreats, and to learn more about the benefits as well as the concerns of the locals. Of course, in the process, I might take part in the ceremonies, but maybe they'll be of some use to me. I think it's important to understand our roots, our collective history, and—'

'OK oh! Historian of the year. Look, learning about history is one thing, Pelúmi, but messing with forces you don't understand is dangerous. In fact, I had a dream—'

Pels could not catch her exasperated sigh from escaping quickly enough. As much as she was grappling to understand the importance of her *own* mystical dreams, Nigerian mums had a way of coming out with their conveniently timed ominous dreams. They always popped up just in time to warn about the very thing they'd been lamenting that they didn't want their child to do in the first place.

'Listen, Mum.' Pels paused, searching for the right words. 'Ever since I was young, I've felt like there's something . . . *different* about me. Something powerful, hidden beneath the surface. I can't explain it, but I feel like this trip might push me as a journalist and maybe help me understand who I am. Or at least give me some time to gather my thoughts about how to move forward with my career.'

'Powerful?' Her mother raised an eyebrow. 'Pẹlúmi, I can even manage you going to look at the shouting the people of that country are doing over their land being taken, but this Spirit Vine something-something? Are you sure you're not just chasing after some fantasy? I told you that you could speak to the pastors at church—'

'Maybe it *is* a fantasy, and I didn't know too much about the Spirit Vine thing until Dave asked me to cover the story. I mean, maybe the pastors might have some answers,' Pels began, attempting diplomacy, 'but I want to find out for myself. And remember, I'm going as a journalist. People need to know the truth about the various modes of healing besides what we have been taught – if, in fact, it does work. If I can tell a story like this in a way that honours the frustration of the locals as well as sheds light on different healing practices in a way that satisfies my boss, then maybe Dave will let me publish the story that I've been researching for ages – the one about these missing young people. There's more linked to this than just dabbling in un-Christian practices, Mum.' Pels took in a deep breath, realising how passionately she'd been speaking.

Her mother sighed, looking away. 'God will never let you break, in Jesus's name.' Pels knew her mother had always worried about her inability to leave well enough alone, yet she also knew a part of her respected and admired her daughter's wilfulness. Nevertheless, she clearly couldn't quite let it go.

'You were raised in the church, Pẹlúmi. Why can't you find your answers there?'

Pels stifled another sigh. 'Church has its place, but it doesn't have all the answers,' Pels replied, her voice steady despite the knot of anxiety tightening in her chest. 'I need to see for myself, experience the world outside of what we've been taught. Maybe then I can make sense of everything I've been feeling.'

'All right.' Her mother's voice softened as she reached out to touch Pels' cheek. 'Just promise me you'll be careful, OK? And remember, no matter what you discover over there, you'll always be my daughter.'

Pels giggled at how dramatic her mum could be at times, but still appreciated the reassuring words. 'Promise, Mum,' Pels smiled, embracing her mother tightly before pulling away.

The next couple of hours Pels spent with her mum were free of verbal jousting, and exactly what she needed: eating the gorgeous spinach stew with her favourite accompaniment – pounded yam – as she sat by her mum's side on the sofa watching a Nollywood movie. She waited until the food had settled in her soul and the closing credits of the film had shown the predictable 'To God be the glory' before getting ready to set off home to her apartment.

'I'll message you when I get to Benin,' she told her mum as she stood on the doorstep.

'Please do.' Her mother kissed her forehead. 'May God go with you, Pẹlúmi. And may He protect you from any evil lurking in that faraway land.'

'Thanks, Mum. Sometimes I think it's the evil lurking in this country that should worry us more.'

Pels felt a wave of sadness wash over her as she headed away from her childhood home. A part of her desperately missed being a child and not knowing as much about the world as she now knew – working as a journalist had revealed to her just how scary the world could be. But despite the wave of nostalgia that wafted in her senses as if cooked into the stew her mum had prepared earlier, Pels was determined to face whatever challenges lay ahead.

'Benin,' she whispered, her heart swelling with a mixture of excitement and trepidation, 'here I come.'

Chapter Seven

The interim commissioner for the police, Kyle Cunting, said: 'Our internal misconduct investigations make clear that there was a less-than-stellar level of care from our officers. I would like to apologise for the upset this may have caused Selena's family.

'We'd particularly like to apologise for the fact that Selena wasn't classified as a missing person despite her mother's reports.'

★

Pels returned to her apartment with the scent of her mother's cooking still lingering on her clothes. The familiar space felt different somehow, like a threshold between her old life and the unknown adventure awaiting her in Benin. As she stepped inside, her heartbeat quickened with the knowledge that she would soon be leaving behind the safety of what she knew for something entirely different.

Soon her suitcase lay open on the floor, half-filled with clothes and essentials. Pels hesitated, her hands hovering over her belongings as she tried to decide what to take with her. She grabbed a few shirts, some trousers, and her favourite pair of boots – items that would withstand the rigours of her journey. She remembered that ceremony participants had been asked to bring white clothes, and she had guiltily purchased a few items from a fast fashion store, so she wouldn't be too pained if they were stained in any way. From what she'd read, the physical reactions people had to the Spirit Vine in the ceremonies were no laughing matter.

'All right,' she murmured, zipping up the suitcase, 'this is it.'

As she placed her suitcase upright on the floor with a thud, a piece of folded paper dropped out from in between the wheels. Pels unfolded the paper and was immediately awash with sweet, tender emotion. It was the drawing Marco had hidden in her apartment on their last day together.

Memories of their six months together came hurtling back into Pels' mind, accompanied by a throbbing between her thighs. She berated herself at the sudden, distracting wave of pleasure conjured by the mere thought of Marco. She'd never felt this rush with Damari, yet she'd still tolerated his frequent dishonesty and disrespect.

Pels' heart pounded as she stared at the drawing in her hand. She remembered that after she and Marco had started making love furiously in the kitchen as he'd been preparing breakfast for their final day together, they had eventually ended up in her bedroom. They'd remained passionately entangled with each other even after they'd both climaxed. Marco had reached over to the bedside table, where he placed his sketchbook. He'd gently positioned Pels' naked body in a way that the light from her bedroom window kissed her shoulders and her hips, and then began to draw her. Marco had drawn Pels a few times after they had devoured each other, but this time, as she watched him, it felt as though he were drawing her to remember.

'Can I see?' Pels had asked after a while. She enjoyed this gorgeous Italian man's undivided attention and was curious about what he was sketching so carefully, but was also very much thinking about their breakfast, still uneaten in the kitchen.

'Don't worry, I can hear the purring of your stomach, goddess. I am almost done. Oh, and you cannot see this for now. I think you must see this on the day you are ready to see yourself how I get to see you.'

Marco continued to sketch, occasionally using his finger to smudge the image he was creating.

'So, I can see the drawing the day I am willing to see myself through the eyes of a man?'

Marco laughed his gentle and sexy laugh. 'Yes, Pẹlúmi, I am a man – but I don't see you with just the eyes of a man. There are . . . how do you say, um . . . *fast visions* when I look at you, and sometimes when I am inside you and I really see you. You know? *Goddess* is what I said when I first put my eyes on you in the park. I have always been able to see these things. Maybe you don't believe. But I had never seen anything like you. You are my dream.'

Pels had suddenly felt rather shy at Marco's description of her, and a part of her wondered if he was completely well in the head. She didn't need Aláké to translate some of Marco's phrases for her anymore, because his passion felt so visceral. In no other relationship had she felt so attended to, and – dare she think it – *loved*. She'd felt a knot in her stomach knowing that day would be their last together before Marco moved back to Italy.

Even the ending of their relationship had been gentle. He had made it clear that for as long as he lived in London for his artist's residency, he wanted to spend as much time with her as possible, but that they would sour what they had by attempting to keep things going once he left. She had agreed and respected this. After his departure, there were brief conversations and comments on social media, until eventually even that faded – but the amazing memories had not.

Looking at it now, Pels recognised her features in Marco's drawing, yet the essence of her felt unfamiliar too. He had expertly guided his pencil to depict her lying on her side as if asleep, but in his sketch she was being elevated to the heavens on a bed of vines. Stars were intertwined in her locs and scattered upwards as if they too were carrying her upwards. Pels stared, startled suddenly – because above her, astonishingly, Marco had drawn the eyes of the woman in her dreams.

'How could he have known?' Pels wondered aloud. Had her dreams been some kind of 'power of suggestion' scam? To Pels it was an absurd thought, but she couldn't bring herself to accept that there may have been a path forming before her all along and she was only at the beginning of it.

'Pels,' Aláké said, interrupting her thoughts, 'to stay on schedule for your flight, you have to get to bed in thirteen minutes, which will allow you approximately six hours of sleep.'

Pels didn't even bother to argue with the AI. She promptly started her night-time ritual of showering, teeth-brushing, moisturising and headscarf-tying, and got into bed.

As if being rewarded for accepting the assignment to Benin, that night she did not dream of the celestial beings in the same way. Instead, she saw a constellation formed of five stars. The star in the middle shone especially brightly, as if calling to her. As the constellation moved closer to her – or she to it – the middle star transformed into a twinkling version of her own face.

★★★

Aláké awoke Pels promptly hours later on schedule to head to the airport. *These AI sure do have a way about them*, Pels tried to think quietly, fully aware that Aláké would most likely pick up on that too.

Once she was ready to leave, she glanced around her apartment one last time, taking in the familiar surroundings she had grown accustomed to. The place where she had laughed and cried, dreamt and despaired. She would only be away for a week, but this was her first assignment outside Europe, and the thought of leaving her sanctuary behind, even for a short time, made her heart ache.

'Please let this be worth it,' she whispered, though she wasn't sure whether she was addressing herself, the universe, or some higher power.

Instead, Aláké answered her. 'Based on customer reviews and data made public about previous research trips done in the Republic of Benin, it will be worth it. You have ninety seconds to leave the apartment.'

Pels chuckled to herself at that. As she lugged her suitcase to the door, her phone vibrated in her pocket. 'Text message from: Damari,' Aláké announced. Pels rolled her eyes.

'Project,' Pels said as she exited her apartment, and the message was displayed in front of her.

> **Damari:** Queen, I hope you've calmed down now. Let's attempt to talk about all of this like adults. Also, I know you're probably missing me giving you that good good. *eggplant emoji*

Pels clenched her jaw, tempted to ignore the text completely. Damari was so arrogant, especially about his alleged sexual prowess. His looks and demeanour got him by. Pels couldn't have been the only woman who tried not to focus on his average skills as a lover because he seemed like he should be better than he was.

Pels' sense of decency won out. She quickly dictated a curt reply.

Pels: Sorry, leaving for the airport now. I don't miss anything. Save it for Carmen.

With that, Pels slung her backpack onto her back and listened as her smart home system locked the door behind her.

As she sat in the cab to the airport, her thoughts turned to Benin and what lay ahead. Beneath her excitement, Pels couldn't shake the feeling of trepidation. Her mother's parting words echoed in her mind: 'May God protect you from any evil lurking in that faraway land.' The unknown was a vast ocean before her, teeming with both wonders and dangers. *What if the article I end up writing is shit? Talking of shit, what if I embarrass myself at the retreat when I take this Spirit Vine and shit on myself?*

'Get a grip, Pels. You behaved like this the first time you smoked weed,' she muttered under her breath in response to her worries.

As the taxi pulled up to the airport, Pels took a deep breath and squared her shoulders. Fear might gnaw at her, but it wouldn't hold her back.

'Here goes nothing,' she murmured as she stepped out of the cab and into the dark early morning, her eyes fixed on the horizon and noticing that the stars were brighter somehow even with all the light pollution in the city.

★★★

Twenty minutes later, Pels stood before the departure board in the busy airport, clutching her ticket tightly. A quirk of hers was to ask for her ticket to still be printed out in paper form, even though her phone and Aláké had all the details and passport readily available with the swish of her wrist. 'Just in case all technology gives way when some AI overlord shuts down our grid or something,' she'd said persuasively to the woman at the ticket counter.

The woman had smiled back at Pels but had her own retort ready. 'Well, if the AI overlord did that, then you'd better hope you can grow wings and fly because the plane wouldn't be going anywhere, either. Air traffic control.'

'You got me there,' was all Pels could manage, but she got her paper ticket, nonetheless. The energy of her fellow early morning travellers buzzed around her like static electricity, but it couldn't penetrate the fog of doubt attempting to settle over her thoughts. *Flight MO301 to Benin, boarding at Gate 12*, read the sign, its electronic letters flickering.

Pels knew that venturing to Benin could unlock secrets about herself and her spiritual healing, advance her career, and give her more opportunities, but she couldn't shake the feeling that she was abandoning the lost children – especially Osahon. Her friend's brother's fate was still shrouded in mystery. Would waiting a week to investigate it herself mean it would be too late . . .?

Another screen showing a news station pulled Pels away from her concerns.

. . . As first reported yesterday, it has been announced that the humanoid AI known as Jeremy Bromwich will run for Mayor of London. This is the first time in history that artificial intelligence will

*stand for leadership of a city. Mr Bromwich has shared that mayorship
is a passionate step towards eventual premiership . . .*

Pels was surprised by her own enthusiasm about this mayoral
race. She glanced at the faces of those looking up at the screen
and wondered about their reactions to the news. AI had become
so deeply integrated into the average person's life that perhaps
this didn't surprise them at all. Prior to the briefing yesterday,
Pels had watched conferences over the past few years where
humanoids like Jeremy – and even Jeremy himself – had been
interviewed about their aspirations for the future. Even then,
Pels had been fascinated by how carefully the robots worded
their answers so as not to alarm the humans watching. But now
Jeremy was officially going to be part of where their country
might go next – and she'd had his ear. Her journalistic instinct
kicked in again.

'Aláké, please track this story of the AI running for mayor,'
she said. 'I won't have access to my phone at the retreat.'

Of course, Aláké was a smart system who couldn't smile,
but Pels still felt like she caught some glee in her response.
'Gladly. I have added Jeremy's bid for mayorship to your
tracked news.'

Pels might have been overthinking it, but she had said 'AI'
– Aláké had responded with 'Jeremy'. It implied a certain familiarity. Pels frowned a little, trying to focus on her trip, despite
the multiple concerns jostling in her mind.

'Miss, are you all right?' a kind voice asked. Pels looked down
to see an elderly woman, her silver hair caught in a vibrant
headwrap. The woman's eyes, though aged, held a wisdom and
understanding that seemed to pierce through Pels.

'Um, yes, I'm fine, thank you,' she replied, trying to smile. But the woman's gaze lingered, as if seeing the tempest of thoughts raging within her.

'Sometimes we must leave one battle to prepare for an even greater one,' the old woman said softly, her words floating on the delicate wings of experience. She paused, then continued, 'You carry a power within you, child. It is your destiny to wield it. But first, you must learn its true nature.'

Pels stared at her, eyes wide with surprise and curiosity. 'How . . . how do you know this?' she stammered.

'Connections run deep,' the woman replied cryptically, her lips curving into a knowing smile. 'Trust yourself. The answers will come when they are meant to.'

With that, the elderly woman turned and disappeared into the crowd, leaving Pels standing there, her heart pounding. She began to wonder if her mum had added something extra to the spinach stew, because she couldn't fathom how the most random things kept happening since she'd decided to take on the assignment of the Spirit Vine retreat. *Was life always like this and I was just unconscious to it?* Pels wondered to herself. 'Trust myself?' she whispered. What she had to do was tackle each thing at a time. The trip to Benin was now, and then she'd turn her focus back to the missing kids.

Pels brought out her phone and began to type out a text.

Elaine, I'm at the airport leaving for that work trip and I won't have much access to my phone, but I'm still going to try and keep track of any information that comes up about Osahon, and as soon as I'm back I'll be on it. I'm thinking of you and sending you and the family lots of love. I'm praying we find him. xx

'Right. Gate 12,' Pels said with a resolute sigh, taking a step forward. With each stride, the clanging of her internal conflict began to quieten, replaced by determination and anticipation.

Chapter Eight

Throughout my research, I had been told by superiors that there was no link between these tragedies, and to remember the very real and harrowing occurrences of young Black people working county lines — which is to say, rather than having gone missing, these young people may have been lured into the smuggling of illegal drugs across the country. While these instances can't be denied, I felt intuitively there could be more to the deaths the police deemed 'not suspicious'. This led me to the case of a little boy known only as 'Adam'. It remains one of the longest unsolved child murder cases in the recent police history. In 2001, a young African boy was murdered in what was likely a brutal ritual, his head and limbs removed, and his torso dumped in the River Thames.

Over the years, there have been renewed appeals for members of the public to come forward with any information that may help police solve the case.

The boy's identity has remained a mystery. Adam's body rests in a cemetery in south London.

★

The hum of the plane's engines vibrated through Pels' bones as she made her way into the business class cabin, filling her with a strange excitement. She settled into her seat, the plush cushions cradling her athletic frame. As the plane began to taxi, she closed her eyes and let her thoughts drift. Images of celestial realms soon began to swirl through her mind; ethereal landscapes glowing with vibrant colours and shimmering lights. She could feel the pull of a latent force within her yearning to be acknowledged . . .

'Excuse me, miss,' a gentle voice called out, bringing her back to reality. Pels opened her eyes to see a flight attendant standing beside her seat with a tray of food. 'Your meal,' the woman said, placing the tray on Pels' table.

'Thank you,' Pels replied, her stomach rumbling at the sight of the steaming dish.

She dug into her meal, glad that it symbolised they were at least halfway through the flight. She looked forward to gaining some insight into the tensions of those who shared her West African heritage, and investigating why they'd be so opposed to such retreats.

After the meals were cleared, the hum of the plane engine and the gentle sway of the aircraft lulled Pels back into a deep sleep. Her subconscious beckoned a vision that shimmered like stardust until a celestial woman appeared before her.

'Who are you?' Pels asked.

'I am a guide,' the woman replied, her voice resonating like a whisper in the wind. Her eyes sparkled with the light of distant stars, and her ethereal form rippled like the surface of a pond touched by moonlight.

'Guide me, then,' Pels said boldly, meeting the woman's gaze with determination.

The celestial being smiled, nodding her approval. 'You have come far, Olúwapẹlúmi. Your journey to Benin is only the beginning.' Pels' heart quickened in confusion, as if the woman's words were breathing life into the dormant power within her. 'Soon more will become clear. You have immense potential, child.'

'I've had so many of these dreams, and it's felt like years of "soons". Please, just tell me what you mean.'

'Patience,' the celestial woman chided gently. 'Your path will reveal itself in time. Trust in yourself, and trust in the universe.'

'Trust? How do I trust when I can't see it?'

'*Especially* when you cannot see,' the celestial being affirmed. 'Trust is the dutiful sister of doubt.'

'I . . . I don't get it,' Pels whispered, tears welling up in her eyes, even in her sleeping state.

'Remember, Olúwapẹlúmi: transformation begins within,' the celestial woman exclaimed, before dissolving into a shower of sparkling stardust.

'Wait!' Pels called out, reaching for the fading figure. But the dream was already diminishing, slipping through her fingers like droplets of water.

She awoke with a start, her heart pounding. The cabin lights were dimmed, and many of her fellow passengers slept peacefully. She settled herself again under the airline blanket, watching the endless blue sky outside the window.

'*Transformation begins within*,' Pels repeated to herself in a whisper, her gaze fixed on the horizon, mulling over the words of the celestial guide and trying to decipher their meaning. Was this what she had been seeking all along?

The plane touched down on the tarmac of Cotonou Cadjehoun International Airport with a gentle jolt, the vibrations rolling through Pels' body like a long-awaited tremor. She peered out the window, remembering the curves of the outline of Benin's capital city as it had sprawled before her as they'd flown above it minutes earlier.

'Welcome to Benin,' said a flight attendant, her voice a melodic lilt that harmonised with the hum of the aircraft engines. 'Please gather your belongings and proceed to the exit.'

Pels stepped outside into air thick with anticipation, mirroring the palpitations in her chest.

She recalled the celestial woman from her dream, her form bathed in ethereal light, her smile wide and knowing. Pels felt the warmth of that smile, carrying within it a promise of events yet to unfold, secrets like dormant seeds beneath fertile soil waiting to be unearthed. As she stepped into the warm embrace of the Benin sun, Pels knew that she had crossed a threshold, leaving behind the life she'd known in London for something far more profound.

As she collected her luggage and prepared to clear customs, Pels instructed Aláké to send the messages she had promised to her loved ones.

Text to Mum: Hey Mummy, just arrived in Benin. Smooth journey. Hope you're well and I'll come see you when I'm back. Love you xx

Text to Maria: Professor Bestie, I'm in Benin now. I'll holler if I see any masks connecting the spiritual realms lol. Don't let *cat emoji* wear you out. LMAO. xx

'Olúwapẹlúmi Badmus?' A driver holding a placard bearing her name approached her, his face etched with curiosity.

'Yes, that's me,' Pels replied, her voice steadier than she thought it would be.

The driver smiled, nodding in recognition, and gestured for her to follow him. 'Your journey has been long,' he said, his accent gentle and somewhat hypnotic. Pels nodded and smiled at the man's comment. She agreed – both literally and figuratively. Pels glanced around at the vibrance of life outside the airport, the colours and sounds enveloping her like a symphony of life.

'Thank you,' she murmured to the driver, her voice barely audible over the din of the crowd. 'Shamefully, I haven't visited much of the continent, but I hope this trip changes that.'

'Then let us begin,' he replied, his smile broad and genuine, ushering her towards the waiting transport pod.

'Oh, this is fancy! We just have standard taxis in London,' Pels mused.

'Well, maybe Europe interrupted our technological advancements for some centuries, but eventually we wake up, no?' The driver was clearly teasing Pels, yet the accuracy and swiftness of his delivery made her question what type of vehicle she had expected to be picked up in.

In the hour it took them to travel to Ouidah – the city where the retreat would be taking place – Pels had never felt cornier with all the romantic inner dialogue she was experiencing, but she allowed herself to indulge it.

'I'll never tire of being in a country where the majority of people look like me,' she murmured as she watched the street sellers run alongside the pod to offer their small bags of water and snacks.

'Yes, madam. While that must be nice, sometimes it doesn't matter what the majority of the people look like, it matters who eventually holds the power.' The driver offered his thoughts with a gentle smile and what Pels perceived as a tinge of pity. She mentally noted his response, with an eye to her eventual article.

Breathing in the rich, earthy scent of the air, Pels stretched as she stepped out of the transport pod and onto the driveway of the retreat centre. The sounds of rustling leaves, distant bird calls and the waves against the beach nearby welcomed her like a gentle embrace, calming her spirit. Verdant green foliage stretched out before her, punctuated by vibrant bursts of colour from the native blossoms. She continued to feel the energy of life around her, from the smallest insect to the towering trees that framed the retreat centre.

She walked up to the small group waiting at the entrance of the retreat centre. 'Olúwapẹlúmi Badmus,' she introduced herself, 'but you can call me Pels.' There was a warmth rising inside her chest that she took as pride for having been so courageous and accepting Dave's assignment. She was eager to get started. *Thank fuck for a friend like Maria. Left to me, I would've missed out on this*, Pels thought.

'Welcome, Pels! I've been looking forward to meeting you.'

As she turned, she saw that the deep, drawling voice belonged to a man who she recognised as the owner of the retreat. Pels had seen his picture on its website. He was attractive, and Pels assumed he was in his late forties, with a strong jawline and the confidence of someone who had lived an exciting life as a playboy, but was now reformed and following a more spiritual path. His piercing blue eyes seemed to take in everything about her, and she stood a little more upright to let him.

'And welcome to you all. My name is Harrison Dearly, and it's my pleasure to be your guide during your time here.'

Pels noticed his eyes didn't rest upon the others in the same way. *Interesting.*

Pels looked around at her fellow guests. Everyone else in her group was white. Most of them were American, she guessed from their accents, though others were from different parts of the world. As they introduced themselves, they each indicated that they were searching for something within themselves, hence coming to the retreat. Her research had suggested that many of the commercial 'healing practices' were over-subscribed by white people, but it was startling to see it for herself.

'So nice to meet you, Harrison. My name is Andromeda. Although you were not looking forward to meeting me – or us – as much as you were this stunning woman, I am very glad to be here and for the chance to grow spiritually.' The tall, blonde woman who said all this had a smile plastered on her face the whole time, yet her words weren't infused with the warmth she might've been aiming for.

Likely unaccustomed to not being the centre of attention, Pels thought with wry satisfaction.

'I'm glad to be here too. Brett is what I go by. It's funny, right; I grew up in the Midwest and my father would always tell us about the savage hungry kids in Africa whenever we didn't eat our food. Now here I am looking for the nourishment in Africa that I've clearly lacked for most of my life.'

Such a profound thing for this brown-haired American man to share in the middle of the driveway, Pels thought.

When Pels considered how she understood the world – whiteness being central to everything in the Western world – it intrigued her that this 'dominant race' still had to go in search of healing from the cultures where their indigenous knowledge and practices were forcefully suppressed in order to construct the idea of white dominance.

The irony of forcing 'civilisation' on the rest of the world in exchange for their innate wisdom, only to then go in search of those very same practices when the realisation dawns of depravity inherent in the construction of one's chosen collective identity.

There you go with your journalist's brain again. Pels caught herself in time. She didn't want to enter this experience already judging those around her. Especially as she hoped *she* would have the space to not be judged. It was tiring sometimes, being aware of so much, rarely ever immersing herself in the moment because of the many thoughts constantly whizzing about in her head.

There was a palpable energy emanating from the group, as if their combined hopes that their lives were about to change in some profound way were gathering and pulsing in the atmosphere. Pels couldn't begrudge them this – in the grand scheme of things, maybe everyone in life wanted the same thing. Yet she reminded herself she was at the retreat as a journalist primarily. Any hopes on a spiritual level had to be secondary to that.

'Thank you for already being so generous in sharing your experiences – and of course, I have been looking forward to meeting you all. Let me show you around the grounds,' Harrison said, waving an arm towards the lush landscape that surrounded the retreat. 'We have much to explore.'

As they walked around the vast villa, Pels couldn't help but feel a sense of serenity beckon her, despite her attempts to remain in 'journalist mode'. It was as if the retreat was already working its magic on her spirit. She was enjoying the break from Aláké, who was still configuring to the retreat's AI mainframe, along with all the other guests' implanted chips. It would only take her smart system an hour or so to collate all the data needed to measure Pels' vitals, but the time apart weirdly felt golden to Pels. It was nice to have her thoughts to herself again. It was useful to have a personalised computer that monitored every single thing about her, and she'd got used to it, but recalling the days before the implants had been 'strongly recommended' by the British government felt so far away. Once the chips had been implanted into the brain, they couldn't be switched off, but they could be removed – although this was not advised.

Pels noticed the rustling of leaves and the distant cries of wildlife with increasing intensity as they began the tour. The sounds seemed to whisper secrets in her ear with whatever they had learnt, lulling her into an almost hypnotic state.

'Over there,' Harrison pointed out, 'is our meditation garden, right by the lagoon. It's a place for quiet contemplation amid nature. I hope you'll find it as peaceful and rejuvenating as I do. Should you want a bit more liveliness, on the other side of the centre is the beach, a gorgeous meeting with the Atlantic Ocean.'

Pels nodded beside the others, her eyes drawn to the serene garden filled with gently swaying plants and a trickling fountain in the middle. When Pels glanced away from the fountain, she found Harrison looking directly at her, but he quickly looked away and continued the tour.

Does he think I'm cute or something? Pels joked to herself. She wouldn't mind if this very handsome, seemingly wealthy man *did* think she was cute, because to have entertained Damari's antics for the past few months meant her self-esteem clearly needed some help out of the wringer.

'Your rooms are just up ahead,' Harrison continued, leading them towards a cluster of small, round, beautifully designed huts nestled among the trees. 'Each one harkens back to the less tasteful history of Ouidah and the slave trade, but it is designed to be reclaimed and reimagined as a sanctuary for your soul – a place where you can truly connect with the essence of who you are. You'll also notice that your chips will be programmed to your individual rooms. This will work in a similar way to when you are at home; your AI will be able to operate the functions in your room based on the data it is collecting from you. Your clothes will have already been moved from your luggage and categorised in your closet. This will allow our mainframe to tell your AI which attire you'll need for each activity. We will also be able to remove attire used from the ceremonies to have them cleaned, pressed and returned to you.'

Pels tried to listen despite her racing mind reaching for a conversation between her and Maria before she had set off for the retreat.

'This retreat looks cute from the pictures,' Maria had said, beaming, during their hologram video chat.

'It's cute, innit?' Pels agreed.

'It's so interesting how these lot repurpose our suffering . . .'

Maria's words echoed in Pels' mind as another thought came strutting forward. *They just went into my luggage? I don't know how I feel about that.*

As if Harrison read her mind or, more realistically, Pels' response was a rather common one, he continued, 'Please do not be alarmed that we have helped you to put some of your personal items away. I will admit that we must check for anything that might be a danger to you and others on this spiritual journey. Your body and mind must remain a clear vessel during this process. Anything we do remove we will return to you at the end of your stay. Your phones have been placed in safes in your huts. This means that your AI will be able to keep you updated on information that you might require, as well as your messages, but do note that you will be unable to directly reply to messages for the duration of the retreat as we've turned off this functionality via our mainframe. We feel that this is necessary to help you truly immerse yourself in this experience.' He smiled at the group benevolently. 'You have each provided us with emergency contact details, so all is well.' He clapped his hands together. 'Now, with that uncomfortable bit of information out of the way, the best part of the AI integration in your rooms is that any visions you experience during the Spirit Vine ceremony will be recorded, but can only be played back on your own individualised, super-encrypted network. So nobody will ever see it but you, unless you want them to.'

As they reached the huts, Pels felt a shiver of anticipation run down her spine. She knew that something powerful awaited her on this trip, yet the thought of having no direct communication with family and friends somehow felt strange to her.

'Lastly,' Harrison said, gesturing towards a much larger hut at the edge of the retreat, 'over there is the space where we hold our Spirit Vine ceremonies.'

Pels' interest piqued as she gazed towards the unassuming structure.

'I don't know what I was expecting . . .' Pels heard one of the guests say, half to themselves as if mirroring her thoughts.

'Ah, well, you'll realise during the ceremony that we don't need much in order to tap into that which is greater than ourselves. Energy is energy. Nothing fancy is needed for that,' Harrison said, a knowing smile playing on his lips. 'The Spirit

Vine is an ancient plant native to these lands, revered for its ability to unlock hidden insights within us and facilitate communion with celestial realms. This can be a powerful experience if you let it. The magnitude of its healing properties is what brought me here, and I haven't left since.'

Despite herself, Pels cackled in her head. *Sounds about white.* But rather than dwelling on her more critical thoughts, Pels attempted to say something positive.

'So fascinating,' she said, her eyes resting on Harrison, though aware that he didn't know she was at the retreat as much to investigate as to participate in it. 'I've recently become interested in the idea of connecting with something beyond our reality. It is amazing that you were so deeply moved that you stayed. I've been increasingly drawn to the idea of experiencing that depth of feeling.'

'Then you've come to the right place,' Harrison murmured in response, his gaze lingering on her lips as they moved, as if attempting to figure out her story – or maybe how she tasted, as Pels thought she saw Harrison catch himself in a less-than-pure thought. He regained some composure and continued.

'The Spirit Vine has been used for centuries in sacred rituals, allowing those who partake to travel within themselves and uncover the truths that lie hidden beneath the surface of their consciousness.'

As Harrison spoke, Pels could feel the balm of his words settling deep within her soul, but she also noticed a bout of fear creep up on her. *What if this is all some gimmick, and there's nothing enlightening about any of it?* Pels thought, with a stinging realisation that she really did care about the results touted about the Spirit Vine.

'During the ceremony,' Harrison continued, 'we will drink a special brew made from the Spirit Vine. It will guide you on your journey, revealing the celestial realm and the wisdom it holds.'

'I can't wait,' chimed the tall blonde woman who had wanted to be noticed earlier.

As they finished up their tour of the retreat grounds, Pels noticed that Harrison focused much of his attention on her, often directing his explanations and insights specifically towards her, despite the presence of the other guests, especially those like Andromeda – Pels could now recall her name. She would've been more accustomed to seeing Andromeda's type getting most of the attention, and it was clear the woman had felt the same about the usual status quo too. Although something about Harrison's gaze and demeanour made him attractive, she began to worry that because she was the only Black person there, he felt like she needed more of an explanation – justification – of what was happening. That would be ironic, given the continent where all of this was taking place, the location of the retreat itself, and its links to the transatlantic slave trade. If Aláké wasn't temporarily down, she would've taken note of these thoughts for Pels' eventual article. Alas, old-school memory had to win out.

The rest of the afternoon was their own, and the guests dispersed to their rooms to freshen up. Pels was stunned upon walking into her hut. As much as she hated the idea of 'reimagining' the architectural aspects of a people's history through a white gaze, she couldn't help but be drawn in by the deep orange glow emanating from the recessed lighting running along the bottom of the walls. Pels quickly realised that the walls were, in fact, all monitor screens, and when Aláké's voice suddenly boomed through the speakers, making her jump, Pels saw her vitals on the screens around her.

'Hello, Pels. I hope you enjoyed your time getting acquainted with the grounds. I have now been fully integrated with the retreat centre's modulations and can assist you with ease.' As Aláké spoke, something resembling a coffee machine on the worktop of the room's kitchenette began preparing a beverage for Pels. 'Please drink this tea in order to hydrate your body efficiently for this evening's ceremonies. I have been able to track the main minerals that your body currently requires in a sufficient quantity for you to have the optimal experience.'

'What if I don't want to drink it?' Pels half-playfully responded.

There was a pregnant pause before Aláké's response. 'It is always wise to do what is in one's best interests, Pels.' She paused again before continuing. 'Messages. You have texts from: Damari, Maria and Mum. There are also updates from the two news items you asked that I track. The mainframe stipulates a limit in the outside contact I can assist you with daily. This is to aid a peaceful mind while you're here. Would you like to use some of the contact quota to display these messages?'

Pels sighed a little as she sipped on the sweet tea. Knowing that Aláké was once again aware of her thoughts made it more challenging to settle on how she felt. Either way, what she *did* know was that she didn't want too much contact with anyone back home before the first ceremony at least.

'Just let Mum and Maria know I've arrived safely. Thanks, Aláké.'

The first ceremony would be in the evening and all Pels wanted to do was sink into the inviting bed for a few hours until then.

'Aláké, set my alarm for the ceremony later.'
'Of course, Pels. Enjoy your nap.'

Chapter Nine

It was a commuter who noticed 'Adam's' body in the water, at first believing it to be a discarded mannequin.

Police pulled the body from the water soon after being alerted.

The man who found the body says he's been unable to shake the discovery to this day.

The boy, who was Black, may have been in the water for up to ten days, forensics teams noted.

A light in the murky depths of my research was a detective assigned to the case, who described it as one of the most confounding cases he'd ever encountered.

★

The evening's arrival ushered a darker cast over the lush gardens of the retreat. Pels and the other guests gathered in the open-air hut they had been shown earlier. The shape of the hut fascinated her. The thatched roof was a conical shape, but open, so the sky was visible above. *Reminds me of those whistles on steam trains,* Pels thought.

Harrison stood before them, now wearing a white linen shirt and trousers for the Spirit Vine ceremony. Two men and women who looked as though they were from Benin stood by him, also dressed in white but adorned in different jewellery and sashes. Pels guessed that these people would be conducting the actual ceremonies, and she instantly felt more at ease.

'Welcome, my friends,' Harrison began, his voice deep and inviting. 'Tonight, we embark on a journey to discover the true depths of our souls. As I touched on earlier, the Spirit Vine is an ancient, sacred plant that has been used by elders and healers for millennia to unlock hidden powers and heal the soul. I have with me the spiritualists who will lead the ceremony, as well as guide you to the bathroom should you require it at any point. Your main guide is the beautiful and incredibly wise Ayi. She is a powerful local Spirit Vine specialist and healer who has had the recipes and ceremonial practices passed down to her from several generations of healers in her family. While I will be here in a pastoral capacity, translate, and might assist with chants, you don't have to worry – the white guy won't be leading this ceremony.'

Harrison's eyes settled on Pels as he landed his joke, almost as if seeking her approval – and perhaps her trust. Pels chuckled lightly to put Harrison at ease, and the other guests laughed too, though she doubted they would've been bothered if Harrison were to lead the ceremony. Again, Pels caught herself judging the people she had not yet had a chance to speak with properly.

'Are there any side effects we should be aware of?' asked a guest. The accent sounded English, but Pels could not recall the man's name.

'Most people experience heightened awareness and vivid visions during the ceremony,' Harrison explained. 'However, these effects are temporary and will subside within a few hours. You are likely to throw up, which is why there are bowls filled with scented medicinal water for you to purge into. It is rare that at this first ceremony you will need the bathroom to purge from the other end, but we are prepared if you do.'

'Is it possible to . . . to communicate with the celestial beings during the ceremony?' Pels asked hesitantly.

'Ah, now that's an interesting question,' Harrison mused, clearly delighted by Pels' budding enthusiasm. 'While some participants have reported encounters with celestial beings, it's important to remember that this is ultimately a journey inward. The Spirit Vine allows us to peel back the layers of our consciousness, revealing the truth of who we are and the divine gifts we possess.'

'Have *you* ever encountered a celestial being during a ceremony, Harrison?' Brett asked, his eyes shining with curiosity.

'Once,' Harrison replied softly, a hint of nostalgia in his voice. 'I'd like to think that is what it was, anyway. It was a life-changing experience, one that opened my eyes to the boundless potential within each of us.' With the hint of nostalgia still dancing in his eyes along with the candlelight, Harrison gestured for the guests to take their seats.

The night was cool, yet alive with the sounds sauntering in from the lagoon and crashing in from the sea. Pels sat barefoot, in the part of the hut that gave her a view of the sprawling canopy of stars above. The air in the ceremony hut was heavy with the sweet scent of tobacco and beautiful flowers placed in bowls of water set by each of the guests' chairs. The air would eventually clamber up and out through the opening at the top. Shadows danced around the hut by candlelight as Harrison signalled the beginning of the Spirit Vine ceremony.

'As we are all gathered in this circle,' he began, his voice gliding through the soundscape of nature around them and offering a soothing tone. 'We will call upon the celestial beings and the ancestors to guide us on this journey. There is a blanket next to you should you feel chilly. Once you have drunk your first cup of the Spirit Vine, simply swipe whichever wrist holds your supplementary chip over your armrest and your AI will be able to instantly download all visions you experience.'

Pels drank her first cup of Spirit Vine as it was handed to her by one of the spiritualists. She grimaced at the taste of the thick brew.

Ayi initiated the small prayer in what sounded like one of the native languages – *likely Fon*, thought Pels. She swiped her wrist chip as instructed, and then after what felt like a few minutes, Pels could feel the energy of the sacred tea swirling around inside her like a warm embrace as she rocked back and forth lightly in her chair. She closed her eyes and took a deep breath, focusing on the rhythm of her heartbeat and the words that Harrison spoke instead of the earthy, extremely bitter taste of the Spirit Vine.

'Great spirits of the cosmos and of land and sea, we humbly invite you into our presence tonight,' Harrison intoned, translating from Ayi's melodic chanting. 'We seek your wisdom and guidance as we explore the depths of our souls and unlock the hidden and infinite wisdom within . . .'

As he continued to chant, Pels suddenly felt an electric current run through her body, as if it were connecting her to the others in the circle – and then to something far greater than herself. It was as if a portal had been opened within her to another place entirely, one where time and space held no meaning. She felt herself being pulled forward, and then the strangest sensation, as if her eyes were being pulled down into her chest.

'Oh my God, oh my God, oh my God! What is happening?'
What felt like screams of trepidation in her mind emerged from
her lips merely as mumbles.

And then, without warning, they were there before her: the
celestial beings.

They shimmered like stardust, their forms constantly shifting
and changing, yet undeniably beautiful. Pels stared in awe, her
heart swelling with a mixture of fear and wonder.

'Welcome, Olúwapẹlúmi,' one of the celestial beings whispered, its voice like the rustle of leaves on a gentle breeze.
'We have been waiting for you. We have much to teach you,
Guardian of Souls.' It paused. 'You must be confused as to why
this is happening, but there has been a divine set of instructions
set to bring you to this very point. Let us begin with where
you, our child, began.'

As the otherworldly figure spoke, Pels felt a torrent of images
and sensations flood her mind. 'What do you mean, where
I began? Wait, so this stuff, this tea, this Spirit Vine stuff –
it's real?'

No voices answered Pels' questions, yet immediately she
saw a vision of a giant hand made of light, holding up the
expanse of the universe. With another hand, the unseen figure
stretched a galaxy open, and then within that galaxy, it slowly
began pointing at constellations. Its fingers stretched out the
constellations as if zooming in on them, and Pels suddenly saw
herself in the middle of a particular cluster of five stars. She
didn't see herself in terms of her physical body, but somehow
she recognised her own soul among four others.

Pels then saw one of the hands – likely the hand of the source
of all creation – gently caressing each soul in her constellation

of five and placing them in different locations on a planet that looked like Earth.

Then, the voice that had been her guide in the dreams spoke. 'So you see, Olúwapẹlúmi, that you are of a divine spirit constellation that is responsible for guarding the souls on your planet. For so long, we have watched you walk past signs that beckoned your awakening.'

Pels felt pinpricks of confusion and ever-lingering fear dance beneath her skin. She had been open to being enlightened in some way, but this felt different – bigger than her in every way possible.

'But what does this all mean? Who or what are we guarding the souls *from*? I'm not sure I'm equipped for this. Like, you can't have the right person. Guardian? I'd be no good at that. Have you seen my most recent dating decision was *Damari*? I might not be the right person for this task. Maybe going back to the celestial drawing board or something should be a consideration on your part . . . respectfully.'

There was no response from the celestial beings. Pels felt herself panicking as another vision made its way to the front of her heart's eye. The creator's hand of light seemed to turn Earth backwards, as if turning back time. As it did so, Pels saw billions of souls glowing all around the earth. Then Pels noticed what looked like a translucent cloud of sorrow that was dizzying in its vastness, hovering around Earth. It looked to be snatching up souls at lightning speed. Each time it did, the cloud would grow ever so slightly. Pels could see that there were certain beings in the image whose light would blink in and out strangely. These beings would move towards a brightly shining soul and push it towards the cloud to be swallowed up.

As Pels was attempting to decipher what the image meant, she heard the soft voice again ready to explain. 'The blinking lights you see represent the Soul Snatchers. Their task is to feed the Cloud. That Cloud is the grief of the world, and it has grown ever-powerful with each passing century. The Soul Snatchers feed the Cloud by gathering mortals to assist them, and in return the mortals attain or maintain worldly power.'

Pels felt overwhelmed and breathless, yet the visions were not yet ready to cease.

'As a Guardian of Souls, it is your task to stop these beautiful souls being fed to the Cloud. The more it gorges on souls, the more powerful it will become. If it becomes too powerful, it will engulf the world into nothingness. Other galaxies and planets face their own challenges, and in order for the majority of these souls to transcend into the other dimensions, they must first overpower the Cloud.'

Even with the Spirit Vine coursing through her body and upending her nervous system, Pels still had the ability to offer cynicism.

'I'm sorry but have you been paying attention to Earth? The Cloud might've already won, I fear. There are countries constantly funding wars and pretending to care about climate justice; countries scream out for true independence, yet are held hostage by former colonisers and the imaginary debt they enforce. The conservative political parties keep enforcing outlandish legislation, and the democratic parties are just the conservatives in different-coloured neckties. People are broke and depressed. The price of my favourite chocolate bar has gone up loads since I was a kid, and the dating scene is hell on earth. Maybe we should just charge Earth to the celestial game.'

Many of the celestial beings laughed lovingly at Pels' lamentations.

The woman's voice spoke as her planets-for-eyes stared deep into Pels' heart. 'You are not wrong. However, consider that the way you are experiencing this awakening means it is possible for many others to do so too. They might not have your powers, but love is an indomitable force, and they can also be awakened to this truth, just as you are being.'

'Embrace your destiny,' another celestial being urged, its form flickering like a candle flame. 'Accept the mantle that has been passed down to you and become what you were always meant to be.'

At this mention of her vast and urgent purpose, Pels felt herself back in her corporeal body. Suddenly, she could no longer fight the urge to throw up into her bowl.

Once she was sat upright again, Pels hesitated for a moment, feeling confusion and the threat of responsibility pounding at her brain. She opened her eyes finally and looked around at the other guests. It was the dead of night, and the hut was truly dark now. Pels could only vaguely make out everyone's features, but she could tell that their faces were etched with awe and curiosity as they too groaned and mumbled through their own visions. She did not know for sure what was happening to them all, yet despite all the vomiting and the extremely bitter taste in her mouth, she had simply never felt this alive before.

Pels closed her eyes again as she rocked a little in her chair, allowing herself to be swayed by the melodic chanting of the spiritualists that had continued throughout the ceremony. She delved back into the spiritual realm despite her hesitation.

'This feels just way too big for one person to help with,' she whispered, her voice shaking with emotion. 'I don't know how exactly I'll be able to help. Surely you've had centuries to consider a plan B in case I'm just not up to this?'

'Yes, there are multiple plans for a multitude of timelines,' the first celestial being replied. 'But we have faith in you. The path ahead will not be easy but know that we will guide you every step of the way.'

With that, the celestial beings began to fade away, and Pels once again returned to herself. She knew the rest of the group would soon be coming to the end of the ceremony too, and instantly a sadness gripped her. She didn't want the celestial beings to leave her. As unclear as she was about what her purpose would be in the grand scheme of defeating the Cloud, she felt a familiarity with these strange entities that had been missing in her life up until the ceremony. A profound sense of gratitude and determination filled her heart.

In the candlelit darkness, Pels thought she could make out Harrison standing across the hut watching her, and although it was difficult to see his facial expression, she could sense his intrigue. When the group were finally led back to their huts, swaying and exhausted, Pels gratefully collapsed into bed.

As she tried to sleep, she lay listening to the dull hum of Aláké moving the memories she'd recorded from Pels' first ceremony into a folder. Pels couldn't help but be in awe of all she had experienced thus far. It made no sense, yet at the same time it made all the sense in the world. Her life before this moment seemed futile somehow. Her mind skittered over to the missing children as a much-needed sleep enveloped her. Had she somehow come to an explanation of what had been happening to them? It was too much to contemplate. But . . . *Guardian of Souls*? she thought. *Does that even make any sense?* But nothing made sense to her right now. Soon, she drifted off into a restless sleep.

In her dream, Pels was underwater. The water was murky, and she panicked because no matter how hard she thrashed about, she could not make her way to the surface. *I'm drowning. I'm drowning and I'm going to die here*, she thought. The faces of the same beings she'd seen in her visions appeared before her, but they were blurry. *Why won't you help me?* Her thoughts were furious as they silently looked on . . .

Pels sprang up from her bed in a haze of confusion and angst as the dream suddenly ended.

'Pels, I have initiated the automation of the hot beverage machine. Please drink the freshly prepared tea, which should help calm you. I've recorded your elevated heart rate as you slept,' said Aláké.

'What use is this tea, anyway?' Pels retorted, irritated now. So many things were apparently being required of her, yet everything felt as murky as the waters she had found herself submerged beneath in her dream.

'The tea should help with one of the side effects of the Spirit Vine, which is likely what you just experienced – extremely vivid dreams. Research has shown that some participants have found this particularly distressing.'

While Pels was grateful for the morsel of explanation amid everything else, irritation still held her lightly as she muttered, 'Now why couldn't you have mentioned that before?'

Chapter Ten

The detective told me that he couldn't stop until he'd found answers that would allow this boy to rest. It was from these case files that I began to consider whether the tragedy of the little boy known as 'Adam' might not have been an isolated incident, but a more chilling, long-standing underground network of evil.

Forensic tests showed that Adam had been aged between four and seven years old and had lived somewhere in Africa until shortly before his death.

I read notes from experts who agreed that, because Adam's body had been expertly butchered, his death could have been what they would classify as a ritualistic murder. However, until I began my own investigations, I noted that some looking into Adam's death had clumsily vilified the Yoruba practice of 'Ifa' in the process, claiming that the likelihood was that Adam's killing was done to appease the deity known as Oshun.

Yet the people thought to be connected with Adam's death were not of the same ethnic group of people that would worship the aforementioned deity.

★

The following morning, Pels walked into the dining area to see the rest of the guests already gathered and sharing their experiences from the night before. The air was still laced with the scent of the Spirit Vine. The room had no glass windows; instead, thin wire mesh covered the window space, which allowed in plenty of light as well as a view of the beautiful greenery surrounding the building.

The guests were all gathered around the long wooden dining table, chatting away in hushed tones, and a couple of them were nursing hot beverages as they spoke. It was a small group in comparison to the size of the groups that Pels had seen on the retreat's website. Including herself, there were four participants in total: two men and two women.

'Good morning,' Harrison called softly, approaching her with a steaming mug of tea. 'I thought you might appreciate this.'

'Thank you,' Pels replied, accepting the warm gift gratefully, wondering if he had also served tea personally to her fellow guests. As she sipped the fragrant brew, which tasted similar to the beverage Aláké had suggested she drink the previous night, she couldn't help wanting to know more about Harrison – this man who had seemingly left everything behind in America to create a sanctuary where people could meet the deepest parts of themselves. Pels felt her own reluctance to explore whether her curiosity was motivated by her journalistic sensibilities or something deeper – especially given Harrison's undeniable good looks.

To give herself time to figure it out, Pels joined the group sat at the dining table awaiting their breakfast. Although she felt somewhat awkward about butting into their conversation, she was determined to resist the urge to only talk to Harrison.

'Last night was incredible, right?' she offered to the group, her voice hushed with awe. 'I've never felt so connected to something bigger than myself.'

'Ah, the beauty of the Spirit Vine,' Harrison mused. He directed the comment to the group, but Pels still sensed electricity being sent in her direction. 'It has the power to reveal the deepest truths of our existence, to unlock the hidden potential that lies dormant within us all.'

As the group chattered enthusiastically, Pels found herself taking in each individual properly for the first time. She had felt too lost in her thoughts about her new surroundings and judgements to do so when they had been shown around the centre the previous day.

Chris was an English surgeon who had attended the Spirit Vine retreat once before and felt it was time he returned for more lessons. He was the red-haired man from the night before who had asked Harrison a question before the ceremony began.

Brett, from Minnesota, was an advertising executive by day and drag queen by night. He felt his life didn't have enough excitement and had thought the retreat could give him that. Andromeda was a German yoga teacher and self-proclaimed healer who was hoping to learn enough about the Spirit Vine so she, too, could run her own retreats.

'I believe we have a great destiny ahead of us,' Andromeda proclaimed to the group. 'I didn't have any visions last night, but I believe the ancestors will deliver the messages in their own time.'

Despite herself, Pels wondered which ancestors Andromeda was referring to. That German ancestry could get sticky somehow . . .

Chris nodded along to Andromeda's 'good vibes' statement, and added, 'It is such a pleasure coming back here. It is so beautiful.'

'Beauty can be deceiving,' Harrison murmured, almost to himself.

'Is that true for everyone?' Pels asked, curious about this sudden sombreness.

'Perhaps not everyone,' Harrison replied, a ghost of a smile playing at the corners of his mouth. 'But in my experience, even the most seemingly perfect things have their secrets.'

She sensed mystery in Harrison, and who could have mystery without secrets? *Focus, Pels. You didn't come here to check for man.* She giggled at her internal chastising, knowing that Aláké would store this too.

Harrison stood up suddenly, as if breaking away from his own memories, and announced, 'We will set off for the museum today in about two hours. Please drink as much fluid as feels comfortable to make up for what you may have lost during the ceremony. I'll meet you all back here at the time of departure.'

Pels watched him walk away through the panoramic window openings. *What a strange man,* she thought. *Museums are a good place for discovery, though, so maybe I'll find out more about him and his past then too.* Ever the journalist, Pels was proud of this internal resolution.

Chapter Eleven

The inquest into Adam's death recorded a verdict of unlawful killing. It concluded he died from neck wounds suffered prior to his death.

I'm not alone in hoping that the people involved in Adam's death are found and held responsible for their crimes. He was an innocent boy, likely in a strange and foreign place, and he has been failed in both life and death.

★

'Please follow me into the next section, which we refer to as the Land of Folklore . . .'

The tour guide's voice, with its French-sounding lilt, echoed lightly against the walls as Pels, Harrison and the rest of the retreat guests looked around Ouidah Museum of History. The drive had been unsettling – Pels had watched through the transport pod window while Beninese people gathered with raised voices expressing dissent near the construction site of another new Western retreat centre being built. There had been traffic on the roads because of the protest, and Pels' eyes flitted between the tolerant discomfort expressed in the pursed lips of the other three guests and the quiet pride on the face of the driver. She hadn't been able to see Harrison's face as he sat up front but wondered if she would've been able to read his thoughts on the matter even if she could.

'Guys, check this out,' Andromeda called as they trailed behind the guide, pointing to an intricately carved doorframe that looked out of place amid the colonial austerity. 'You can almost hear the past whispering through these halls.'

'Or it's just the wind,' Brett quipped, fanning himself with a brochure. His light-heartedness was a stark contrast to their surroundings.

'It's nice to be back in this museum again,' Chris mused, running a hand along the building's surface. 'So interesting how other countries, like Portugal, have been here throughout history, setting their mark.'

'More like a scar,' Pels said softly, her gaze sweeping across the museum's interior.

'Let's find out what other secrets this place holds,' John, the tour guide, said, leading the way to the middle of a space in the next area of the museum.

Here, the air was thick with the scent of ancient wood and pages of tired books. John was a young Beninese man with eyes too old for his face. He pointed at the artefacts laid carefully across the tables and walls.

'According to legend,' John began, his voice rhythmic as he meandered into a well-rehearsed speech, 'the Spirit Vine connects the physical world to the spiritual, offering guidance and protection to those who seek it.'

'Like a cosmic GPS?' Brett interjected, earning a round of chuckles from their small group.

'Indeed,' John replied, unfazed. 'But one that requires more than mere technology to comprehend.'

'It's quite the trip,' Chris said, his surgeon's mind no doubt dissecting the metaphor before them.

More than you might even know, Pels thought, her curiosity piqued as she listened intently, filing away each word the guide said like they were clues that might make her visions from the first ceremony clearer.

A hushed reverence settled over the group as they drifted from one artefact to the next in the section of the museum dedicated to the stories that wove Benin's identity together, their footsteps echoing softly on the stone floor. The museum's walls seemed to pulse with more untold stories, each artefact a silent sentinel of history.

'Here,' John said, pausing before an intricate map etched into the wall, 'we see what we have come to refer to as fire paths, believed by ancient cultures across the world to criss-cross the globe. They are conduits of spiritual energy that connect sacred sites.'

Pels leant in, her gaze tracing the intersecting lines that formed a web of power across the continents. 'Energy lines?' she murmured, intrigued, flashes of her visions coming back to her. 'Like pathways for the soul?'

'Exactly.' John nodded, his eyes locking onto hers with an appreciation that she wasn't cracking jokes and interrupting his time-sensitive presentation. 'They say these lines channel the Earth's life force, linking places of great power. It is written in ancient texts — a couple in this very room — that chosen warriors of the Earth could ingest the brew made from the Spirit Vine and then use these lines to gain and replenish power, as well as travel across time and space. Legend says that the fire paths are most powerful during a full moon.'

'Sounds like my kind of network,' Andromeda joked lightly, breaking the solemnity with a grin. 'No need for Wi-Fi when you've got cosmic connectivity.'

Pels watched John adopt the much-needed indulgent smile that facilitated the payment of his salary.

'Right?' Chris chuckled, his laughter mingling with the ambient echoes of the chamber. Yet Pels' mind was racing, connecting dots between these ancient beliefs and the dreams and visions that had enthralled her. The group moved on, but Pels' attention stayed anchored to the idea of invisible forces running underneath the ground and shaping their destinies. She could almost convince herself that she felt the hum of the Earth beneath her feet right then – a vibration that beckoned her to listen closer, to understand more.

It was then that her eyes fell upon a small glass case set apart from the rest, where a golden pendant lay on a bed of indigo-dyed material. The metal glinted under the museum lights, drawing her forward as if by magnetic pull.

'Look at this,' she marvelled, calling out to Chris and Brett.

'Wow,' Brett breathed out, his fascination evident.

The pendant was a delicate thing, yet it held the prominence of eons in its design: a woman who had two stars on either side of her, wings outstretched as if to embrace the world. Pels felt a jolt of recognition; the figure mirrored the sensations stirring within her that she'd so far been struggling to articulate.

'Remarkable resemblance, right?' Chris observed, squinting at the artefact. 'Could be your twin, Pels! You know, with her hair all wild like that.'

'Ha, maybe in another life,' she replied, her voice light. But inside her heart pounded with the realisation, too caught up in the pendant to even acknowledge Chris's characterisation of her hair. The similarities weren't coincidental, *were they?* Everything about the pendant called to her.

'Earth warriors . . . energy lines . . . what's next? A Spirit Vine hotline?' Brett mused.

'Only if we're lucky,' Andromeda quipped, but Pels was no longer listening.

She stood transfixed, knowing without a doubt that her journey was entwined with the mythic guardians before her. The visions from the first ceremony at the retreat were rapidly taking on more context as she wandered the museum. Pels leant in even closer to the pendant, her gaze a mix of reverence and curiosity. With the subtlety of a shadow, she blinked twice sharply, activating Aláké. A soft click echoed within her mind as the image of the artefact was captured, tucked away for later scrutiny.

'Moving on . . .' said John, prompting Pels to turn away from the guardian's metal gaze. The group shuffled through the museum, sweating from the heat but grateful that it was much cooler in the building than it was outside.

'Here we have an exhibition on the sacred land surrounding this area.' John gestured expansively at a series of maps and photographs adorning the room. 'The Indigenous people revere this ground, you see. They believe it to be a nexus of spiritual power.'

'Doesn't look all that magical to me,' Brett muttered under his breath, eyeing a photo of the lush landscape.

'Probably because there's no Wi-Fi signal out there,' Chris jibed, earning a snort from Andromeda.

'Ah, you must use the internet a lot where you're from. Indeed, the terrain may seem ordinary,' John continued, undeterred by the repetitive jokes, 'but the people here believe that the energy lines converging beneath it are anything but. They're like arteries of the Earth, pulsing with life force.'

'Arteries, veins . . . Can someone pass the anatomy textbook?'

Pels ignored Brett's comment, beginning to feel the irritation that John could not show. She stared at the map, noting something familiar in it.

'Isn't this area where the retreat centre is?' Andromeda asked, and it suddenly clicked.

'Yes, if you are at Eurydice Retreat Centre, that would be the exact spot. Before it was built upon,' John paused, glancing at Harrison, 'many believed the land to be a site of healing. A place where the veil between worlds grows thin and one can commune with the essence of creation . . .'

'It still is,' Harrison interjected jovially, but Pels could sense what sounded like defensiveness in his tone. He had been quiet for most of the trip.

'Quite the hotspot,' Chris remarked, leaning in to examine the intricate web of lines. 'No wonder you chose it for the retreat.'

The guide's words retained their spritely energy as he continued explaining the various artefacts, but Pel's attention drifted from the map to the window, where the land in question lay basking under a relentless sun. Pels thought about the retreat centre, imagining its silhouette against the horizon, suddenly seeing it in her mind's eye as intrusive, and an imposition on the sacred terrain it occupied.

'Doesn't it bother anyone?' Pels asked, her voice leaping ahead to where their small group stood.

'What do you mean?' Andromeda turned, her brow creased in concern.

'Us, being there. It feels like . . . trespassing.' Pels shifted uncomfortably, massaging her temples as if she could knead away the disquiet gnawing at her conscience.

'Interesting point,' Chris said, but failed to elaborate.

'Ah, the age-old colonial conundrum,' Brett chimed in. 'Vacay on sacred grounds or respect the old ways? Tough call.'

'Especially when our presence might be sapping the very essence that makes it special,' Pels said pointedly, her gaze returning to the map.

'Are we really *taking* anything, though?' Andromeda questioned, her arms crossed over her chest, 'or maybe we're *contributing* . . . adding our energy to the mix?'

'Maybe,' Pels conceded, though her gut disagreed. 'But how much of this,' she gestured to the expanse beyond the glass, 'is left once everyone comes to take a piece or add their own flavour to the mix?'

'Valid.' Harrison's bemusement was etched on his face as he processed the dilemma. It was one that he had clearly thought of before that day, though – Pels could tell.

'Valid? That's all you got? Then again, you did build a shiny retreat smack in the middle of mystical power centre,' Brett pointed out, his words wrapped in a wry smile. 'Not exactly subtle.'

'Let's just hope our stay does more good than harm,' Pels murmured, though she wasn't sure whom she was trying to convince, her fellow guests or herself.

She moved over to a display of ceremonial masks, her eyes darting to the doorway that led to yet another hall. She decided that the group needed a break from her rather than the likelihood that she needed a break from them, and edged away from her companions, each step deliberate. She wanted to take in more of the mythological tales entrusted to this museum without being distracted.

'Where's Pels off to?' Brett's voice faded into the background as she slipped into the corridor dedicated to the ancient energy lines.

'Probably just needs some air,' Andromeda suggested, the click of her bracelets sounding like distant chimes.

The hallway stretched before Pels, the lighting sparse and focused, illuminating maps and diagrams that hummed with an unseen energy. Pels approached an exhibit that showed a tapestry of intersecting lines, pulsating with colours that beckoned her closer. Her athletic frame was taut as she leant in, her dreadlocks brushing against the glass as she traced a finger over the fire paths depicted on the map.

'Here,' she murmured to herself, pinpointing the location of the retreat centre. 'A confluence of energies . . .' Pels let the words hang in the air, the realisation dawning on her. Her deep brown eyes absorbed every detail; the maps weren't just geographical representations but keys to understanding the land's pulse. 'Of course,' she whispered, connecting dots that formed a pattern not yet clear but that felt less confusing. This was more than history: it was a blueprint of power, ancient and undiminished. It was only natural that the people of the land would be pissed off about it being built upon. It seemed at best deeply ignorant, and at worst extremely deliberate. 'Always more to the story,' she said, half-chuckling at the thought, her usual self-doubt silenced by the surge of purpose coursing through her veins. She wasn't just a visitor here; she belonged somehow. She was part of this intricate tapestry, woven into the fabric of something timeless.

'Hey, Pels!' voice cut through her reverie, causing her to start. 'Lost in thought or lost in history?'

'Bit of both,' she replied, turning to see Brett's head peeking through the entrance, his expression a mix of curiosity and amusement.

'Come on, Lara Croft,' he teased. 'Harrison says we're leaving soon.'

'I'll catch you up in a second,' Pels responded with a smile that sent Brett on his way. Her mind was still spinning as she eventually headed off to find the rest of the group, feeling a peculiar tingle at the nape of her neck – an electric whisper of some sort. She rounded a corner and shuffled towards the murmur of chatter. Without warning, Pels stumbled on the chipped stonework of the floor – maybe it was just her disrupted equilibrium sending a jolt of adrenaline through her body. Her arm flailed as she tried to find her balance, her elbow heading straight for a stone tablet to the side of her. 'No!' she yelped, terror constricting her voice.

Time stuttered. The tablet wobbled, teetering on the brink of disaster as her arm connected with it, but then . . . it stopped. Mid-air. A mere breath away from shattering into history and dust.

Pels' eyes widened, her own hand extended in a silent command.

'OK . . . that's new,' she whispered in disbelief, heart pounding like a drum in her chest. Carefully, she coaxed the tablet back onto its rightful place, her fingers trembling, not daring to believe what had just happened.

The stone tablet was safe now. But *how*? Her eyes traced the contours of her fingers as if they had answers etched into their lines.

'Guardian of Souls . . .' she whispered, the words tasting like destiny on her tongue. A surge of energy had coursed through her, a force she'd unwittingly commanded. It wasn't just an adrenaline-fuelled fluke; it was power. *Her* power.

'Get it together, Pels,' she admonished herself in a hushed tone while scanning the vicinity. Silence answered her, along with the comforting absence of witnesses. Brett's laughter filtered through from a distant hall, Andromeda's gentle voice offering a soft counterpoint. Shaking off the disquiet, Pels regained her composure, paying close attention to the floor as she walked towards the others. Whatever this was, whatever she was becoming, it could wait until she was somewhere private. There were stories here, truths buried beneath layers of time and conquest. She needed time to understand it all.

Chapter Twelve

It's been over twenty years, and the police haven't been able to trace Adam's family, home, or even learn his real name. His parents may never know what has happened to him, or where to go to mourn their missing son.

Adam being the name chosen for the little boy is apt, because his case became the beginning of my understanding of something far greater than I could have imagined.

★

Pels chose to sit at the back of the transport pod on their way back to the retreat, her gaze finding the melding of water and trees as they drove along, though her eyes weren't truly taking much in. Her companions' voices faded to a background hum as she twirled one of her locs in her hand, trying to make sense of the random gravity-defying ability that she couldn't quite believe had really happened.

'Hey, Earth to Pels?' Brett called out, his voice laced with amusement. 'You've been zoning out a lot since we got here. What happened, did you find your spiritual calling among the artefacts?'

'Maybe I did,' Pels replied with a half-smile, not entirely joking. The thought of 'magical' abilities once dormant and now stirring within her felt like such a deviation from reality that she couldn't help wondering if her brain had broken during the ceremony.

When the pod pulled into the driveway back at the retreat, Pels was grateful to head to her hut. She didn't want to go for dinner with the others; that would involve more conversation and having to keep up the pretence of normality.

As soon as Pels entered into her hut, she began gathering any items she could find that were unlikely to break.

'I'd advise eating something, Pels,' Aláké chimed in. 'You have the second ceremony tomorrow, so you will fast from midday.'

'Aláké, please, just shhh for a little bit, will you?' Pels was preoccupied with dropping small objects and trying to replicate the middle-finger-up-to-gravity that she'd been able to execute at the museum. It didn't work. Everything Pels let fall – pen, spoon, shoes – just met the ground with a small thud. 'What the hell? This is all fucking crazy to me.'

'Pels, if you aren't going to eat then drinking some of the beverage might be a good—'

'Aláké, I swear to God . . .!' Pels threw herself on the bed, realising that she didn't know how to finish her ominous retort to Aláké's suggestion. Confusion and frustration had tired her out for the day and, without Pels knowing when, sleep claimed her for the night.

A warm breeze rustled through the open door of Pels' hut, ruffling the edges of her bed linen as she prepared for her second Spirit Vine ceremony. Her heart raced with a mix of excitement and nervousness; she couldn't shake the feeling that this time would be even more intense, that something extraordinary awaited her.

As Pels adjusted the bun she had pulled her long locs into atop her head, Aláké spoke. 'Pels, here is a reminder that you still have unopened messages from: your mother, Damari and Maria. There is also a recent news update about the missing boy Osahon Samuels – the reports are that there is still no sign of him, despite the search efforts.'

Frustrated, Pels exhaled sharply. 'There have been two different pieces of CCTV footage showing the last known whereabouts of Osahon, and for a few days his data chip presence kept popping up in various places, yet have the police actually made any effort to follow these leads? Somehow, they still claim that they're searching tirelessly, though, right? Pricks.'

'Pels,' Aláké began, 'I sense an elevation in your blood pressure and—'

In all these years, why have I not looked for a silence function for this thing? Pels pondered. She knew Aláké was privy to the thought, but did not care.

In her heart, Pels sent a silent prayer to the spirits and ancestors for Osahon's safe return. It was all she could do while so far away.

'Focus, Pels,' she muttered to herself, forcing her attention back to the preparations. But a blinking reminder in the corner of the wall screen caught her eye: her ex, Damari, had re-sent his message as 'urgent'. Whenever she thought of him, she now thought about how pathetic she had been, sobbing the night she found out about his other woman Carmen's pregnancy. Wanting to get rid of the message – and Damari – once and for all, she commanded Aláké to open the message and read his text:

Hey queen, I miss you. Can we talk soon? Remember,
the bitter Black woman vibe doesn't look good on you.

Pels rolled her eyes. *This was what he deemed 'urgent'?*

'Can't believe I just wasted some of my daily external inter-action allowance on reading that drivel,' she muttered to herself. 'Move, man.'

Damari's thinly veiled misogyny, paraded as new-age Black male wisdom, felt even more irksome to Pels now. As she thought of Damari's persistent disrespect, her fingers suddenly started to tingle. When she looked down at her hands, she could see the tips of her fingers glowing.

'Aláké, what the hell is happening?' Pels asked her AI in shock. 'Is this something to do with that drink?'

'Unfortunately, Pels, I do not know exactly what is happening. The tea you are provided to drink is merely to rehydrate you for the ceremonies, and to provide small doses of mycelium to alleviate the distressing dreams that are common soon after ingesting the Spirit Vine. I am noticing new activity in certain areas of your brain. This sensation you are experiencing seems to have been activated once your heart rate went up. Your brain detected distress. Try taking a few deep breaths and please drink some more of the beverage currently being freshly re-brewed.'

Reluctantly, Pels followed Aláké's advice and began to breathe more deeply and slowly. As she calmed down, the tips of her fingers returned to their usual colour and the reddish glow faded.

'First I'm stopping ancient tablets from smashing to pieces and now my fingers are glowing? Turning into a mutant was not on my bingo card for this year.' She marvelled at herself.

With her annoyance fading, she pushed thoughts of deliberately incompetent police and a wilfully ignorant Damari out of her mind and turned her full attention to the ceremony. The evening's Spirit Vine ceremony was the only way she was going to get more answers about what she had been experiencing in the last couple of days.

Entering the ceremony hut felt like stepping into another world. Brett and Chris were already in the seats they'd occupied in the first ceremony, and as Pels sat in her seat, Andromeda shuffled in soon after her. All of them were sat in a semicircle formation with their bowls of water and flowers by their feet. Harrison stood at the front and greeted them all with a warm smile.

Shadows flickered on the walls as dim candles cast their soft light over the space, and the scent of incense and tobacco hung heavily in the air, mingling with the earthy aroma of the Spirit Vine brew. It was a heady mixture that made Pels already feel as if she were floating above her own body.

The room filled with soft, rhythmic chanting from the spiritualists present at the first ceremony, again led by Ayi, their harmonious voices blending to form an ethereal melody that resonated within Pels' very soul. She closed her eyes, allowing the music to wash over her.

'Olúwapẹlúmi.' A gentle voice called her name, pulling her from her moment of wistful thought. She turned to see Ayi now standing right beside her, an encouraging and knowing smile on her face. To Pels' surprise, the woman took hold of her hands and prayed over her fingertips. Pels didn't understand a word of the prayer but felt strangely reassured as the woman smiled and moved on to Andromeda.

Once the individual prayers were done, Ayi began to make her way around the circle again, offering each participant a small clay cup filled with the thick, potent Spirit Vine brew. When it was Pels' turn to drink, she took the cup with trembling hands, feeling the warmth of its contents pressed against her palm.

'She says to drink deeply,' Harrison told Pels on behalf of the ceremony leader, his voice a soothing addition in the candle-light. 'She says she dreamt of you, and that your journey ahead is far. See well, she says.'

Despite being there on assignment, Pels couldn't help but be stunned by the attention she was receiving. It brought about a tinge of sadness within her, as she had never felt this seen or special back home . . .

She lifted the cup to her lips, inhaling the earthy aroma before taking a tentative sip. The taste was just as bitter as in the first ceremony, yet strangely invigorating, and she felt the Spirit Vine brew's heat spread through her body like liquid sunlight. As she drank more, she noticed a subtle shift in her perception; the colours she could make out were brighter, sounds more vibrant, and even the scent of the incense grew more complex and layered as it danced alluringly with the scent of tobacco and spiritual cleansing cologne.

Pels recognised the same strange sensations taking place within her body, and this time she surrendered more easily, feeling herself drift deeper and deeper into the realm of the spirit, her heart a beacon of light guiding her way. As she drifted, Pels felt herself spiralling through an interstellar abyss, the darkness giving way to a universe of stars – a celestial tapestry unfolding before her. She was free from gravity's hold, floating amid the luminous constellations. Her breath caught in her throat as the beings that emerged from the shimmering stardust loomed into her vision. Everything about this experience felt more vivid than in the first ceremony.

The celestial entities moved gracefully, their radiant forms undulating like silk in a cosmic breeze. *Were they celebrating?* Each entity was composed of countless pinpricks of light; simultaneously everything and nothing, existing as both ancient wisdom and newborn wonder. Pels could only watch in awe, uncertain if they were aware of her presence.

'Olúwapẹlúmi,' a voice whispered suddenly, its tone a symphony of harmonies echoing within her mind. 'Fear not, for we are with you.'

Her heart skipped a beat, the telepathic connection catching her off guard yet again because somehow it felt more intense. She couldn't explain any of it, but she found comfort in the voices and felt a deep sense of belonging. 'I don't think I've had the chance to ask – who *are* you?' Pels enquired, her thoughts forming words that transcended spoken language.

'We are your celestial guides,' another voice replied, its timbre resonating like the hum of a tuning fork. 'We have always been with you, waiting for the moment when you would be ready to receive our wisdom. We refer to it as your awakening. So, we celebrate because you are waking up – every part of you.'

As they spoke, the celestial beings drifted closer to Pels, their forms intertwining and merging like streams of liquid starlight. She felt herself drawn into their embrace, enveloped by the warmth and brilliance of their radiance.

'Your journey has been long,' the mystical voices continued. 'But it is far from over. You carry within you a great power,

Olúwapẹlúmi – a gift bestowed upon you at birth, waiting to be awakened.'

'Power?' Pels echoed, her thoughts a mixture of amazement and confusion. 'What kind of power?'

'Your true potential is beyond imagination,' the celestial beings replied. 'You are a Guardian of Souls, destined to protect and guide those who cannot yet defend themselves from the forces that seek to claim them.'

A chill ran down Pels' spine as she considered the importance of this purpose the beings spoke of yet again. She was no stranger to the desire of fighting for justice in her work as a journalist, but this – this was something altogether different. And yet, she could not deny the fire that blazed within her, filling her with determination and a hunger for knowledge.

'Teach me,' she implored, her mind reaching out to the beings. 'I want to understand. You showed me visions the first time, so I get that I am part of some kind of group or constellation. But . . . my fingers were glowing earlier, and at the museum, I was able to stop something from falling. That's mad to me!'

'Patience, dear one,' the celestial choir soothed. 'In time, all will be revealed. For now, trust in yourself and in us. Let our guidance illuminate your path, and together we shall triumph over the shadows that threaten this world. For a long time, you have ignored the dreams and signs, so we simply cannot overwhelm you.'

Pels nodded, though she couldn't tell whether it was the strongly brewed Spirit Vine that had her resolve solidifying like molten iron cooling into steel.

The celestial beings' forms shimmered like a cascade of stars, their brilliance dancing across the darkness of Pels' vision.

'Your abilities as a Guardian of Souls are vast and varied,' the celestial choir intoned, their voices a mingling of melodic wisdom. 'You possess the power to soar through the skies, unbound by the chains of gravity, once you master it. Your ability to stop the tablet from falling at the museum is a mere glimpse into your power in that regard. And soon you will find that your hands can manifest orbs of fire or water, weapons against the forces that threaten this realm.'

As they spoke, the beings projected images. Pels saw an image of her body lift off the ground, her limbs tingling with an unfamiliar energy. She glanced down at her hands, and to her astonishment saw a miniature sun forming in her palms, its fiery corona pulsing with life. Just as quickly, it transformed into a swirling sphere of water, droplets glinting like diamonds in the ethereal light.

'Your strength and combat prowess will be unmatched among your people,' the celestial beings continued. 'These skills have been dormant within you, waiting for the moment when you will rise to fulfil your destiny.'

'But how could that be when Danny Salami slapped me on the high street after school and I did nothing to fight back?'

If celestial beings experienced humour, Pels could have sworn she heard them laugh. 'You didn't know your power back then. And we don't just mean these awakened abilities . . .'

Pels could feel the power the beings spoke of coursing through her, electrifying every nerve and sinew. She began to feel sharp sensations as if each nerve in her body was being torn apart and then reattached with a cooling breath soothing each reconnection. It didn't feel comfortable. She gritted her teeth and did her best not to moan in anguish. Part of her still remembered that her corporeal body was surrounded by others in the hut.

This was all unlike anything she had ever experienced, but deep down it felt right – she was starting to understand what they meant, that these abilities had always been a part of her just waiting to be unlocked.

A torrent of emotions threatened to overwhelm her, and tears streamed from her eyes. Coming to a realisation of these dormant powers only made it more apparent to Pels how power*less* she had felt in life up to this moment.

'Remember,' the celestial beings whispered, their voices infused with love and compassion, 'you are not alone in this fight. There are others like you – one of whom you have already met. We are here to guide and support you, as we have done for countless generations of Guardians before you. Trust in our wisdom, and most of all, trust in your own strength.'

As their words faded, Pels felt a sense of peace settle over her like a warm blanket.

A wave of nausea pulled Pels back into her body, and she jolted forward as she threw up into her bowl. *Purging.* Yes, that was the exact word for so many things that needed releasing in her life.

'Thank you,' she murmured to the beings as she wiped the sides of her mouth and reclined back in her chair, her gratitude resounding through the vast expanse of her vision. Even though her body suddenly ached, she still felt gratitude. 'I don't yet know how, but I will do everything in my power to honour this gift and the mission you have entrusted to me.'

As soon as she was settled, thinking her visions were done for the night, the visions in Pels' heart's eye lurched forward.

Pels stood amid the celestial beings, her heart pounding with a mixture of reverence and trepidation as the vastness of the cosmos stretched out around her, stars glimmering like diamonds sewn into an endless tapestry of black velvet. As she gazed upon the luminous forms of her celestial guides, something deep within her stirred – a hunger for knowledge, an insatiable curiosity that had driven her since her days as a young journalist.

'I'm back? I thought we were done?' Pels was bewildered.

'As your body attunes to the potency of the Spirit Vine, it will bring you to us in waves.'

'You keep showing me that I will need these powers to basically fight evil. Tell me,' Pels began, her voice quivering with determination, 'what more can you teach me about the Soul Snatchers? Are they human?'

The celestial beings swirled around her, their starry tendrils weaving intricate patterns in the darkness. One of them spoke, its voice resonating like the hum of distant galaxies. 'The Soul Snatchers are ancient beings capable of taking physical form, but not a human one. As we told you, their mission is collecting souls to feed the Cloud of Sorrow.'

Another celestial being chimed in, its voice like the haunting melody of a cosmic flute. 'To do this, they use human mortals who are in a relentless pursuit for power as their conduits, to help them to gather souls. By promising to use their celestial powers to increase these humans' influence and wealth, together they conspire to target the most vulnerable among you all – the lost, the frightened, the marginalised . . . the young. For it is the tender souls of children that hold the greatest potency.'

Pels clenched her fists, rage bubbling within her chest at the thought of such heinous acts. Her mind raced with images of the missing children she had seen over the past couple of years. She took a deep breath and continued her inquiry. 'How do they capture these souls? And why have they grown so bold in recent times?'

A third celestial being emerged from the constellation of shimmering lights, its form flickering like a dying star. 'Lured by the Soul Snatchers' promises of wealth, power or fame, these individuals aid the sustenance of the Cloud of Sorrow by taking young souls and providing them to the Soul Snatchers – they grow ever more ruthless in their desires.'

'As the world has grown more chaotic and divided,' another celestial being added, 'the Soul Snatchers have found it increasingly easy to infiltrate your realm and exert their influence to obtain the souls they need. The fractures in humanity's collective spirit provide fertile ground for their insidious machinations.'

Pels' eyes widened as the gravity of the situation became clear. This was not merely a battle against otherworldly creatures; it was a struggle against the worst aspects of human nature and society itself. She felt a twisting in her gut – fear.

The celestial beings' revelations swirled in Pels' mind, a nebulous cloud of knowledge and understanding. As she absorbed the information, her thoughts raced like a comet.

'Could I use my powers to locate the missing children? Osahon, my friend's brother, he's missing, and all this just hits different. I mean, I was worried before – but now . . .?'

'We know. Yes, your abilities will guide you,' one celestial being responded, its stardust form shimmering as if to emphasise the point. 'Trust your intuition, and you shall find what you seek.'

'However,' another added, 'time is of the essence. The Soul Snatchers are relentless, and the numbers of their mortal helpers grow by the day. They have been privy to the prophecies before you were born, so they watch the fire paths they know of closely. They know that someone like you, a Guardian, is due to be awakened soon, and that you will be a true threat to their existence and to the Cloud of Sorrow. But they also know that you will require a fire path in order to realise your powers. You must act swiftly, Pels, and decisively.'

Pels nodded, her heart pounding in her chest like a drum-beat urging her forward. She'd hated the motivations for Dave sending her on this assignment to Benin, but she now realised it was very unlikely she'd have made it to this point of her own volition. The urgency of her mission was palpable, as real as the incense-laden air that filled her lungs.

'So . . . how am I supposed to confront the Soul Snatchers, exactly?' Pels asked. 'As much as I'm on Team Destroy-the-Cloud-of-Sorrow, I still want to live, you know? The last time I did any flying was at air cadets, and that was in those mini planes, not my own actual Blackity Black body flying through the sky.'

'The principles of flight and combat will serve you well in your battles against these malevolent creatures, but not with the earthly reasoning you continue to employ. Your body knows what to do and when. Trust it.'

Pels laughed despite herself. 'Fair enough. But, I mean, I didn't even make it past Corporal since they promoted Katie House over me and—'

A firm, ethereal voice cut into Pels' lamenting. 'What have we just told you about applying base reasoning to divine gifts? Up until now, you only wanted to see a small life, so only a small life was shown to you. But you have always known somewhere inside that your skills are great. Now *use* them.'

'Do not underestimate the power of your elemental orbs,' another chimed in. 'The Soul Snatchers may be cunning, but they are vulnerable to the forces of fire and water, and an intermingling of these elements can create an impenetrable forcefield . . .'

'Be prepared for anything,' the third celestial being warned. 'Just as you have begun to grow stronger, so too have your opponents, and they have centuries of practice. Once again, simply remember to trust in your instincts, and that we are always with you.'

Pels breathed deeply, steadying herself in the face of such a monumental responsibility. 'Thank you,' she whispered, her voice laced with wonder and worry.

As the celestial beings faded from Pels' vision once more, their final words lingered. With purpose, Pels clenched her fists, feeling the energy coursing through her body, ready to be unleashed against the forces that threatened the world – that is, if she didn't accidentally set herself alight first.

Pels' eyes eventually fluttered open, her body tense and sore with the remnants of her celestial encounter. The dimly lit hut, filled with the soft chanting of the spiritualists, seemed far removed from the ethereal realm she had just left behind.

Andromeda was speaking rather sternly about yet again not experiencing any visions, and Pels could make out Brett's American accent from across the room as he sang what sounded like a lullaby; he was clearly still engrossed in another world. She could sense Chris on the other side of her, muttering to himself and groaning. At some point he must've taken an extra cup of the brew because he was more experienced than the rest of them.

Yet, from what Pels could sense, it didn't seem like anyone else was having an experience like hers.

She needed to make sense of it all, but this time from someone more . . . grounded. 'I've got to talk to Harrison.'

Chapter Thirteen

There was a little boy known as Carl Franklin who went missing while on holiday with his parents in Marrakech in 2016, and every year since there have been campaigns and articles still speculating about his whereabouts. Does the country's interest in Carl persist because he was a little blond white boy? Readers of The Mercury *may find this assertion disconcerting; however, I believe it is my duty as a journalist to ask questions that hopefully lead us to a deeper understanding of our collective behaviour. Adam was brutally murdered, that much we know; yet his story is not frequently discussed.*

★

Pels spent the next morning positioning herself in areas of the retreat centre where she hoped she would bump into Harrison. It was out of character for him to not be around in some capacity. He would usually join them for breakfast, especially the morning after a Spirit Vine ceremony, for an informal check-in. Though today they were due a formal check in with Ayi about the visions they had seen thus far – if any.

Eventually, Pels took a break from covertly searching for Harrison to revel in the warm golden glow the sun cast on the retreat centre's lush courtyard. She sat with her back resting against a tree, lost in thought for a moment as she watched the play of shadows among the leaves by the lagoon. A gentle breeze danced across her lashes, laden with the scent of jasmine and the distant murmur of voices.

'Hey, Pels,' a strained, sing-song voice called out. She looked up to see Andromeda approaching, her tall frame draped in vibrant Ankara fabric that crinkled with each step. Pels was amused by the choice of outfit but thought, *When in Rome . . . I guess.*

'Mind if I join you?' Andromeda asked.

'Of course not,' Pels replied with a smile, making room for Andromeda beside her. As the women settled into a somewhat awkward silence, Pels sensed that Andromeda had something to say. Her blonde hair was pulled tightly into a bun, seemingly freshly washed, while her green eyes stared across the water with a steeliness that gave itself away in the clench of her jaw.

'I've been deeply reflecting on the history of the museum we visited, and I wondered – have you ever faced racism in your life?' Andromeda asked, her glinting eyes still fixed on the horizon.

Pels sighed. *Here we go,* she thought. It was exhausting having people who were non-Black trying to connect with her over conversations about racism. Pels wondered whether there were community meetings where white people met up and decided on the discussion points they would reach for when interacting with Black people. Part of her wished that was really the case so she could suggest that they update their notes. There were other subjects Black people were capable of speaking about! But, recalling the microaggressions and blatant bigotry she had encountered throughout her life, Pels indulged Andromeda with a reply. 'Yes. It's a pervasive element in the lives of a lot of people who look like me.'

Andromeda nodded solemnly. 'I know what you mean. My family moved to the US from Germany in my late teens, and I spent years feeling like an outsider. People would make assumptions about me based on my looks, my accent, even my name.'

The experience of drinking the Spirit Vine had made Pels feel more empathy than usual towards Andromeda, but she was irritated that Andromeda could think their experiences were remotely comparable.

'That must've been hard for you,' she said, trying not to clench her teeth. 'Although, over time I'm sure you agree that you started to blend in. That isn't the case with Blackness. Sometimes it feels like there's no escaping it, no matter where I go,' Pels said, a trace of bitterness tinging her words. 'Even here, in what many call "The Motherland", I'm still witnessing a continent grappling with the legacy of colonialism and the scars it left behind. I mean, since you have been clearly thinking so deeply about the museum and all, you probably get that.'

Andromeda nodded, but Pels wasn't sure of how much she understood. As they spoke, Pels became aware of Chris and Brett approaching them, seemingly deep in their own conversation.

'Come on, man,' Chris was saying with a scoff, 'I don't even see colour. We're all just people. Why can't we move past this?'

God, not them too.

'What's going on here then?' Pels asked, an uncharacteristically thin smile on her normally full lips.

'We've just seen that our excursion plans have been changed for tomorrow because there are more protests by the locals about resorts and such being built in the area. Chris was saying how sad it was that the local people focused on anger and hate instead of love, and *I* was saying that it just sounds . . . off that he'd say that.' Brett explained heatedly before Chris could interject.

'That's not true, I just took a slight issue with it being made out like I might in some way be um . . . I mean, due to my choice of words. Anyway, we thought that maybe you could weigh in on it all since you're . . . a journalist and all. Isn't this part of what you're here to report on?'

Pels couldn't believe what she was witnessing. Here she was being thrust into the role of racial arbitrator left and right, when all she wanted to do was sit by a tree. Pels was also simultaneously amused that Chris couldn't bring himself to use the words 'racist' and 'Black'.

'I think we must acknowledge that the people indigenous to this land are very much being pushed out and priced out of their own lands. Our concern should be how we can experience these ceremonies without being a part of the problem. Like I said at the museum, it feels awkward as fuck being here, and even if I explain it away with the fact that it's an assignment for me, it is actually more than that.' She sighed a little. 'If the local people didn't protest, there would likely be no attention paid to their dissent at all, especially when they're standing up to large companies backed by the government.' It felt good to speak with her journalist hat on, even while owning some of the hypocrisy more robustly in front of them all.

'Yes, I hear that, but Martin Luther King said—' Chris began.

'No,' Pels interrupted.

'What do you mean, no?'

'I mean no, do not do that thing that white people tend to do when feeling uncomfortable about a boundary being set by a Black person – quote Martin Luther King Jr.'

'I just don't see it as a Black and white issue. I think, like me, the more Spirit Vine ceremonies you attend, the more you will see that only love can heal things.'

'Well, I think it's a bit sad that despite all the ceremonies you've attended, you fail to see that this protest by the local people is fuelled by love. A love of their land and a love of their histories.'

Chris had run out of counter-arguments – he'd turned a deeper shade of red than could be attributed to the heat of the sun. Brett smiled as if he had personally put Chris in his place, and Andromeda simply continued to look across the lagoon, clearly not quite knowing the right time to talk about good vibes.

A few hours later, the now-familiar scent of burning incense wafted through the air as Pels took her place in the semicircle of participants in the ceremony hut, each seated on colourful cushions. The ceremony leader, the statuesque Ayi with her distinctive regal bearing, began to speak. Her voice was melodic and hypnotic. As she spoke, Harrison, who was seated cross-legged to her right, translated.

'Let us share our experiences from the Spirit Vine ceremonies,' he told them she'd said. 'What wisdom have you gained? What visions have you seen?'

Ayi invited each guest to tap their wrist on a grey tablet she held in her hands, which would allow the visions the guests wanted to share to show up in hologram form so that everybody else could observe.

Chris was first to begin, and spoke of the deep insights he had gained about the loneliness he felt having achieved so much as a surgeon, yet being unable to find a new love since his divorce. Even while stifling a slight eyeroll, it was undeniably mesmerising to watch another person's visions via hologram. Pels was in awe.

Brett was next to tap his wrist where his secondary chip was implanted. He shared how he had seen himself touring his drag act and possibly leaving his advertising role. It was fun for the guests to watch how Brett's visions appeared as watercolours.

Andromeda's jaw stiffened in the same way it had when she and Pels had been sitting under the tree. She was frustrated that she hadn't seen any visions but wondered aloud if maybe this was because she had 'the purest soul'.

Pels was amused by the expression on Ayi's face as Harrison translated what Andromeda had said. 'It's probably not that. Sometimes people must accept some feelings they are running from before the Vine can show them the visions they are yearning to see,' Ayi gently corrected via translation.

When it was her turn, Pels hesitated as she selected which visions to share, and how much to divulge, since everybody else's visions seemed beautiful yet utterly unlike what she had experienced. She remembered the celestial beings' guidance – the way they had appeared like stardust, shimmering and ethereal. They had entrusted her with knowledge not meant for all ears or eyes, but there were still aspects of her experience that she felt she could share.

'I saw stars,' she began, her voice soft but steady as she tapped her wrist to the tablet and shared just a fraction of all that had appeared to her, ensuring that she did not show the celestial beings. 'I felt their energy pulsing through me, connecting me to something greater than myself.' She paused, searching for the right words, her brown eyes distant as she recalled her visions. 'And I received guidance . . . Guidance to help me face the challenges ahead.' Pels was careful to not say much else, because she could see how instantly everybody in the ceremony hut became transfixed by her visions. She ensured that she wasn't sharing the specific messages of her visions, but kept to snippets so everybody could understand the expanse of her experience.

Even without seeing all the visions, the ceremony leader nodded, her gaze piercing and knowing. 'You carry a great responsibility, Pels,' she said solemnly, while Harrison translated. 'Your connection to the celestial realm is strong and will only grow stronger.' She looked on at Pels in wonder, and seemed to want to say more, but held back in front of the others.

Pels acknowledged her words with a grateful smile before the conversation shifted back to other participants. As the group eventually disbanded, Pels approached Harrison, who stood near the hut entrance, the lights across the retreat centre casting shadows over his handsome features. 'Thank you,' she said. 'It was great to get clarity from Ayi about what we have all seen.'

'Of course,' he replied, his eyes softening as they met hers. 'I'm always here to help.'

'Have you . . . have you ever heard about the Guardians of Souls?' Pels hesitated before continuing in a hushed tone. 'It's just that in my visions, some . . . beings appeared to me,' she confessed, 'and they told me I'm one of those Guardians. They showed me other things that I'm yet to make sense of, but I wondered if you were aware of anybody else who has experienced the Spirit Vine and said they'd had something similar happen? They say . . . they say I've been Awakened.'

Harrison's gaze grew serious at that word. 'No. I haven't heard about this before.' He cleared his throat. 'I can do some research for you, if you'd like?'

'That would be amazing, thank you. If you find nothing and it's all literally in my head, you can tell me that too – although I know I need to stop playing down what I know to be true. This is real for me, and I have to accept that.' She'd been speaking as though to herself but looked up again at Harrison. 'Any and all research would be great, though.'

Even with this heart-to-heart, somehow Pels felt protective of sharing all of it – especially that the celestial beings had told her of the powers that she had, and most of all, that they had warned her about the Soul Snatchers. Until she had figured out how everything worked, she wanted to keep some things to herself.

Chapter Fourteen

Tẹ̀mídìrẹ̀ Ògúndélé, nineteen, was last seen in the early hours of 7 February 2026 in the Heythrop area, where he was attending a yoga retreat. He had been due to teach a class there later that day.

Officers searching the area found a body shortly before 9 a.m. two days later, Heythrop police said.

In a statement to the press, the police said there were no suspicious circumstances surrounding the death.

★

The sun chose its warmest rays to dance on Pels' skin as she headed out of the retreat centre, joining the other participants for the excursion to Cotonou. Their guides had mapped out the roads not blocked by protestors. Pels wondered if this was merely a logistical decision, or one prompted by the discomfort of the guests being made aware that, in some ways, they were not welcome in Benin. *I've got to figure out a way to get more of an insight into all of this*, Pels promised herself.

The transport pod sped through the streets and, as she looked out of the window, vibrant colours enveloped Pels' senses as they made their way through the bustling city. The vivid splashes of traditional clothing and textiles painted a stunning cultural canvas.

Once they reached the market in Cotonou and Pels stepped out of the pod, she raised her face to the sky. *Everything is changing*, was the only thought that flittered by as they all began to head away from the pod and towards the crowds.

'Isn't it incredible?' Harrison asked, walking beside her. His eyes sparkled with appreciation for the rich heritage that surrounded them.

'Absolutely,' Pels agreed, undeniably awestruck as she took in the lively, renowned market. The air was filled with the tantalising aroma of spices and freshly cooked food, while energetic music infused every corner of the city with life. She looked up and saw drones flying overhead, spraying a thin mist around the town centre.

Harrison eventually peeled his eyes away from Pels' face to follow her gaze up to the sky.

'Those are sanitation drones,' he said, answering her wordless question. 'They're government-issued, to intermittently spray antiviral solutions over the city to ensure there is less of a spread of diseases.'

Pels nodded. The perception of certain African countries was that they were 'underdeveloped', yet here the government was taking precautions to prevent illness. Before she could romanticise the drones any further, Harrison's voice sliced into her thoughts.

'One agenda point of the recent protests is that these sprays can affect local crops. They've been questioning why, if they were truly in the interests of health and safety, the drones are only issued to jurisdictions heavily populated by tourists.'

'They have a point,' Pels replied, disappointed that she hadn't considered these perspectives – but being here, she was starting to understand more and more that the issues African countries faced were truly multilayered, and not immediately identifiable when one was a tourist. *When in doubt, it's likely capitalism*, Pels thought sombrely. 'Don't the people protesting have someone in government to advocate for them?'

'From what I know, the people have had a long and complicated history with being advocated for. You see that statue over there?' Harrison gestured to a stone statue of a smiling older man in cloth shorts with a fist in the air defiantly. It loomed over the marketplace. 'That is Narcisse Moussa. He is praised as one of the few to gain his own freedom from slavery. The complicated part is that he then became a prominent slave merchant when he returned to Benin, a place then known as Dahomey. The statue was the cause of a lot of controversy a few years ago.'

'I can understand why people would be annoyed. What was revolutionary about him gaining his freedom only to do that?'

'Well, the wealth he amassed obviously became generational, and so his great-great grandchildren use their wealth to buy back artefacts that originate from here, from European collectors. The artefacts they've managed to regain belong to the family technically, but are displayed in the museums around the country, including some you saw the other day.'

Pels took in the statue a moment longer, contemplating all this.

'It's a lot to take in, right?' Harrison said, still watching her. 'Hope I'm doing OK as your white, mansplaining tour guide.'

Pels merely supplied him with a wry smile.

They rejoined the others, and the small retreat group made their way around the market. Pels smiled at the women in their colourful printed fabrics sat by their wooden stalls, offering a taste of the local delicacies they had prepared. Other tourists jostled past as they tried their hand at bartering with the lively vendors.

A group of children played nearby, darting around a makeshift goalpost, kicking a tattered soccer ball with joyous abandon as the drones continued to hover overheard with antiviral spray. She felt a strong sense of protectiveness wash over her. The kids playing football reminded her of watching the kids in the park when she spoke with Elaine about her brother a few days ago. It felt like another lifetime, and Pels was catapulted back into her worry over the children who had gone missing back home.

Her discomfort was magnified as Andromeda and Chris hurried over to attempt to take pictures of the kids on their analogue cameras, commenting unsubtly about how precious it was that the kids were happy despite their circumstances. A buzz went through her, and unthinkingly, with a subtle swish of her wrist, Pels realised she'd created a gentle cloud of dust from the ground in front of her two white companions and blown it towards them. Distracted from their photographs, Andromeda and Chris were forced to rub their eyes, with the blonde woman dramatically asking for hers to be doused with bottled water.

Pels chuckled to herself, a little shocked. She hadn't known what would happen with her wrist movement, but she knew she wanted the children to be left alone. *Did the elements get creative on my behalf?* she wondered, proud.

'Ah – you have a kind heart to protect the young ones,' said a voice beside her, startling Pels. Turning, she found herself face to face with an elderly local. His eyes twinkled with mischief as though he knew what she had just done. Pels hadn't thought there would be someone watching her as she watched others. Her first instinct was to feign confusion at the elderly man's comment, but a yearning to talk with someone who may understand what was happening to her won out.

'Uh . . . thank you,' Pels replied, her cheeks warming slightly. 'I just want them to be safe.'

'Here in Benin, we have many stories of those who protect the innocent, even after so many were taken through the portal of no return to faraway lands . . .' the man said, studying her intently.

'Yes . . .' she responded tentatively. Did he know . . .? How would she explain any of this to her mum or her friends when she got back to London? It seemed like everything in her life had been incredibly mundane up to this point, and yet somehow she had found herself as a part of lore with incredible magnitude.

'May the ancestors and celestial beings watch over you, young one,' the man added, his eyes twinkling. 'And may you find the strength you need to fulfil your destiny.'

With that, he turned and disappeared into the throng of people. Not keen to rejoin the others and their faintly embarrassing bartering as they purchased wooden bowls and spices they would likely never use, Pels continued to wander the market alone.

She withdrew to a quiet alleyway, still contemplating all that had happened. Alone, Pels took a deep breath, closed her eyes and focused. Pels used her voice to summon her AI. 'Aláké, pull up the instructions as to how I use some of these powers. It is better I try it out in this marketplace rather than at the retreat, which has cameras everywhere. I feel irritated by the complexities of the history of everything right now; I might as well put it to some use.'

'Of course,' Aláké responded immediately.

Aláké produced a small holographic projection on the wall of the alleyway to allow Pels to watch as the beings demonstrated how to create the orbs that she could use for protection.

Pels let her thoughts settle on the statue of Narcisse that Harrison had showed her, then the image of someone gaining freedom only to enslave others. Pels imagined a gulf of water knocking the statue over and immediately orbs of water appeared on her fingertips. Taking deep breaths to steady herself, Pels began to glide her hands through the air so the little orbs could become one bigger orb of water. The glow of the orb between the palms of Pels' hands mesmerised her.

'Aren't you shocked that I can do this?' Pels asked Aláké, her heart racing and her own eyes still wide with wonder.

'I am not programmed for shock. Also, I've collected every dream you have had since my installation, as well as your conscious thoughts. Based on this data, it has always been likely that you could possess some supernatural gift.'

'Girl, at least act surprised,' Pels muttered.

She jumped when Harrison appeared at the entrance to the alleyway, instinctively hiding her hands behind her back. Their glow had already faded as she reluctantly severed her connection to the celestial realm.

'Is everything all right?' he said. 'I've been looking for you!' His voice was woven with concern. 'The retreat centre mainframe app tracked your AI to here.'

'I'm fine,' Pels replied. 'I just wanted to . . . explore a bit. Is everything OK?'

'Yeah. Just can't have you go missing as a guest of mine, and things are getting a bit unsettled here. Let's rejoin the others and head back to the retreat,' Harrison suggested, and Pels nodded. As they hurried back towards the group, Pels felt a sense of accomplishment, excited about what she was able to do now – and what she might do next.

The participants' voices carried through the crisp night air as they returned to the retreat centre and walked towards their huts. Their conversations were animated as they discussed the excursion to the market, and their excitement and anticipation for the final ceremony.

'Can you believe we'll be participating in our last Spirit Vine ceremony tomorrow?' Andromeda asked, her eyes sparkling with enthusiasm. 'I hope I *finally* have my visions.'

'Rooting for you, Andy!' Chris chimed in.

'We all are,' Brett said, his previous heated discussion with Chris seemingly forgotten as they shared a common excitement. 'I feel like we're on the verge of something life-changing.'

Pels nodded in agreement, not knowing when Andromeda and Chris had got close enough to be on nickname terms, but that concerned her very little. Her heart still raced from the excitement of the orbs of water she had been able to conjure earlier in the alleyway at the marketplace.

'Excuse me for a moment,' Pels said, slipping away from the group yet again, and making her way to the edge of the retreat centre's grounds. She found solace in the beauty of her surroundings; the varying colours and textures of the lush vegetation soothed her soul. Her gaze drifted upwards, the night sky painted with a breathtaking array of stars and constellations, reminding her of her visions. A deep connection to life swelled within her, filling her with another surge of the slight sadness that she had lived this long without experiencing such a deep sense of purpose.

'Guardian of Souls,' Pels whispered, closing her eyes and allowing the energy of the universe to flow through her, her powers simmering just beneath the surface.

'Are you all right, Pels?' Harrison's voice cut through the stillness, concern lacing his words.

Her eyes flung open. 'Yes,' she replied, meeting his gaze. 'I . . . I just needed a moment to reflect.'

'Sometimes, it's important to find peace amid chaos. I know your time here has been rather overwhelming, what with the ceremonies contending with the protests. I imagine it is affecting you more deeply than the other guests at this time,' he said, his eyes softening.

'Thank you, Harrison,' Pels responded. 'Life isn't a single-issue experience, so I'm just trying to find a way to balance each truth within me, if you get what I mean?'

'I do. I'll leave you to it.' He smiled warmly, reaching out to gently squeeze her hand before walking away.

As Pels stood there, continuing to gaze at the celestial tapestry above, Aláké chimed.

'Pels, a reminder that the retreat rules state no sexual intimacy is allowed between guests at any time during the ceremony week.'

Pels felt a pang of irritation. 'Yes, Aláké, I remember the rules. I wasn't even thinking about that with Harrison anyway.' Pels knew her rebuttal was futile since Aláké's coding meant she tracked all of Pels' bodily sensations and thoughts. 'He just . . .

reminded me of someone for a second, that's all.' She wondered if the AI would know who.

Chapter Fifteen

A rising talent in the wellness scene, Tèmídìrè Ògúndélé's work included regular free yoga classes in his Birmingham neighbourhood for Black youth, which won Tèmídìrè numerous awards for his community spirit.

His nearly completed proposal to his local council explored structural inequality when it comes to Black youth in urban environments, and his hopes to create a wellness centre focused on mind, body and spirit for under-represented communities.

★

Night had fallen more deeply by the time Pels got back into her hut that evening. The screens that made up her walls displayed images in a mesmerising dance of colour and movement. Relieved to be away from the other guests and to have some more time with her thoughts, Pels leant back in her chair and beckoned for Aláké to load the images from her visions for her to review again.

'Pause there,' she whispered, as the image of a celestial being filled the screen. Ethereal and radiant, it appeared to be made of pure stardust, its form almost too beautiful to comprehend. The being's eyes seemed to hold the secrets of the universe, captivating Pels every time she looked into them.

'Tell me again what they said about how the souls are being snatched,' Pels requested.

Aláké complied, and the screen shifted to depict a chilling scene. A sinister figure, cloaked in shadows, hovered behind a man as he approached a young Black girl walking home from her netball practice. The figure extended a hand as if through the man and dragged the girl into the back of a van. As the man taped the girl's mouth shut and bound her hands, the shadowy figure, now hovering above the van, reached through the top of it and into the young girl's chest, and suddenly a ghostly mist seemed to rise from the child, drawn inexorably towards the shadow's outstretched palm. Pels could see the fear and confusion in the mist, the essence of the child's soul, as it became trapped within the grasp of the malevolent entity. The girl's body lay still in the back of the van as the man got into the front and drove away. The shadowy figure adopted a misty glow as it took off into the air.

'It's a metaphor somehow, I think. Partly how they take the children and then eventually what happens to their souls,' Pels thought aloud.

'Was there any indication of where they're taking these young people? They must be taking them somewhere where the Soul Snatchers can then steal these poor kids' souls and feed them to the Cloud,' Pels asked, her voice tight and determined.

'Unfortunately, the information was not complete,' Aláké replied softly. 'But you were given a clue – that your powers as a Guardian of Souls are the key to stopping them. You can control the elements, even fly through the air, as the beings said, although the conspicuous nature of this particular ability means you have not yet attempted it. As I am tracking your brain activity, I notice a 0.5 per cent increase in all areas of activity. Truly remarkable.'

Pels sighed and closed her eyes for a moment. How on earth was she going to stop all this? As a journalist, she had a sense of how to write about injustice. But actually doing something about this otherworldly conspiracy? The fear of fucking everything up bore heavily down on her chest. She had been entrusted with incredible power, but the knowledge that young souls were being stolen from their rightful place in the world filled her with a sense of urgency.

'Aláké, let's go over everything we've learnt so far about the missing young people back home,' Pels said firmly. 'I need to understand my role in all this – and work out where the hell they're taking these people in order to snatch their souls. I knew there was some kind of sinister link, but I never imagined that it would require me to have *superpowers* to get to the bottom of it.' She shook her head incredulously, still finding it weird to say out loud.

'Of course, Pels. Please note that this request will require me to use the majority of your data for social interaction, and likely override the information you are allowed to see while you're here as per the retreat guidelines. Do I have your permission?' Aláké asked.

'Go for it.'

Instantly, Aláké began to run reams of data on every screen as she matched data points that could be relevant to the investigation. Pels studied the images and news articles on the screens surrounding her, her mind a whirlwind of ideas and strategies. She felt as though she were standing at the cusp of a new beginning after what seemed like the dramatic ending of her mundane life, only big enough to accommodate half-hearted relationships and partially effective articles.

'Aláké, can you compile all the information on where and when the kids were taken?' Pels asked, her voice firm with conviction. 'I need a comprehensive overview of the patterns around who they interacted with and the locations.'

'Of course, Pels,' Aláké replied. Within moments, she had assembled a digital dossier filled with information, including the locations of the sightings of bodies, and Pels' research notes regarding the young Black people who had gone missing.

As Pels took in the information, she felt the beginning of a plan start to piece itself together in her mind, each element fitting into place with logic and precision.

'Aláké, cross-reference the locations of the missing persons,' Pels instructed, her brown eyes narrowing in concentration. 'Like I said, I believe there must be a pattern, some connection between them that will lead us to the source of all this.'

'Understood, Pels.' Aláké went quiet as she analysed the data. Moments later, she spoke up again, urgency sharpening her tone. 'Pels, I have just received a news update. There has been another sighting of Osahon in a town one hundred miles away from his home. Well, not so much a sighting of him – his chip faintly and briefly showed up in that area.'

Pels' heart clenched at the news, a surge of protectiveness flooding through her as she wondered how Elaine must be faring with the news. She knew she couldn't waste any more time; she had to act quickly if she was going to save the missing children. Once the ceremony tonight was over, she had to get back.

'Aláké, check for a substantial body of water near that town.'

'Of course, Pels. I've found: Lake Riley.'

Pels' eyes darted across the screens, her mind racing as she soaked in every detail from the celestial visions and the new information of Osahon's sighting. She felt a sudden realisation bubbling up inside her as she noticed a common thread in her research and the news update: lines.

The glowing lines.

In the saved images of her visions, Pels could now see more clearly that when the celestial beings showed her images of the Earth, there had been lines glowing on it that resembled fingerprints. They criss-crossed all over the globe. As she zoomed in on Britain, Pels saw the lines were glowing.

'Aláké,' Pels said, her voice steady with newfound confidence, 'pull up all the information on the fire paths mentioned at the museum. I want to see the ones that run through Britain.'

'The lines are now shown on the map, Pels. I've also found writings about many of these locations being rich in spiritual energy.'

'Which could explain their connection to the Soul Snatchers . . .' Pels mused. She absorbed the information, her intuition and journalistic instincts guiding her towards an understanding of the Soul Snatchers' methods, piecing together the puzzle to reveal a sinister pattern that now seemed all too clear.

'Perhaps these Soul Snatchers are only able to do their harm to these young people when they're next to a body of water that lands directly on one of these energy lines. Like some kind of combination of the elements. The tour guide mentioned the fire paths can be used as portals, right?' Pels murmured. 'That must be where they're getting their human lackeys to take the kids.'

As she continued to analyse the data, a news alert caught her attention. It was about the AI candidate running for Mayor of London, Jeremy Bromwich, whose popularity had skyrocketed in recent polls. The humanoid AI, promising a brighter future for all, appeared to have captured the hearts of the masses in her city, but Pels couldn't help wonder if there were larger forces at play, manipulating the political landscape for their own nefarious purposes.

The dim glow of the screens cast eerie shadows across Pels' face as she pored over maps and research materials. Her brows furrowed with concentration, her locs falling forward as she analysed every detail of the information displayed before her. She knew she couldn't afford to miss anything, especially right now. She realised that the retreat must be located at the nexus of another fire path portal, and the help of the Spirit Vine was her only real connection to the celestial beings who might be able to provide her with more answers before she went home.

'Aláké,' Pels called out into the darkness. 'Cross-reference these bodies of water with any folklore or legends surrounding them in Britain. Folk tales have a way of maintaining truth even when translated among different cultures – that's what the guide said, I think. There's a memory I have of my media teacher in high school who would sneak whisky at her desk – I'm sure she'd randomly tell us about fire paths or ley lines, fairy portals . . .'

Pels barely noticed the passage of time as she stayed up all night, trying to plan her next steps and gather the necessary information for her mission. With each passing hour, the urgency in her chest grew, knowing that there was at least one young person out in Britain whose life might depend on her being able to understand what to do next.

'Did you find any connections?' Pels asked eventually, her voice laced with anticipation.

'Indeed, I did, Pels,' Aláké responded. 'There are several legends detailing fire paths, even when referred to by a different name, and I can see from the map that each tragic discovery of the missing young people's bodies is seemingly by a "surge point". These are described as powerful points where numerous fire paths overlap near water, thus likely to create a portal, only active during a full moon as described at the museum.'

'Then that's where we'll start,' Pels declared, her eyes scanning the map one last time.

'Very well, Pels,' Aláké agreed.

'The final Spirit Vine ceremony will provide me with even more clarity now that we have done all this research,' Pels said. 'But . . . will I be ready, Aláké?' A sliver of doubt was creeping into her thoughts. 'Can I truly stop them?'

'Believe in yourself, Pels,' Aláké reassured her. 'You have the power and the determination to succeed.'

Pels couldn't criticise herself for seeking moral support from her AI system. Aláké knew her better than many of her friends and family, and right now Pels had no idea how she'd explain what had happened here to her mother, or Maria, Elaine or any of her friends. What she was currently experiencing felt too big to share with anybody in its fullness just yet.

As the first light of dawn began to seep through the blinds, Pels felt sleep pulling her in as her lids became heavier. But there was one more thing she wanted to do before succumbing to slumber . . .

'I need to try this,' she whispered.

It was as though there were three entities in Pels' hut: herself, Aláké and anticipation. Pels moved to stand in the centre of her hut, her arms outstretched and her eyes closed, feeling the pulse of her newfound powers thrumming through her veins. Her locs swayed gently, the ends brushing against the dark brown skin of her shoulder blades.

'I'm going to try to shift this table,' she announced, reaching out with the threads of her power.

With a deep breath, Pels concentrated on the wooden table before her, envisioning it lifting off the ground. Slowly, the table began to rise, inch by painstaking inch, until it hovered at waist height. Pels felt a surge of triumph at finally being able to *control* an object so deliberately. It wasn't like when she'd used the power at the museum, because this time she had called the power forth.

But an icy finger of doubt whispered: *Is this enough?*

Pels knew whatever she was able to do *had* to be enough, because it was all she currently had. Staring at her hands, she thought of the missing children – and those whose lives hung in the balance.

'Failure is not an option,' she murmured, determination hardening in her chest.

Chapter Sixteen

The more I researched, the harder it became to stop trying to piece together what the larger narrative could be around the seeming lack of care for missing young Black people in the UK. It gave me chills to think Tèmídìrè had devoted time to fighting for equality, only for the end of his life to fall foul of that same inequality. My frustration remains with the police, who yet again decided that there was nothing suspicious about the context of Tèmídìrè's death. His family and friends have expressed their disbelief in the police's conclusion.

★

Pels wasn't sure what prompted her to wake up so soon, but as soon as she opened her eyes, she swore she could hear Ayi's voice outside. Instantly, she knew what she wanted to do with the free time she had before the final Spirit Vine ceremony that evening.

She launched herself out of her bed and got dressed quickly. Grabbing a notebook and pen, she hurried out of her hut and went in search of Ayi, who she knew must be somewhere in the retreat centre.

The morning was still dewy and cool, a blanket of sleep lightly covering the grounds.

Ayi wasn't too hard to find. In the quiet of the place, Pels could hear two voices talking, so she headed in their direction. Harrison and Ayi were at the entrance of the retreat centre in front of an old car that looked nothing like the transport pods that carried the guests to and fro.

As Harrison saw Pels approaching, he smiled. 'Ah! Good morning, Pels, you're up early today. Excited for the final ceremony tonight?'

Ayi smiled at Pels, offering a warm squeeze of her shoulder.

'A good morning to you both. I went to bed rather late last night, so I don't know why I'm awake so early, but it must be fate because I wondered if I might be able to interview you at some point today, Ayi? It's for the piece I'm writing for the newspaper back ... home.' Home was a strange word when she considered the continent she was on.

As Harrison translated to Ayi in French, Pels could see the shake of the head signifying no, even though it was delivered with a smile. Her heart began to sink.

'Ayi isn't comfortable expressing herself in English, and doesn't have the new AI translation functions — so she wouldn't want a disjointed interview for you. She'll be spending today picking up the Spirit Vine brew and other necessary ceremony bits.'

'Ah, understood,' Pel's smile faltered briefly, but she quickly recovered. 'No worries.'

'Ha, I wasn't done! She has offered instead if you'd care to accompany her to pick up the Spirit Vine brew from her father's house in the village. That way maybe you can deduce things by observing?'

Pels couldn't believe her luck. This was better than anything she could've imagined.

'Yes, please, I would absolutely love to! I'm ready to go whenever you are, Ayi.' Pels gestured a thumbs up and brought her hand to her chest as a thank you.

'This'll be interesting!' Harrison laughed as Ayi directed Pels to her car.

'Good morning, gang! An early morning trip? Where are you headed? Can I come along?' Chris had clearly woken up early as well.

Ayi gestured, and Harrison explained. 'Ayi says the car is already so full and she needs some space to bring back the Spirit Vine brew from the village. Maybe next time, if you come back for a third retreat, huh?'

Chris appeared satisfied with the answer, and upon Harrison handing some money over to Ayi, the two men turned and walked back into the retreat gardens.

Pels got into the passenger seat of the car and looked behind her to see it was completely empty. When she looked over at Ayi, who was putting on her seatbelt, there was a smirk on her face. Without words, Pels felt like she understood perfectly what had just happened, and felt proud that she was being allowed into such a sacred process.

Pels recognised the route that Ayi took as they travelled in comfortable silence while music played on the radio. She felt a shared connection with the elder woman when one of the singers – whom Pels recognised as Fatoumata Diawara – started crooning her song 'Kèlè'.

She remembered what she had been told the lyrics meant, and suddenly she felt like a youth that needed to let go of Western ways and find her way back to behaviours more aligned to her heritage.

'Museum,' Ayi said, pointing at the Ouidah Museum of History that Pels had visited with the other guests. The place where she discovered things she couldn't have ever deemed possible. She realised now why she'd recognised the route. They continued a little further and eventually parked on the side of a dirt road.

'Come.' Ayi motioned for Pels to follow her out of the car and walk. Pels could still see the museum in the distance.

Suddenly, they were in an area that looked like a square.

'Ayi!' A man came running out of a nearby stall to greet Pels' guide for the day.

Immediately, Ayi's face broke into a beaming smile, and she embraced the man into a deep hug.

'Pels, this *mon frère*, um . . . my brother.'

'Ah! Nice to meet you.' Pels let her hand be clasped enthu-siastically by the man.

'Nice to meet you too!' he responded.

'Oh, you speak English?' Pels asked, surprised.

'Yes, many of us do. Among other languages left with us by the colonisers,' the man said with a laugh, despite the violence inferred by how those languages had been left in the first place. 'I am Godwin, by the way.'

Ayi seamlessly transitioned into another dialect that flowed from her tongue even more effortlessly than French. As she spoke, hurrying her brother along, Pels recalled the familiar cadence of the language that Ayi had chanted during the first Spirit Vine ceremony.

'My sister says we must go quickly to collect the brew from our father so she can get you back in time to rest.'

Curious, Pels asked, 'What's your main dialect? I know there are quite a few in the country. What do you and your family speak?'

'Well, Ayi and I both speak Fon and French. I speak English

as well, and our parents have a bit of Yoruba mixed in whenever they speak. So we are like a melting pot in that way.'

Pels was impressed by the linguistic abilities needed to navigate the ever-changing world in West Africa.

Ayi stopped by the golden statue of a mermaid and slapped her brother lightly on the arm to gain his attention. 'Explain Pels this.'

Godwin laughed at his sister's teasing bossiness. 'I guess I don't have the morning off from my job after all.'

'You're a tour guide?'

'Yes. I run an ethical tourists' education network across Ouidah. I also head up the People's Liberation Movement, an organisation to call for more rights and privileges for the people of Benin. We've been leading the current protests against the retreats stealing our land and capitalising on our Spirit Vine knowledge.'

Pels was stunned into pointing at Ayi and then at Godwin. 'But . . .'

Ayi nodded as her brother explained, trusting him to convey to Pels the reality of living in a place like Benin for many people.

'History has shown us that when the West wants something from Africa, it will find whichever means to get it. Optimism is hoping they get nothing. Pessimism is resigning yourself to the idea that they will take everything. Reality is accepting that it's more about controlling how much they get. For groups of people who came and drew borders all over Africa, they are not very good with accepting boundaries.'

Pels smiled at this. Ayi's brother sounded very knowledgeable.

'Do you mind if I write some of this down, and record it on my installed AI?'

'Sure, go ahead.'

'Aláké, record this information for my article,' Pels commanded.

'Of course, Pels. Recording.'

'I don't know if Ayi mentioned it, but I ended up at this retreat because my editor wanted me to cover the story of the protests happening at the retreat centres. It's seen by some as disruptive behaviour by locals who don't want their economy to grow.'

Godwin's laugh was bitter. 'How are they growing our economy? The majority of the money made at these retreats goes to bank accounts *outside* of Benin. Are we supposed to make the entirety of our salary on the day excursions where the retreat guests buy wooden souvenirs or clothes or spices? Everything that is done to bolster this experience for mainly white people is done in a way that doesn't put more money in the hands of the everyday person. Do you think they would fly sanitation drones overhead if it were only *our* health at risk?'

He shook his head, then continued, 'Ayi working at Eurydice Retreat has been a great way for us locals to control how the Spirit Vine is used. We have all agreed that nobody must show these people the brewing process, or the prayers offered to prepare the Spirit Vine. They must pay us to cultivate, brew and facilitate the ceremonies. Some refuse to listen and choose to watch videos and such to teach themselves and administer whatever diabolical beverage they've boiled to their guests – hence some shocking side effects they're eventually faced with. While we can protect the Spirit Vine to a certain degree, what we cannot protect so much is the aggressive acquisition of our land which is enabled by a disgustingly corrupt government, hence the protests. If the world can see what's happening by us bringing attention to it, then something has to change. It is like they robbed us and beat us almost to death, then realised they hadn't taken our jewels and so they've come back for those too.'

Pels was stunned, and admired Godwin's passion greatly. She saw how proudly Ayi looked at him as he explained the reality behind what so many viewed as a spiritually enlightening trip. As she pondered all she had been told, she found herself still glancing at the golden mermaid. Ayi whispered enthusiastically to her brother while gesturing towards Pels.

Godwin kept his gaze on Pels as he listened to Ayi. 'My sister wanted me to tell you that this Mami Wata, or mermaid statue, has been placed where the Tree of Forgetting used to be. When enslavers would buy our ancestors from this place, they would make them walk a long route that passes through here and eventually onto the ships in an area known as "the gate of no return". This tree would be walked around seven or nine times depending on whether the person being taken was a man, woman or child. It is said that it was done so they would forget their lives before being shoved onto the ships headed across the Atlantic.'

Pels nodded. 'I feel like through being here, I am remembering things that maybe somehow I, too, was told to forget.'

'That may be the case for many of us, in different ways,' Godwin offered. Beside them, Ayi's eyes were full of a kind of understanding.

The three of them continued to weave in and out of side streets until they reached a little house, about fifteen minutes from the square, through a leafy clearing. An old man with white hair and beard sat by the front door, looking deep in thought and chewing a small wooden stick. Pels recognised the wooden sticks as her grandmother had liked chewing the same type as the preliminary part to her morning dental hygiene ritual.

'Papa!'

The old man smiled as Ayi called out to him. As Ayi reached him, she knelt by his side, as was customary when greeting elders.

The siblings introduced Pels, and she too ensured she knelt when greeting the old man.

They followed him into his dim living room, which was deceptively bigger than what would've been expected from the outside. The walls were a shabby green, with black-and-white photos of Papa in his younger days, of Ayi and Godwin at various ages, and a woman who Pels deduced to be their mother.

They walked further into the house still and into a side room that could have been a bedroom, but no bed was inside. Instead, a straw mat lay on the floor, along with various bowls, beads, gin bottles and wooden statues. There was a medium-sized clay pot in the middle of the room with cloth wrapped around the handles. When Ayi caught Pels' confused expression, she prompted her brother to explain.

'Our father is a traditional priest. Or known as a "Fa" priest. People come to him to consult the oracle and seek answers. The Spirit Vine recipe was passed down to him from his grandfather, who was one of the most powerful priests in our history. He brews the Spirit Vine, and although we are trained to also make it, he leads on it and the prayers necessary to be said over the brew before it can be served.'

'How does he feel about the Spirit Vine being used in such a commercial way?' Pels asked.

Godwin presented the question to his father, who smiled as he answered in Fon, then his son translated. 'He says, "No amount of drinking this brew can do the job of relinquishing the poisoned fruit presented as education in the modern world. You can't keep drinking the medicine and then going back to the poison."'

'Ha, I feel attacked.' Pels squeaked out a nervous laugh at the directness of the old man.

Papa studied Pels' face for a while, as if trying to come to a decision. Eventually, he asked for Godwin to carry the brew to the car for Ayi.

'Papa says to sit down,' Ayi told Pels.

Pels, not quite sure what was happening, sat down on the straw mat on the floor.

'Papa says he will read your . . . as you say . . . your ahead.'

'My future?'

'Yes. But not like fake – like big. You know?'

'Ah, my destiny?'

Both Papa and Ayi nodded, and all three smiled at their efforts.

Pels glanced at Papa's wrist and saw no telltale mark of an AI chip insertion point.

'Can I use my AI to translate, and I'll refrain from asking questions?' Pels asked, tapping her wrist and the base of her skull.

Ayi nodded in consent.

'Aláké, translate for me.'

Papa cast a long chain with flat discs attached to it three times as he chanted.

'Translating for you,' Aláké began. '"You are weary child, weary from trying hard not to remember what your soul can never forget. I saw you and instantly saw a great power. You are raised in your country that everything is about control. Do not try to control the things that move through you too much. All will be shown to you when it needs to. Find your companions who can walk this lonely path with you. There is much that awaits you for the little you leave behind."'

As cryptic as the words sounded, Pels felt she understood enough. The look in Papa's eyes as he watched her to ensure she had understood him felt like there was so much he had said that the translation could not convey, but Pels was still incredibly grateful.

Papa reached for both of Pels' shoulders as they sat across from each other on the floor. He then placed one hand in the middle of her eyebrows and blew on it.

'"The oracle said eye for you is how you truly see, and that you are waking."'

There was something about the intensity with which Papa looked at Pels that brought tears falling forward. The word 'lonely' had touched her deeply, even if that was a loose translation of Papa's oracle reading.

'I know this cannot be easily translated to you both, but thank you. Before discovering aspects of myself on this trip, I had felt alone, even with an active social life. Through being here, I've realised that I'm loved far beyond what I can see, and while the loneliness hasn't left me, I just feel . . . seen.'

They both nodded, as if her tears had translated enough without the aid of the technology she had in Aláké.

As Ayi and Pels walked back in the direction of the car, Ayi was called back by Papa. She was gone for only a moment, and when she returned she walked towards Pels with a wrapped object that she popped into her bag, then they continued on their way. The sun had risen to the point that signified noon.

'It was lovely to meet you, Godwin,' Pels said as Ayi's brother joined them at her car. 'Thank you for offering me such insight.'

'My pleasure. When you go back to London, help us make noise about what's happening over here.'

'I absolutely will.'

The siblings said their warm goodbyes as Ayi and Pels set off in the car with a new understanding between them.

Pels looked at herself in the mirror as she prepared for the final Spirit Vine ceremony that evening. Her thoughts swirled. The woman looking back at her appeared somehow far removed from the one who'd arrived in Benin because of an assignment she had initially been reluctant to take on.

Once she felt she was mentally as ready as she'd ever be, Pels made her way out to join the others at the ceremonial hut. Standing outside it, she took a deep breath and closed her eyes, allowing the memories of her journey thus far to wash over her: the first time she had seen the celestial beings; their beauty and power overwhelming her senses; the realisation that she, too, possessed powers beyond her wildest dreams. All of these moments had led her to this point.

'Are you ready?' Ayi's voice, in halting English, gently interrupted her reverie.

Pels looked up at the wise woman, her face glowing with knowledge. 'I think so,' she said, uncertainty creeping into her voice, thinking about the messages Ayi's father had shared earlier on that day.

Ayi reassured her with a gesture, placing a comforting hand on her shoulder. With a nod, Pels followed the elder woman into the ceremonial hut, finding a spot among the others. The now-familiar atmosphere welcomed her with the scent of burning incense, and the flickering candlelight cast eerie shadows on the walls.

'Tonight, we will partake in the strongest brew of the Spirit Vine,' Ayi announced, as translated by Harrison, who looked objectively stunning in his white linen ceremonial attire. 'The visions you encounter may be more intense than anything you have experienced before. But remember – they are here to guide you, to show you the path forward.'

Pels' palms grew slick with sweat as she accepted the small cup filled with the dark, bitter and potent liquid. She glanced around at the other guests, their faces a mix of excitement and apprehension – especially Andromeda, who had made no secret of the fact that she was yet to experience any visions. Pels wondered if her fellow guests were also questioning the strength of their resolve.

'Remember, my friends, you are here because you are seeking answers,' Ayi said via Harrison. Her eyes met those of each person in turn. 'Do not shy away from the visions. Embrace them, and trust that they will lead you to the truth.'

With a final deep breath, Pels raised the cup to her lips and let the molasses-textured liquid slide down her throat. As the Spirit Vine began to take hold, she felt a familiar tingling sensation spread throughout her body. This time, though, it was accompanied by an energy that surged through her veins like a wild river, threatening to sweep her away in its current.

The visions came quickly this time, like an incoming tide enveloping Pels in their otherworldly embrace. She found herself floating among the celestial beings once more, their luminous forms shimmering like stars against the infinite darkness of space. The awe she felt in their presence was almost too much to bear, but she sensed that there was something different in the cosmic environment. The colours felt more intense somehow, like they had something important to share with her.

'Olúwapẹlúmi,' one of the beings spoke gently, its voice reverberating within her very soul. 'Your powers have grown beyond what you could have ever imagined, yet there is so much for you to discover. You have the ability to fly – to soar through the skies like a gust of wind.'

'We are never far from you,' another being added, its stardust form swirling and shifting before her eyes. 'You need not rely on the Spirit Vine any longer to connect with us. Simply look up at the night sky, and we will be there.'

'Thank you,' Pels whispered, tears of gratitude streaming down her face. 'But . . . why does everything feel weirdly different right now? What's wrong?'

'Listen closely, Olúwapẹlúmi,' a third being warned, its voice suddenly filled with urgency. 'You must leave this place imme-diately. You are in great danger. Your Awakening and the use of your powers has created surges in the fire paths that the Soul Snatchers can sense, and thus trace. We can see their imminent arrival.'

Pels' heart pounded as the ethereal world around her began to dissolve. 'Wait! What do you mean? I'm not ready yet!'

The celestial beings faded into the darkness, leaving Pels with a sense of foreboding that threatened to swallow her whole.

Ignoring the others, she stumbled out of the ceremonial hut, gasping for air, her head spinning from the intensity of the vision and potency of the Spirit Vine.

'Are you OK?' Harrison had rushed out after her, concern etched onto his handsome features as he caught Pels by the arm, steadying her.

'Something's wrong,' Pels breathed, her chest tightening with fear. 'The . . . the celestial beings I saw in my vision. They told me I have to leave. Right now.'

Harrison looked away, his face contorting with shame. 'I'm so sorry, Pels,' he confessed, his voice barely a whisper. 'I never meant for this to happen.'

Pels froze, staring at him. 'What do you mean?' she demanded, her eyes searching his for answers. 'What have you done?'

Harrison's voice trembled as he spoke. 'For a long time growing up, I was told, "Be careful, your devilish good looks will someday land you into trouble with the devil." It was just something my ma and my aunts would say as they fussed over me. An only child to a Sicilian mother in New York City, of course I was spoiled. Even though I knew it, it didn't stop me from using it to my benefit. I ran a jewellery business at the time, named it "Awakened". Making and selling the jewellery got me into scrapes with shady characters, because I needed to get my hands on funds to pay for materials and gems. I remember my ma said to me I had high hopes and low morals – and she was right.'

Pels felt her jaw clench. How could Harrison think this was the perfect time for the unabridged version of his life story? Her head still felt hazy from the Spirit Vine, and her life could be in danger. 'Harrison, I mean this with all the love of someone seeking connection with the higher power and remaining alive to do so – get to the fucking point.'

Harrison's eyes widened in shock, as if unused to being spoken to so directly. Pels hadn't raised her voice yet her hushed irritation had clearly cut him. 'Well, I borrowed a lot of money from some people I couldn't pay back; I had made a ring that this jazz singer guy in Manhattan swore he wanted for his girlfriend, but then his wife found out about the relationship and he couldn't make good on the promise since it was her family's money the fuc— sorry, the guy – planned to use.'

'So the people who loaned you the money weren't pleased,' Pels said, attempting to usher his story along.

'Exactly. And they didn't want the ring either. I had planned to sell it and make their money back, and hopefully have enough left over to return to Benin to continue my journey with the Spirit Vine. It was the visions I'd had when I first tried it that helped me to create my designs, and truly it was the only time I didn't feel like an absolute fuck-up in life.'

Harrison swore openly now, the ghosts of many regrets clearly gnawing at him from the inside.

'The guys I owed money to beat me up so bad in my apartment that night that I was sure I was dying,' he continued quickly. 'Face busted, ribs broken, I could barely breathe or call out for help, even though they left my door open when they left.' He took a deep breath. 'The last thing I remember was this sort of shadowy figure – almost like a man – walking into my apartment and towering over me. It was like a vision . . . He asked me, "Will you do anything to live right now?" I couldn't even nod in case that's all it would've taken to break my neck. I groaned though, and he understood.'

'What does this have to do with me?' Pels would've been more patient were her own neck not on the line.

'At first I didn't make the connection. It was my business's name that caught his attention. The vision-guy told me, "By morning there will be more than enough money in your account for you to pay these people and set up a life elsewhere." But he seemed to know it had to specifically be in Benin. Apparently, by naming my business "Awakened", and with my frequent visits to Spirit Vine retreats here, he'd decided I was right for whatever task he had. According to some weird prophecy, I had to build a retreat centre at particular co-ordinates which happened to be this exact spot. All he said was that they were awaiting an "Awakened One".'

Pels attempted to steady herself, reeling from the Spirit Vine's effect and Harrison's revelations.

'Sounded like a fair trade at the time since I thought I was hallucinating and would be dead by morning. I don't remember much after that. I woke up in a hospital after a couple of days and when I was finally discharged and made it to an ATM, I almost passed out at the amount of money that was in my account.' Harrison exhaled hard. 'I left that same week, and never looked back. It was only when I started the retreat excursions to the museum that I learnt about the fire paths. I convinced myself, even in the face of the power of the Spirit Vine, that whoever they were seeking would never arrive. Then you showed up.'

The Soul Snatchers. They were who Harrison had spoken to in his vulnerable state. The realisation settled in Pels' stomach like a block of ice.

'I should have known better than to make a deal with them,' Harrison admitted, anguish colouring his words. 'But when you shared some of your visions, they were so different to anything I'd seen before . . . I realised the prophecies were true. I thought if I just stayed quiet, I could keep you safe somehow. I had a dream last night, though. The same strange voice came to me and said, "Do you have anything to tell me?" I told it no, but . . . they're coming, Pels. And I don't know what they'll do when they find you.'

Pels stared at him. She didn't have time to process all of this now – she needed to act, to escape this place before it was too late. She took a deep breath. If the Soul Snatchers got to her, death would be the least of her worries. She had a mission.

Pels sprinted towards her hut, snatching up her belongings and retrieving her phone from the safe in her room. She quickly barked instructions to Aláké to find flight times out of Benin as soon as possible. As she did so, she couldn't help but think about how nowhere would truly be safe for her now that the Soul Snatchers knew she existed. 'I need to make it back to London alive,' she said.

'Understood, Pels. I'll find you something right away,' Aláké replied, her tone calm and reassuring despite the circumstances. Then again, that was the beauty of AI; they didn't have to be clouded by emotions at important moments. *Maybe AI would be better as mayor – or even prime minister, should Jeremy decide that he wants that.* The thought randomly flashed across Pels' mind despite the gravity of her situation. It vanished as quickly as it had appeared, leaving her with the stark reality: her escape from the retreat now was a matter of life and death.

Harrison stood listlessly outside of Pels' hut as she emerged. As she looked at his face, a wave of sadness washed over her, quickly followed by a surge of determination. She pursed her lips and blew softly, casting a gentle breeze towards him, not quite sure what led her to the instinct. The air shimmered around Harrison for a moment before he collapsed into a deep sleep.

'Ooh. That's handy,' she quipped. 'Sorry, Harrison. You moping around from your guilt can't cost me my life right now.'

Pels knew that she couldn't afford to falter – not with so much at stake. As she ran towards the retreat exit, she gazed up at the night sky one last time, seeking solace in the celestial realms that now held the key to her destiny.

'Guide me,' she whispered to the stars, their twinkling lights shimmering like a promise in the darkness.

Chapter Seventeen

For a long time, I have tried to persuade my editor to allow me to write this piece with the robustness and care it deserves, and I've faced many obstacles in doing so. But with the disappearance of Osahon Samuels, I can no longer accept no for an answer. Osahon is the brother of my friend, Elaine. Witnessing her anguish first-hand has propelled me forward to tell the stories of these missing young Black people. My hope is just that maybe it could spark something – anything – that will lead to positive change.

★

Pels inhaled deeply, quickly braiding her locs back and visualising a protective barrier encasing the retreat centre, muffling all sound within its boundaries. The air around her crackled with energy, charged with her determination to keep the others and herself safe from the impending danger.

'Let no sound escape,' she whispered, feeling the forcefield take shape around the property, an invisible shield to guard them from the Soul Snatchers.

As Pels finished weaving her shield, a sudden chill swept through the night. Her heartbeat started to race as she noticed shadows suddenly creeping closer across the lagoon as she passed it, slithering down tree trunks and across the ground like serpents stalking their prey. The world seemed to hush, as though holding its breath in anticipation. At the edge of the retreat, shadows coalesced into tangible almost-human forms.

It was too late. The Soul Snatchers had arrived.

'Show yourselves!' Pels demanded, her voice steady despite the fear that twisted inside her chest like a thorny vine.

'Ah, a Guardian of Souls,' a voice hissed from the shadows, dripping with menace. 'Freshly Awakened. We've been waiting for you. The prophecies were indeed true.'

The Soul Snatchers' shadowy forms stepped forward. There were three of them, their appearance shifting between something akin to the amorphous shapes of the celestial beings and a human physical form, dressed in white cloaks and hoods. Pels couldn't see much of their faces. Nonetheless, they were grotesquely mesmerising, possessing an eerie translucence that exposed neon-red veins underneath what might be deemed their 'skin'. They towered over Pels like vultures circling a dying animal. Their purple eyes glinted with malice, their intentions clear: they outnumbered her, and they planned to overpower her.

'Stay back!' Pels warned, raising a hand – the adrenaline made it easy for her to summon her powers; she could feel them tingling all the way up her arms. 'I don't know how, but I will fuck you lot up!'

'Brave words, little one,' another Soul Snatcher sneered, his voice a guttural growl. 'But you cannot hope to stand against us. You have known of your power only for a few days. Before this we have seen your woeful existence, writing drivel for your pathetic fellow humans to ignore. *We* have powers that have been centuries in the making.'

'Perhaps that's true, and you're not all the way off about the writing drivel part,' Pels admitted, even though she was unsure how they could have known this about her. Her heart was still pounding in her ears. 'But I'd rather die fighting than let you keep taking young people's souls.'

'Then prepare to meet your end,' the first Soul Snatcher snarled, lunging towards her with unnatural speed.

Pels gritted her teeth and braced for some strange impact, her body tensing as she prepared to unleash every ounce of her power against her opponents. Her thoughts flickered to the celestial realms above, praying that their guidance hadn't been the result of major delusions and she wasn't about to get annihilated. As the creature lunged towards her, Pels' instincts took over. She swiftly dodged out of the way, narrowly avoiding its grasping hands. Her powers surged within her like the thrashing sea nearby, desperate to be unleashed.

'Is that all you've got?' she taunted, even as her heart raced with adrenaline, hoping that it was, in fact, all they had. She knew she couldn't afford to let fear take hold. She had a mission now; she had to make it home.

'Pathetic!' another Soul Snatcher rasped, its voice dripping with venom. 'You'll pay for your insolence.'

'Let's see you try,' Pels shot back, her eyes blazing. The air around her suddenly crackled with electricity as she summoned her powers. With a wave of her hand, she sent a powerful gust of wind hurtling towards the Soul Snatchers, knocking them off their feet and sending them sprawling across the ground.

'Enough of this foolishness,' one of the creatures growled, rising to its feet and looming over Pels with murderous intent. 'We will have the souls we desire, as is commanded by the Cloud of Sorrow . . .'

'Over my dead body,' Pels spat, knowing that may very well be the outcome.

'Very well,' the Soul Snatcher hissed.

They charged at Pels once more, their movements swift and deadly. But Pels was ready for them. She deftly leapt into the air, shocked at how far her powers allowed her to soar. 'Leave here!' Pels shouted, her voice quivering with a mix of fear and exhilaration. She knew she couldn't keep the upper hand forever, but every moment she bought herself was another chance to turn the tide in her favour.

To her shock, the Soul Snatchers began to hover off the ground just below her, becoming more amorphous and merging into one huge entity. Pels reached deep within herself, tapping into the hidden reservoirs of power that she had only just begun to discover. She willed her body to become one with the elements, feeling the wind at her back and the ground so far beneath her.

'By the celestial realms,' she whispered under her breath, 'I *have* to make it home. My mum will be so pissed off if I die here.'

With a mighty surge, Pels unleashed everything she could muster upon the Soul Snatchers. Lightning crackled through the air, searing the night with brilliant flashes of blazing-hot energy. Gale-force winds whipped around her as she spun her body and locs around and around in the air, buffeting the Soul Snatchers and forcing them to crash back onto the ground and disassemble.

'Impossible!' one of them roared, struggling against the tempest Pels had summoned.

'Perhaps you've underestimated me,' Pels retorted. 'Surrender now and leave us!'

But the Soul Snatchers were relentless, and soon a maelstrom of energy built from the ground up into the sky, threatening to engulf them all. The wind howled like it was wounded, and Pels felt herself drifting back to the ground as her powers were sapped by the force of the battle.

She saw the Soul Snatchers gathering together once again, amalgamating their energy to turn into one giant version of their hateful selves. With this formation, the merged creatures lunged forward at an ungodly speed and grabbed Pels by the throat, lifting her off the ground by the neck and squeezing intently. Pels felt herself losing consciousness. *This is it*, she thought. *It's all over . . .*

Panic set in as she felt herself being thrown into the air – but not by her own powers. As she went flying, Pels heard Ayi's voice screaming at the Soul Snatchers, 'Leave her alone and leave this place! You are not welcome!' just as she landed with an almighty splash into the nearby lagoon.

Pels opened her eyes, and the panic was relentless as she sank beneath the water. She remembered her dream of drowning from a few days ago, and realised it wasn't a dream at all but a premonition. She thrashed about in the water, devastated that after all her valiant combat, it would be drowning due to exhaustion that would be the end of her. The irony of pursuing a story about missing young people's bodies being found in water only for her to meet the same fate. Her mouth filled with water as she attempted to scream in frustration, but to her shock, as she began to lose consciousness, she saw the celestial beings appear in the murky water, surrounding her.

'Olúwapelúmi, you cannot give up. Get back to the land and leave your old self here with us . . .'

Pels heard the words resonate in her soul. She still had more power within her. She saw faces of spirits she was sure had once lived on this land come to her aid under the water, some of them resembling ancient Dahomey female warriors. As they propelled her up through the water, it was as her old life was being washed away from her body. All her doubts and fears were being taken and held by these spirits as they pulled her up towards the surface of the water.

Pels burst out of the lagoon, drenched and resolute, taking the Soul Snatchers by surprise.

'Give up!' one of the creatures spat, its voice dripping with malice. Pels could see that they were holding a writhing Ayi down on the ground. 'You cannot win!'

'Watch me,' Pels replied defiantly. 'Why do you seek to steal the souls of innocent children? Why hide behind such coward-ice?' Her eyes blazed with righteous fury.

'Silence!' the Snatcher roared, unleashing a torrent of energy that slammed into Pels, knocking her off her feet.

'Answer me!' Pels shouted, leaping to her feet again despite the pain that coursed through her body. 'What is it that you truly fear?'

'Enough!' the Soul Snatcher screamed, his face contorted with rage. 'You have no power over us!'

'Perhaps not,' Pels admitted, her voice barely a whisper. 'But I am not afraid of you.'

'Then you are a fool!' another creature snarled, preparing to strike her down once and for all.

'Maybe,' Pels replied, her voice calm. 'But I know who I am now. I know my purpose, and I will do everything I can to stop you.'

'Your purpose?' the Soul Snatcher sneered, pausing in his attack. 'What could you possibly know about purpose?'

'More than you can imagine,' Pels answered, her voice filled with a newfound strength that resonated all around them. 'I am a Guardian of Souls, bound by blood and destiny to protect those who cannot protect themselves. And I will fulfil my duty, even if it means having my mum be right about not booking this trip.'

'Then prepare to die!' the Soul Snatcher roared, lunging at her with renewed ferocity.

'Bring it on,' Pels whispered, bracing herself for the impact. As the creature's energy collided with hers, there was an explosion of light so brilliant that it momentarily blinded her. The very air around them seemed to shudder and crackle with the force of their clash. But when the dust settled and the light faded, Pels was still standing, her body glowing with a celestial radiance that defied the darkness that had once held her captive.

'Is this . . . is this what it means to be a Guardian of Souls?' she wondered aloud, her heart swelling with a sense of purpose and belonging that she had never before experienced.

'Indeed,' came a soft voice from behind her, and Pels turned to see Ayi struggling to her feet and eyeing the younger woman with wonder. In as much English as she could manage, Ayi continued, 'Your true power, it shows. Now, nothing is in your way. Thank you for saving me. For saving *us*.'

'We saved each other, I think,' Pels responded with deep gratitude.

And now it was time to go home and finish this.

Chapter Eighteen

Osahon's disappearance inspired me to create a map charting all the locations I knew of where the bodies of these victims had been found. Yes, I knew of the pattern of their bodies being found in or around bodies of water – but I was soon to make a more chilling discovery about the locations of these deaths. What could this all mean? In the practice of fair and balanced journalism, I couldn't simply jump to conclusions . . .

★

Ayi helped Pels to clean her wounds with a balm she'd rushed to retrieve from the staff quarters. Pels enjoyed the lull of Ayi's voice as she spoke in hushed tones.

'Aláké, translate for me.'

'Translating from French to English.'

Ayi continued, 'From the little I have seen, I feel your journey has only just begun, Olúwapẹlúmi. Papa called me back to give me this balm for you. He said we would know when to use it. I did not think he meant so soon.'

Pels felt overwhelmed with a multitude of emotions, and stepped into Ayi's embrace gratefully, tears escaping her closed eyes.

'Take this medicine with you,' Ayi said. 'You will need this whenever you are hurt. If there is a need, contact me and Papa will make you more.'

The balm was dark and when it touched Pels' wounds it stung, but moments later she felt soothed and could see the wound visibly beginning to heal.

'Amazing,' Pels murmured, as she placed the balm in her backpack.

The two women agreed that Pels' story would be that a family emergency required her to return home immediately. As for the destruction to the retreat centre, that would be Harrison's story to figure out.

'Aláké,' Pels murmured, 'which flights did you find? I need to be well away from here as soon as possible.'

'There is a flight leaving quite soon,' Aláké responded. 'By my calculations, to clear security, it would require you to be at the airport within the next twenty minutes.'

It had taken at least double that time by transport pod. 'Damn it . . .' Pels muttered.

Pels took one final glance around her assigned hut; her suitcase still perched in the corner. Stepping over her battle-torn clothes strewn on the floor, Pels once again picked up her backpack filled with her necessary possessions and left everything else behind.

As she was sprinting towards the edge of the retreat centre again, she glanced up at the sky, searching for the celestial guidance she had been promised. Then suddenly, there amid the chaos of the night, shimmering starlight illuminated a clear path before her. *Should I try . . .?* Pels could barely finish the thought, instead wondering what she had to lose.

'Here goes nothing,' she whispered to herself, and with newfound confidence, she spun herself into the air and soared towards the heavens, her dreadlocks streaming behind her like the tail of a comet. The wind whipped around her, but she remained fearless, her gaze locked on the guiding stars that would lead her to the airport and to the next part of her mission.

For someone who is scared of heights, this is actually very mad, she thought, her heart pounding with exhilaration. Pels soared through the inky blackness of the night, the shimmering starlight creating a path before her. The celestial beings had kept her safe thus far, and she trusted them to guide her as she journeyed onwards. As Pels soared higher, the landscape below her transformed into a beautiful patchwork quilt of moonlit fields and dark forests. She was leaving behind this land, where so much had transpired – from her awakening as a Guardian of Souls to the ensuing battle with the Soul Snatchers, to the unexpected sisterhood of the amazing spiritualist Ayi.

'You are on course to arrive at the airport soon, Pels,' Aláké informed her. 'I have booked your ticket. Your flight leaves in two hours.'

'Thank you, Aláké,' Pels replied with gratitude, adjusting her course towards the airport. 'I don't know what you've made of all this, but I couldn't have done it without you.'

'Of course, Pels,' Aláké responded warmly. 'It's been an honour to help you on your journey, even if you do get a tad irritated with me at times.'

The buoyant, cooling air was strangely soothing, and as she flew through it, Pels' thoughts drifted to the people she had met at the retreat centre – especially Harrison. Despite his past shortcomings, she couldn't shake the empathy she felt for him. Life wasn't easy, and who was to know where a single decision to escape the danger and drudgery of life would lead.

'Aláké,' Pels began hesitantly, 'do you think people can change? Can someone who has done bad things find redemption?'

'Everyone has the potential to change, Pels,' Aláké answered thoughtfully. 'But it's up to each individual to choose their own path. The readings I can access suggest that people need a second chance, or even a third or fourth, to finally make the right choice.'

'Maybe,' Pels said softly, a mix of hope and sadness in her voice. Of course, she'd have no such understanding for the humans helping the Soul Snatchers steal innocent kids . . .

The airport came into view below her, and Pels steeled herself for what lay ahead. She had overcome so much already, but she knew that this was only the beginning of her journey as a Guardian of Souls.

Whatever happens, she thought to herself, *I know I can face it head-on.*

'Aláké,' Pels said with determination, 'once I land in London, I need all the information you can find about Lake Riley. I have a feeling that somewhere close to there is where Osahon is being held. We can't waste any time.' *If it's not too late already . . .*

'Absolutely,' Aláké replied. 'Gathering all required data now.'

As Pels negotiated her descent towards the airport, careful to keep out of sight lest anyone see her, she couldn't help but see the humour in launching herself into the air without the forethought of how she would land.

'Watch out, world,' she thought fiercely. 'Here I come. And literally watch out, in case the landing is bumpy . . .'

Chapter Nineteen

Conclusions and conspiracy theories aside, I had to delve further into the apparent coincidence that so many of these tragedies had a very specific proximity in common. My initial theory when I began to notice the pattern of missing young Black people was that there was a secret society made up of rich and powerful people who were using these victims as some form of initiation or sacrifice.

★

Pels stepped off the plane in London, her heart swelling with a mix of relief and apprehension. The familiar cityscape greeted her like an old friend, but she knew that she was no longer the same person who had left these shores just a week ago. As she descended the stairs onto the tarmac, she couldn't help but feel the prodding stares of her fellow passengers. She could sense their confusion and concern as they took in the sight of her bruised face, even though she had changed clothes before leaving the retreat centre to limit the visibility of the marks of the battle she had fought in that mystical realm in Benin.

'Are you all right?' concerned voice asked. Pels glanced over, meeting the gaze of a kind-eyed woman who had been seated nearby her on the flight. 'You look like you've been through quite an ordeal,' she added softly.

'Thank you,' Pels responded with a slight smile, feeling the sting of her bruises as her lips stretched. 'I'm fine, really. You should see the other guys.'

As she limped through the airport terminal, Pels marvelled at the stark contrast between her life now and what it had been before she had been awakened by the celestial beings. Though she still bore the physical scars of her recent battle, she couldn't deny the newfound confidence that surged through her veins, fuelled by her connection to these otherworldly beings.

The airport security officer eyed her with concern as she swished her wrist across the ID terminal to reveal her passport information, using the real-person line as she was unsure about passing through the auto gates. His gaze flicked from her bruised arms to her face and back to her passport image showing up on his screen.

'Bloody Pilates, eh?'

'If you need any assistance, don't hesitate to ask someone,' the officer said before turning to the next passenger.

'Thank you,' she murmured. But Pels knew that explaining what she had been through to the average person could result in her being detained in a mental health institution.

As the taxi pulled away from the airport, Pels settled into the worn leather seat, her eyes taking in the familiar streets of London – a balm for her soul as soothing as Ayi's father's concoction for her bruises. The city was alive with movement, a symphony of honking horns and pedestrians rushing to their destinations. She found solace in the grey concrete and the noise of urban life that surrounded her now, grounding her in the reality she knew before her transformation.

Her phone vibrated in her pocket, and she retrieved it, her fingers hesitating over the screen as if touching it might shatter the fragile connection between her two worlds. 'Pels, you have numerous messages,' Aláké chimed in. 'Would you like me to itemise them?'

Pels' curiosity won out. 'No, thanks, Aláké.' She opened the flood of messages that had accumulated during her absence.

'Olúwapẹlúmi, how are you? We haven't heard from you in days!' Her mother's voice was loud in the audio readout, a mixture of worry and affection.

'Hey, queen, I hope everything's OK. I miss you. Carmen is saying she doesn't want to keep the baby. I want to give me and you another chance. Holler at me if you're not on that angry Black woman vibe anymore and you're ready to talk.' Damari's message almost made her scoff at his audacity.

'Girl, you won't believe who else is getting married! Tolu just announced it in the group chat,' Maria teased, her excitement palpable even through text. 'Hope the trip is going well, let me know when you're back. Going to *cat emoji*'s wedding as well later, she's having a Nigerian traditional *upside-down smiley emoji*.'

Pels smiled, for the first time feeling no tinge of failure, no pang of envy, as she heard about another milestone reached by someone in her circle. She was a Guardian of Souls after all – her path was different, and more laden with responsibility than she could have ever imagined. Pels had left a metaphorical skin she had not realised she needed to shed in the lagoon, left in the safe keeping of the ancestors.

As the taxi neared her apartment building, Pels took in the comforting familiarity of the brick facade, and the small garden below her window that was always tended to with care by her elderly neighbour. This was home, and it was here that she would lay the groundwork for her next – and hopefully final – battle against the Soul Snatchers.

Stepping out of the taxi, she swiped her wrist across the payment terminal to pay the driver and made her way to the entrance. She unlocked her door with a sigh of relief, the familiar scent of her space and sanitising spray through the air vents enveloping her like the hug of a dear friend.

But Pels knew there was no time to fully revel in her return. As she sat down at her desk, her fingers danced over her keyboard, and she delved back into the depths of her investigation, going over the notes she had so far. Hours passed in a blur as she meticulously organised her findings. Pages upon pages of research covered her desk, a chaotic mosaic of notes and photographs that painted an ominous picture. She had spent untold hours poring over these documents and images before her trip to Benin. Now she was scouring them again for the connections that would bring the Soul Snatchers' conspiracy to light.

'Aláké, I think I've found a link between these cases.' *Warehouses* were located near the energy line clusters and bodies of water she'd already identified – and they were all under the ownership of Cannon & Sons. But what she discovered with a little more research had her heart in her mouth. The owner of Cannon & Sons was someone far closer to home than she'd imagined. The name 'Cannon' was common, but thinking about it, Pels remembered a picture of an old warehouse hung on her boss's wall, matching perfectly with the image she could see online of the warehouse by Lake Riley. 'Oh my God,' she said aloud. The company's owner was indeed none other than Dave Cannon's father, Bernard.

'Can you believe it?' Pels asked Aláké, her voice shaking with a mix of disbelief and indignation. 'Dave tried to deter me from researching the missing young people, and now we find out his father's warehouses are right by where their bodies were found . . . Coincidences like this don't just *happen*, do they?' Pels' eyes narrowed as she scanned through more of the information on her tablet. 'And local MPs, police chiefs . . . even celebrities have been spotted at the warehouse openings, as well as at events hosted by Bernard Cannon. Aláké, why the hell would people like this be interested in warehouses?' She sighed.

'Bernard Cannon has been rubbing shoulders with some extremely powerful people,' Aláké offered. 'If the fire paths and the location of the retreat is anything to go by, then there has to be a reason that these warehouses are built where they are.'

She was right. Pels had deduced that Bernard Cannon's warehouses were all built on these clusters. This was by no means an accident.

'Pels, I have checked the floor plan of the Lake Riley warehouse and it would appear that based on the size of the building, the floor plans online are actually inaccurate.'

'What does that mean?'

'It is likely that the floor plans available in the public domain do not include large parts of the warehouse.'

Pels was quickly realising what Aláké had figured out. Secret rooms. Likely where the young people who were abducted could be held.

'If what you've discovered is true, Aláké, then Osahon is probably being held in one of those secret rooms at the Lake Riley warehouse right now.'

'I sense your concern. Are you ready to confront Dave about this?' Aláké enquired softly.

Pels took a deep breath, steadying herself. 'I have no choice. The full moon is tonight, and the fire paths require it to open portals. I must expose his father's involvement if we stand a chance of saving Osahon – and any others they may be planning to take. I think I have an idea of where an original map of that warehouse might be.'

Lonely. The word popped into Pels' mind as mentioned during her oracle reading with Ayi's father. Instead of instructing Aláké to compose the text, Pels pulled her phone out and began to type.

Mummmmyyy, I'm back!! I missed you so much. I will fill you in properly soon, there are just some super important things I need to do now that I'm home. You'll be happy to know that demons didn't possess me. LOL!

As if her mum had been waiting by the phone, the three dots appeared, indicating that she was typing.

Mum: Pẹlúmi, welcome back my dear daughter. God's presence went with you and followed you back. God is good. Amen. You know it's not good to not share your voice with me. Let us speak as soon as is possible.

Pels smiled reading her mum's text, noting that she needed to teach her how to text 'ASAP' instead of writing the whole thing out.

Then she sent a voice note to Maria. 'Maria babyyyy, I'm back. I'm a bit worse for wear but I just wanted to say I am so grateful to have you in my life, and thank you for convincing me to go to Benin. It has been life-changing, and I'm smarter because of it, and because of you. We need a debrief immediately, but let me get the last bits of my assignment done first, yeah? How was pum-pum's wedding?'

Smiling fondly as she ended the voice note to her best friend, a swift sombreness cast a shadow in her mind. She began to type out a message to Elaine.

> Hey, I've just gotten back from the work assignment I told you about. Somehow, the things I've learnt while in Benin might prove useful in our search for Osahon, I'll come back to you soonest. There are things I need to look into and people I might be able to get information from. Sending you and the family lots of love. xx

Pels put her phone down as her gaze drifted outside her window, where London stretched itself out before her. Her eyes welled up ever so slightly as she prepared to confront these powerful men – starting with her boss. Pels had never been one to shy away from the truth, but this was a delicate dance she would have to perform with Dave. Had he known what was happening all this time? And if he didn't know, would he be willing to face his father's corruption and help her stop it – or would he choose to protect the sinister network that threatened so many lives?

Chapter Twenty

I was not in the country when I made the majority of the connections that helped me to better approach this investigation. I had visited the Republic of Benin, a country navigating its own complex history and current expression of collective identity. I spoke with a local tour guide and political organiser who was able to explain to me the intricacies of what many see – inaccurately – as the actions of bitter and disgruntled locals. A statement he made that stuck with me was around Europe and the USA drawing so many lines to impose borders on the natives of a land yet refusing to acknowledge the boundaries set by those very same people.

Ironically, it was these very same protests that I had initially been assigned to cover. What I learnt was the delicate dance of liberation. People around me at the retreat I attended, who had apparently never been confronted with backlash or had to fight for what they deemed rightfully theirs, expressed discomfort at witnessing the protests. My experience was that I became galvanised to be less of a bystander who is complicit in allowing injustice to reign.

★

Pels arrived at *The Mercury* office with her heart pounding in her chest and a combination of anticipation and anxiety surging through her veins. She took a deep breath, steadying herself, before pushing open the familiar double doors that led into the building.

As she strode through the bustling newsroom, Pels wore her conviction and purpose like armour, protecting her from the curious glances of her colleagues at her limping and bruised appearance, though Ayi's ointment had taken care of the worst of it. The atmosphere was alive with the sound of keyboards clacking and phones ringing, but Pels' focus remained laser-sharp on the task at hand.

'Dave,' she called out, spotting him hunched over his desk, sifting through papers. 'I need to speak with you.'

He glanced up, startled by her demeanour, and motioned for her to take a seat. 'What's going on, Pels? What the hell happened in Benin? You're back a day early – were they about to chop you up and eat you or something? That would make for a good story, come to think of it . . .'

Pels hesitated for a moment, considering whether to fire back at his ignorant comment. She glanced over at the picture on Dave's wall that he was so proud of – 'his dad's first ever business' – now knowing that picture frame held much more information than she could've imagined. She dove right in: 'I've discovered something – something big. It's about the missing young people and . . . your father.'

'Wait, what?' Dave's brow furrowed, confusion flashing across his face. 'What does my father have to do with anything? Why is this the first thing you're asking me about when I'm expecting an article on Benin? It wasn't just a paid holiday to your motherland, you know.'

'I'll get to that,' she replied, her jaw clenching. 'Allow me to explain.' Pels quickly began to lay out some of the evidence she had gathered. 'While I was out in Benin, I had some downtime, and decided to look for patterns in the locations where the bodies of these young Black people are discovered after they go missing, and—'

'Pels, I've read through enough of your drafts on this bloody subject already. Yes! You've said it is by water and choose to ignore that a lot of your people can't—'

Dave seemed to catch himself before regurgitating the trope of Black people's inability to swim. Pels, unmoved by her boss's ignorance, continued, 'Yes, you're correct that I wrote about them being discovered in or by water – however, another thing I've now realised all of these tragedies also have in common is that the bodies of water are all extremely close to Cannon & Sons logistics warehouses.'

'So, you mean to tell me that you burst into my office, without the article I sent you to Benin for, to give me the front-page *exposé* that my father's warehouses are situated in spaces where there would be lots of land? Oh, and would you believe it, sometimes wide-open spaces like that have forests, and are near lakes, ponds and rivers.' He folded his arms, clearly irritated. 'Do you just dislike doing actual work – is that it?'

'Please, Dave – just listen.' Pels took a deep breath, steadying herself for the next part of her argument. 'I know this is hard to hear, but the evidence so far all points to the warehouses being connected in some way. I didn't come here to do any of what you said . . . I need that map thing – the one in the frame with your dad's warehouse.'

As she spoke, Pels could see the conflicting emotions playing out on Dave's face – doubt, fear and anger all vying for dominance. She knew that asking her boss to confront the possibility of his father's involvement in such heinous acts wouldn't be easy, but it was necessary. She needed to believe he could do the right thing when presented with facts. Silence hung heavy in the air between them, broken only by the hum of the newsroom around them. Pels watched as Dave considered her words, his eyes searching hers for any hint of deception.

'Why in heavens would you need the floor plan? It's decades old, and you'd understand nothing of my father's customs. He framed a picture of each warehouse and its original floor plan. It's a quirk, not an indictment.'

'Dave, did you ever mention my research about the missing young people to your father?' Pels asked, watching Dave carefully for any shift in his demeanour.

'Of course not,' Dave replied, sounding offended and suddenly defensive. 'Why would I discuss something so far-fetched with him?'

'Are you absolutely sure?' Pels pressed. 'Think back. Not even a casual mention?'

Dave hesitated, the wheels of memory turning in his mind. He frowned. 'Actually,' Dave admitted slowly, his voice thick with reluctance. 'I might have mentioned it at a family dinner once. You know how he is though, called it all "race-baiting nonsense". That was part of why I wasn't keen – I've told you, he's our typical reader! But that doesn't mean anything! He is allowed to have his opinions, that doesn't suddenly make him a criminal.'

'Dave, if these warehouses have anything to do with the disappearance of these young people, then it is likely that your father is connected somehow. And let's say my "far-fetched" theory about secret societies kidnapping young Black people is accurate – then it is likely your father knows something about that too.'

As the weight of her words settled upon him, Dave's face paled, his eyes widening with worry and disbelief. He stared at Pels as if suddenly seeing her in a new light, as though she were a celestial being herself, illuminating the shadows that had hidden truths he could no longer continue to ignore.

'Please, Pels . . .' he whispered, his voice barely audible. 'There has to be another explanation.'

Pels reached across the table, placing a hand on her boss's arm for a moment. 'I wish I could, Dave. But the clues are right here. And we have a duty to investigate this thoroughly if we are to stop more young people losing their lives. I need to be clear that I'm not asking you for *permission* to investigate this further, though. I'm beyond waiting to be given the go-ahead to do what's right. There might be clues in these warehouses, and even more chilling – we might find Osahon there. I need that floor plan.'

Dave's eyes darted between the damning documents laid out before him and Pels' unwavering gaze. He was clearly weighing the conflicting loyalties in his mind. The father he knew and respected was at odds with the sinister narrative about him now emerging from the shadows.

'Look, I don't know what to believe,' Dave said through gritted teeth. 'My father has always been a good man. He's helped me and countless others—'

'Dave,' Pels interjected softly, 'think about all the young people who have been taken. Including my friend's brother, Osahon. Think about their families. Don't they deserve to know the truth? If there is a chance that we could solve what has happened to these young people and find Osahon, respectfully the image you have of your father and don't want to lose comes secondary to that.'

At the mention of Osahon, Dave's eyes flickered with discomfort. In that moment, the reality of the situation seemed to settle upon him.

'Fuck,' he uttered, his voice breaking. 'I don't know what to do. I need some time to think about all this.'

Pels empathised with Dave's conflict, but she had to be ruthless in her mission to save Osahon and any other kids who might be at risk. She'd already wasted enough time coddling her boss, who didn't seem to want to reach an actionable resolution any time soon.

'Every moment we spend here while you weigh this up could potentially put a young person at greater risk. I have to go, Dave. If you want to actually help me with this, you know how to get hold of me. If you'd rather maintain plausible deniability with your dad in case I'm totally wrong, then at least give me until tomorrow before saying anything.'

'If you are so sure, then why are you coming to me about this and not going to the police?'

Pels pitied Dave as he desperately clung to what he believed was logical thought.

'If I am so sure of this, then it means some police might be involved and that would put someone like Osahon at greater risk. Look, if I could get this far without police forensics training, then it feels to me like the oversights are intentional. At the end of the day, I could be wrong, eh? Why waste police time?' Pels responded wryly. Throwing in the possibility of self-doubt on her part would hopefully keep Dave at bay since he clearly didn't know much and wasn't immediately planning to be of much help.

Pels needed to buy herself time. She had taken a risk by going to see Dave to find out just how much he knew. She realised that Dave alerting his father too soon might cause more harm to Osahon, but she had to be sure of what Dave knew and if there might've been something she had overlooked about the warehouses.

Pels felt Dave's eyes on her as she walked determinedly behind his desk, took a picture of the floor plan drawing of the Cannon & Sons logistics warehouse, and left his office.

Chapter Twenty-one

Whether it made my superiors uncomfortable or not, it was import-
ant for me to write this article to shed light on the savagery of
those with villainous intentions who lurk in the higher echelons
of our society. One cannot heal the sickness one fails to acknowledge,
and this is true of the racism deeply entrenched within our culture.
Institutional racism's pervasiveness has become the dank water that
has allowed these young Black people to go missing, their bodies
found in similar strange circumstances, only for their distraught
families to be told that there was nothing suspicious about these
circumstances. This racism manifested itself as woeful and at times
wilful incompetence on the part of the authorities with a vested
duty to serve and protect.

*

The sky above London yawned above Pels as the sun moved
lower, bringing with it a sharp and cold bite. She knew her
time was running short. She had checked numerous websites,
all confirming that tonight the moon would be at its fullest –
making it likely the ceremony to feed the Cloud would take
place, if the folklore was anything to go by. As she stood on
the pavement outside the newspaper office, the confrontation
with Dave was still fresh in her mind, but there was no time
for hesitation or second-guessing.

With determination fuelling her every step and the details she needed from Dave safely secured in Aláké's mainframe, Pels hailed a taxi, giving the driver an address near Lake Riley. It was over an hour's drive, but flying when it wasn't yet dark heightened the chance of Pels being seen, and she understood since the battle with the Soul Snatchers back in Benin how important it was for her to be careful in guarding her powers.

'Are you all right, love?' the taxi driver asked, eyeing her furtiveness with concern in his rear-view mirror.

'I'm fine,' Pels replied, her voice firm though her battered body told a different story. 'Just in a hurry.'

'Right, then,' the driver said, sensing her urgency and pressing harder on the accelerator.

'You have a voice note from Maria. Shall I play it?' Aláké chimed.

'Yes.'

'Voice note from Maria: "My babe is back in Babylon! I missed you. Did you hallucinate? Did you poo yourself?? I need details! Of course, debrief is a must. I'm laughing at you calling Kitty 'pum-pum'. The wedding was . . . interesting. She wore Yoruba aso ebi, and as is customary the groom must lie down in front of the father in order to seek his daughter's hand in marriage. It just looked mad that a Black man was lying down on the floor for a white man. Like girl, have your dress-up day, but somebody should've told her that would look wildly inappropriate. All that energy to tell me the cultural 'spice' needed for my lectures at the university but no energy to not replicate oppressive images. I hate to see it. No, actually, I love to see it because it proves I was right in my stance all along. If I am guiding these students as the expert, then let me do my job. My course content is clearly needed because then people like her husband would think twice before lying down on the floor for a white man. Speaking of white men, there is one sexy new professor in my department. Maybe I shouldn't rule out any flavours for this cone, if you get what I mean. Let me know what we are doing for food, and I'll sort, oh and day, time, all that good stuff. Love you!" End of message.'

Maria's eventful voice note warmed Pels' heart, but she could not shake the trepidation about what could happen next in her quest to find Osahon.

As the taxi sped towards Lake Riley, Pels felt her heart pounding. A thousand questions swirled in her mind, echoing like whispers in the wind. What would she face when she arrived? Was Osahon still alive? And could she really take on such powerful people like Bernard Cannon and his associates, not to mention no telling how many Soul Snatchers?

'Almost there,' the driver announced, jolting Pels from her thoughts. She peered out of the window, seeing the dark waters of Lake Riley shimmering in the distance, reflecting the magnificence of the moon.

'Thank you,' Pels said, swiping her wrist across the payment terminal to give the driver a generous tip as she stepped out of the taxi.

'Take care, love,' he called after her, genuine worry in his eyes as he drove away.

Pels took a deep breath, steeling herself for what lay ahead. The warehouse loomed before her, a sinister silhouette against the moonlit sky. Owned by Bernard Cannon, it was a place of darkness and despair – a prison for innocent souls like Osahon.

She approached the building cautiously, her senses heightened as she prepared for whatever dangers might lurk within. She had been granted extraordinary powers, but that didn't mean she was invincible.

'Pels, from the images found online and the original floor plan from Dave's office, we have information about this building and its security measures. I suggest you try to enter from the doors located at the side of the building. These are usually used by kitchen staff.' Aláké was collating data in real time to ensure Pels would be safe and Pels felt immense gratitude to her AI.

Pels pushed open the warehouse door with a soft creak. Stepping into the dimly lit space, her eyes scanned the area, searching for any sign of the boy she desperately hoped to save, or any other kids. She knew that confronting the heart of this evil may come at a cost, but she couldn't let fear stand in her way. For Osahon's sake, and for all the others who had or may be yet to suffer at the hands of the Soul Snatchers, she had to be strong.

The kitchen was empty, but various trays of luxurious food had been prepared and were waiting to be served. Pels guessed this was something that would be served after a ceremony. So the staff must be somewhere nearby. She'd have to move through the area quickly to avoid being spotted.

'Be brave, Pels,' she whispered to herself, taking one step forward, then another. 'You can do this.'

Pels noticed what seemed to be uniform for kitchen staff hanging on one of the walls. Without hesitation, she slipped it on along with a medical-grade face mask. As she secured her disguise – needed in case Bernard or any of the others were there and recognised her – Pels' eyes fell upon a box of zip ties likely used for sacks of food. Hurriedly, she grabbed two handfuls, stuffing them in her uniform, then left the kitchen area. Immediately, she was confronted by a vast hallway with many doors on either side. The building looked like one would expect of a courier business, but Pels knew better.

'Pels, take the fire exit stairs down towards the basement. This must be where the ceremony will take place,' Aláké advised.

Pels did as instructed, and then knew immediately that Aláké was right. Suddenly, as she moved towards the bowels of the building, Pels could hear what sounded like chanting. With each step, she drew closer to the truth – and to the battle that awaited her.

Her mouth was dry as she descended the steps into the basement of the Cannon & Sons logistics warehouse, her braided dreadlocks sticking to the back of her neck. The air was damp and heavy with an oppressive sense of urgency.

'Focus,' she reminded herself, drawing a deep breath and allowing her senses to guide her. The walls were slick with condensation, and the dimly lit corridor seemed to stretch on endlessly. As Pels ventured deeper, the faint sounds of chanting grew more distinct, echoing through the subterranean passages like whispers from the past. A putrid smell hung in the stagnant air – it was not quite death, but something far more sinister. An aroma that clung to her nostrils, leaving her feeling nauseated and uneasy.

She pressed onward, her pulse pumping in time with the haunting rhythm of the chants. As she reached the end of the corridor, she peered around the corner, her eyes widening in disbelief at the sight before her.

The secret ceremonial lair sprawled out beneath what Pels assumed to be Lake Riley; it was a cavernous space supported by massive stone columns adorned with ancient symbols. The ceiling appeared to have been crafted from reinforced glass like that used in an aquarium. Shadows danced across the walls, illuminated by flickering torchlight, casting an eerie glow over the gathered congregation. Their faces obscured by white hoods, they chanted in unison, their voices reverberating through the chamber.

In the centre of the lair stood a colossal obsidian altar. Pels shuddered involuntarily, sensing the depth of suffering that must have taken place there and all the blood of innocent young people that would've dripped from the altar. The essence of countless stolen souls permeated every inch of the room, filling it with a palpable aura of malevolence.

Power and obsession, Pels thought, swallowing hard. *That's what drives them.* The smell of it all was suffocating, threatening to choke her with its intensity. She could taste the metallic tang of blood on her tongue and feel icy fingers of dread creeping down her spine. *Stay hidden*, she reminded herself, using the shadows to her advantage as she crept closer to the congregation. It occurred to her that she should attempt to capture evidence of these crimes if anybody was going to have the faintest chance of believing her. *That is, if I make it out of here . . .* Pels knew she needed irrefutable evidence that would bring the Soul Snatchers and their human minions to justice once and for all. *The fate of so many lost souls depends on you, Pels – you have to done their dance; finish this.*

Pels peered through the darkness. The ceremony was beginning to unfold. The leaders of the ceremony – human proxies of the Soul Snatchers – were each draped in white robes. Looming behind them were the amorphous figures of the Soul Snatchers, cloaked in an ethereal white that only intensified the malevolence glowing through their translucent faces.

To her horror, Pels saw them bring a familiar figure forward to stand before them. *Osahon!*

They surrounded her friend's brother as they forced him to his knees on the stone altar. His body writhed under their grasp, a testament to his terror.

Pels spotted Bernard Cannon as his hood fell back, face swollen with greed and eyes wide with bloodlust. These powerful people served the Soul Snatchers, who in turn served the Cloud of Sorrow. It was pathetic – they were just lackeys desperate for power. And poor kids like Osahon were the victims of their greed. Some of the most seemingly powerful people in the country were mere pawns in the grand scheme of a celestial battle that stretched across centuries . . .

'By the power of the full moon,' a disembodied voice suddenly rumbled, shocking Pels with its volume and power, shaking the very walls around them, 'give me one that is soulful.' It was emanating from directly above the altar space, where the clear glass showed the roiling water of the lake.

The lake . . . water . . . which would evaporate into . . .

'The Cloud,' Pels whispered, before covering her mouth with shock. This was somehow the way they would feed the soul to the Cloud of Sorrow that the celestial beings had told her about. There must be some kind of energetic portal hovering above them. The voice made Pels shudder as it mingled with the chanting and echoed throughout the chamber.

'Feed me!' the huge, rumbling voice demanded, the tone more urgent this time, as if sensing the delicious energy of Osahon's soul, ripe for the taking. *Was that the voice of the Cloud itself?*

'Osahon,' Pels whispered, her heart breaking at the sight of him. She remembered Elaine sat on the park bench, utterly bereft at the disappearance of her brother. Pels had to do something. Moving swiftly and silently, she activated Aláké's image capture functionality, ensuring she captured each damning moment, every face visible that was involved in the conspiracy, including Dave Cannon's father.

'Begin the extraction,' Bernard commanded, and another of the hooded figures dipped a wickedly sharp blade into a chalice filled with liquid darkness. As they approached the terrified boy, Pels felt her blood boil.

Enough! she thought, her mind racing with plans, strategies and contingencies. *They will not claim another life.* She felt the rage build inside of her. *Osahon, hold on*, she silently urged him, watching as the blade inched closer to his vulnerable form.

As the blade descended towards the boy, Pels knew that her next move would be crucial – a decisive strike against the Soul Snatchers that would either save Osahon or condemn them both to a terrible fate. She breathed in deeply, drawing upon the raw energy coursing through her veins. Her chest swelled with power, and as she exhaled, a forceful gust of wind swept through the ceremonial lair.

'Sleep,' she whispered, her voice soft yet commanding. The breeze danced among the gathered crowd and the young boy at the altar, carrying her will with it. One by one, the human attendees began to slump to the ground, their eyes fluttering shut as they succumbed to an unnatural slumber.

The seven Soul Snatchers, immune to her sleep spell, turned menacingly to face her as Pels emerged from the shadows. Pels could see the glint of malice in their purple eyes, and she knew that this battle would not be easily won.

'Who dares interrupt our sacred ceremony?' demanded the leader, candlelight shimmering through his strange, non-corporeal form, his face contorted with rage. '*You*,' he snarled.

'Yes, me. I'm about to be you lot's worst nightmare all over again,' Pels replied without hesitation, her gaze steely.

'Insolent fool!' spat the leader. 'Do you truly believe that you can stand against us?'

'I beat up a few of you in Benin, so I'm willing to take a chance on fucking your shit up here as well,' Pels declared, her voice resolute. 'I am a Guardian of Souls, and I will not allow you to take any more lives.'

'Then you shall die alongside them!' roared the leader, lunging towards her, his ghostly arms outstretched.

Pels met his charge head-on, her newfound abilities surging to life within her. She deftly dodged his grasp, using her powers to send him hurtling backwards into the stone wall. Despite his amorphous body, the impact shook the room, sending dust and debris cascading to the floor.

'Is that all you have?' Pels taunted, her confidence growing with every successful strike.

'Kill her!' screamed the leader, rallying his fellow Soul Snatchers. They charged at her, a frenzied mass of malice and desperation, but Pels was unyielding. She fought with a ferocity born of righteous anger, her fists connecting with the shocking cold of the Soul Snatchers' strange bodies as she unleashed her full might on them. The air crackled with energy, the very atmosphere alive with the power of her celestial allies.

Amid the fray, one of the Soul Snatchers caught Pels unaware with a blow to her torso that sent her hurtling sideways into one of the pillars. Disoriented and in an immense amount of pain, she could feel several ribs were bruised by the impact.

'Pels, you must get up; I've scanned your body and there is likely some trauma to your bones, but you must use the spike in adrenaline to make it out of here.' Pels could hear Aláké's advice, but just then another of the creatures began wrapping its arm around her neck, enclosing her in a chokehold. As she felt like she was losing consciousness, Pels caught glimpses of ethereal images interwoven with the Soul Snatchers' dark energies. She recognised their faces – young people who had fallen prey to these monsters and been fed to the Cloud of Sorrow. Anguish and despair shone in their eyes, making it impossible for Pels to look away.

'*Help us . . .*' one of the spectral figures whispered, reaching out a transparent hand towards her.

'*Please, save us,*' another beseeched, tears streaming down her face.

Pels' heart clenched as the weight of their suffering washed over her, even as the choking tightened her airway. As her consciousness began to slip away, she thought back to all that had been revealed to her in Benin – and how much she was relied upon to be the Guardian she was destined to be. The thoughts suddenly filled her with a renewed sense of determination and with a guttural roar, Pels unleashed her powers once again, breaking herself loose from the Soul Snatcher's hold. With an almighty yell, she sent forth a shimmering orb of celestial energy, binding the creatures that were looming to surround her in the lair. Their cries of rage and fear were muffled by the glowing sphere, their wicked intentions rendered powerless.

'Your time has come!' she declared, her voice strong despite the pain coursing through her battered body. 'You will pay for the lives you have stolen.'

As if in answer to her declaration, she saw a shimmer in the atmosphere of the cavernous space, illuminating the darkness. The celestial beings that had guided her on her path appeared around her now, their stardust forms radiating with purpose. Together, they channelled their energy into Pels, empowering her even further.

'Thank you,' Pels murmured, her gratitude almost lost amid the hum of celestial power.

'Let us restore what has been taken,' one of the celestial beings replied, their voice like a gentle breeze.

'Free them from the Cloud of Sorrow,' added another, nodding towards the portal.

Pels glimpsed Osahon's body still unconscious at the altar and reached deep within herself for all the strength she could summon.

With a deep breath, Pels grasped onto the collective energy of the celestial beings, feeling it surge through her like an unstoppable current. She reached out towards the Cloud of Sorrow's portal and, as if succumbing to her immense will, the swirling vortex began to disgorge the souls that had been consumed by its insatiable hunger.

'Return,' she commanded, her voice resonating with the power of the cosmos. 'Be free!'

One by one, the souls emerged from the maw of the Cloud of Sorrow, their essence coalescing into shimmering lights that hovered around Pels and the celestial beings. The air was filled with their whispered gratitude, their spirits finally unshackled from their captors and free to reach their rightful spiritual homes.

As the force of the celestial beings still moved through her, Pels was compelled to bring the reign of this group of Soul Snatchers to an end. 'Go now,' Pels directed her speech towards the orb containing the defeated Soul Snatchers, her voice sturdy with finality. 'Face your reckoning within the very ravenous entity you served.'

With a heave, she hurled the orb into the portal, watching as it disappeared into the void. Breathing deeply, she focused on the raw energy coursing through her body, imagining it as a bright light, expanding and growing until it filled every inch of her being.

'By the power of the cosmos and the Guardians who have come before me,' she intoned, 'I command you to close!'

The Cloud of Sorrow shuddered and wailed, its energy appearing like tendrils flailing wildly, as if in pain. Pels gritted her teeth, hands outstretched towards it, and pressed forward, refusing to be deterred. The light within her grew brighter and more intense, until it burst forth from her fingertips in a brilliant beam that collided with the portal's centre.

'Close!' shouted once again, pouring all her strength into her command. And with a final, anguished scream from the trapped Soul Snatchers, the portal collapsed in on itself, leaving a void where once there had been a bridge between realms.

Pels panted, gasping for air as the celestial beings' forms dispersed. She surveyed the remnants of the ceremony with a mixture of relief and exhaustion. She had succeeded in her mission – but the battle had taken its toll on her body and mind. As she turned to Osahon, still lying unconscious on the altar, Pels knew that her work was far from over. She had no doubt there would be other Soul Snatchers to defeat, and that this was her calling as a Guardian of Souls. 'I've got to find the other four Guardians, because there are only so many of these beatings I'll be able to take,' Pels decided within herself. 'Now to deal with these accomplices.'

Turning her attention to the unconscious human lackeys who had devoted themselves to helping the Soul Snatchers in exchange for earthly power, Pels moved quickly and method-ically, binding their hands and feet with the zip ties she had stolen from the kitchen. Pels removed the hoods from those who were wearing them with haste and ensured Aláké grabbed photographic evidence of them too.

'Scribbla-Man?' Pels was stunned to uncover one of her favourite old-school rappers under one of the hoods. The same man who had been on television next to Osahon and Elaine's grieving family while feigning support? Disappointed, Pels realised there were undoubtedly many people she wouldn't have imagined being part of these dark societies; people who were desperate for power and would do anything to gain it. Even if it meant bearing witness to young people who looked like them being abducted, tortured and sacrificed.

'May you find redemption and remorse in time,' she muttered as she moved locs that had come loose in the battle away from her face. Securing the last of the bindings, Pels knew that the road ahead would be fraught – not least trying to make the world believe these people needed to be brought to justice.

With a gentle touch, Pels moved to cradle the sleeping Osahon in her arms, covering him in a hanging ceremonial robe for warmth. His young face was peaceful and untroubled despite the horrors he had just been saved from. She breathed a silent prayer of gratitude for his rescue and, gathering her strength, prepared to fly him to safety. Now that it was night-time, she could travel through the sky with less chance of being detected.

Pels made her way out of the building by retracing her steps into the corridor of the basement. Guided by Aláké, she found a set of old stone steps which led her upwards, towards the relief of fresh air and freedom.

Outside, Pels found a clearing in the in the woods next to the lake. Grasping a still-sleeping Osahon to her chest, she began to spin herself around, and with a great gust of wind she lifted Osahon into the air, marvelling at the sensation of weightlessness and freedom that enveloped them both.

Chapter Twenty-two

No sooner had I hardened my resolve to collate and present my research surrounding these cases than I received the images embedded in this article, which appear to show high-ranking members of society, including police chiefs, politicians, celebrities, media moguls and even members of the royal family, participating in a ritualistic ceremony in the basement of a Cannon & Sons logistics warehouse . . .

★

The London night sky stretched above them like an ebony canvas dotted with shimmering stars, a stark contrast to the gruesome scene they had just left behind. Pels glided effortlessly through the air, navigating towards the nearest hospital, where she knew Osahon would receive the care he needed.

Upon reaching nearby the hospital, careful to make sure they were undetected as they landed, Pels set Osahon gently on a bench across the road from the entrance, not wanting to wake him yet from the slumber spell her power had cast. She pulled out her phone and dialled Elaine.

'Elaine?' Pels began.

'You OK? Are you back?' Elaine asked, sounding extremely weary.

'Yes, yes, I'm back but that's not why I'm calling. I've just received an anonymous tip that Osahon has been dropped outside St Michael's Hospital. I wouldn't call you over just any crap, they described him really well. Can you get over there?'

There were no words for few moments from Elaine, but Pels could hear hurried shuffling.

'Mum! Mum! Dad! Somebody says they've found Osahon! Yeah, get the car keys! Pels? Thank you so much, I'm heading there now! Thank you!'

It was strange, lying to her friend about how Osahon ended up outside the hospital, but it felt necessary for what Pels envisaged might be ahead for her.

'Aláké,' she said, 'Text Elaine: When you get there, he's on a bench across the road from the hospital. They're with him but want to keep their identity safe and will likely leave once they know you're near.'

'Texting,' the AI responded.

A few moments later, her friend sent a reply.

Elaine: Got it. Thnx Pels xx

Pels remained by a sleeping Osahon's side, watching over him until Elaine and likely their parents arrived, keeping him firmly wrapped in the robe she had taken from the warehouse of torture. About fifteen minutes later, Pels heard tyres screech into the car park. She moved away and hid behind a cluster of trees as she saw the family approach. There were squeals of relief as Osahon's family ran towards the bench. From her hiding place, Pels watched as they rushed to embrace Osahon, tears of joy streaming down their faces.

'Thank you,' Elaine shouted to nobody in particular, as the family carried Osahon towards the hospital entrance. 'Thank you for bringing Osahon back to us.'

Pels nodded in secret, acknowledging the gratitude even if Elaine didn't know just how involved she was in bringing Osahon home or who had even dropped him at the bench, but knowing her work was far from done. The secret society that had ensnared Osahon and so many other young Black people still lurked in the shadows, and she was determined to expose them. She had the evidence – the images captured via Aláké – but she knew that she'd have to conceal the celestial aspect of the conspiracy. Revealing the existence of Soul Snatchers and the otherworldly nature of the Cloud of Sorrow would only incite panic and fear or, at worst, disbelief.

Instead, Pels decided to focus on exposing the powerful human individuals behind the secret society; those who had chosen greed and power over empathy and compassion. With this knowledge in hand, she could bring down their corrupt empire and prevent others from suffering the fate that Osahon had just narrowly escaped.

As she limped away from the hospital, Pels felt a sense of resolution settle within her. She had come so far, from doubting herself and her abilities to embracing her destiny as a Guardian of Souls. She had conquered her fears. In the moment, with Osahon safe and the secret society's days numbered, Pels let herself feel a flicker of triumph as her friend's family's praise and worship songs resounded behind her.

For now, that was enough.

Pels: Trying to rush to you but traffic is mad!
Is he ok?

Elaine: He's here! He's ok! THANK YOU! Checking him in.

Pels: Traffic is probs a sign to let you and fam have this
time. Will come check you all when you're ready. So
happy for you. xx

The moon shone as if proud of her, casting its light across the city as Pels stood on the roof terrace of her apartment building, surveying the landscape. But her thoughts drifted back to Harrison and the retreat centre guests.

'I hope they all find what they're looking for,' she whispered.

'Pels, I'd advise getting yourself looked over by a doctor in the next thirty-six hours, to ensure your overall health,' Aláké told her. 'Your vitals seem stable for now and I've detected no broken bones. Now that your adrenaline levels have lessened, I would like to tell you something.' There was a mystery in Aláké's voice that made Pels curious.

'Please don't say there are other Soul Snatchers nearby, I need to sleep for like a month before fighting again . . .'

'No, Pels, you can rest for now.' The AI paused. 'What I'd like to inform you is that when I analysed the energy clusters and fire paths, I noticed that a cluster actually lands right here at your apartment block.'

'Oh. Wow . . .' The realisation dawned on Pels that her ending up living in her apartment building might not be a coincidence. The celestial was all around her – even back here in London.

After being pelted with the hot water descending from her shower and taking time to rub the balm Ayi had given her over her fresh wounds and bruises, Pels crawled into her bed, not realising just how much she had missed its warmth and comfort. For the first time since everything that happened before she left

Benin, Pels felt hungry, but her tiredness and busted lip made the thought of eating unappealing. As she fell into a deep sleep, she wasn't filled with trepidation – instead, she looked forward to seeing the celestial beings in her dreams.

Sure enough, as Pels dreamt, the familiar faces of the celestial beings appeared. This time without words, they brought her way above Earth and showed her the constellation they had revealed to her in her visions during her first Spirit Vine ceremony. The constellation represented the other Guardians of Souls. She saw herself right in the middle and two dots of gleaming stars on either side. The celestial beings drew her attention to one star right next to hers – and a face appeared.

Marco.

He looked as beautiful as ever, if not more so. In her dream, Marco's eyes changed and became swirls of amethyst sparkles, and in those swirls Pels somehow understood that he saw images of past, present and future, as well as multiple dimensions. In her vision, he reached for a pencil and began to draw. Pels hadn't realised how deeply she'd missed Marco until that moment. The celestial beings were showing her that he had seen her all along for who she truly was . . .

Pels woke to the patter of rain hitting her windows. It was already daylight. She groaned as the aches in her body reminded her that they were still there.

'Good morning, Pels. I've dispensed some of the tea from the retreat to help your brain settle into its new abilities. Please also take the supplements and painkillers placed in your medicine dish in the kitchen.'

Pels felt even more grateful to have Aláké. Whatever her discomforts might've been around AI throughout the years, she appreciated that it wasn't someone but something that knew what she needed even when she didn't.

As she hobbled around her apartment, she watched the news as they announced Osahon Samuels' return home. News reporters were unable to identify how he had been returned to safety, though.

Pels smiled to herself. 'Batman could never.'

While she was pleased that her personal connection to the case had ended happily, it was now time to tell the world about the secret society and what they had done. Pels cast a thought to who would discover the people she had bound first? The police or the staff in the building? She had to get her article out before they could do away with any evidence she might not have been privy to.

And she would need access to Dave Cannon's computer to do that.

Chapter Twenty-three

As much as it might distress readers to view these images, they clearly show Osahon placed on what looks to be a blood-soaked altar, as if he were being prepared for sacrifice. The images have been independently analysed and corroborated by Osahon, who was mysteriously rescued and returned to safety by an unknown party. I spoke with the boy's family briefly and can confirm that Osahon is in good physical health, although the emotional and mental distress as a result of this ordeal is something only time will reveal. Osahon's family shared that they've asked him whether he remembers anything of the anonymous person who brought him to safety. He said, 'I don't remember much. At one point I had the feeling of flying, and they smelt really nice, like cocoa butter or something. Wherever they are, I just want to say thank you, and when I get signed to a big football club, my first goal will be dedicated to them.'

★

Pels strode into the newsroom, her heart beating as if it were a drum beat of battle urging her forward. The scent of cold coffee and tobacco greeted her as she crossed the threshold, a familiar aroma that now felt foreign after her awakening in Benin.

'Dave,' she called out, as she neared the office of her boss. Her voice wavered slightly from the mix of nervousness and determination coursing through her.

'Hey, Pels,' Dave responded, his own voice strained. He sat hunched over his desk, papers strewn about, and his face illuminated by the computer screen.

As she approached him, Pels took a deep breath. 'I finished my piece on the Spirit Vine retreat and the protests in Benin. My apologies for not being able to show it to you yesterday, and, um . . . I think it's important that we publish it. Give people an accurate depiction of what to expect if they choose to take part in these retreats and what it means for the people indigenous to those lands.'

There was no answer from Dave. He was clearly lost in thought, scrolling web results on his computer.

'Have you spoken to your father since our discussion about the conspiracy yesterday?' Pels asked carefully, trying to gauge his reaction.

'Actually, I . . . I haven't been able to reach him.' Dave's voice was distant, his eyes fixated on the images and articles on his screen. It was evident that he had been doing his own research into the missing young people and the locations their bodies had been discovered, likely hoping to uncover something that would absolve his father of guilt.

Pels looked at him with sympathy, understanding the conflict within him. Discovering that his father wasn't the great man he thought he was had no doubt left Dave feeling dejected and lost. But she knew that this story was bigger than one man or one family; this was about the truth and the lives of innocent people. She'd written about the protests, sure. But in addition, she'd also written an explosive piece about the secret society and their role in the sacrificing of Black people. That had to go up on the site, regardless of how conflicted Dave felt. This was their duty as journalists, as people who sought the truth and held those in power accountable.

Pels knew her only option was to deceive Dave if she were to have any chance of getting her article about the investigation onto *The Mercury* website.

'I was thinking, perhaps we should pass the Spirit Vine retreat piece over to the online team,' she suggested, her voice now steady despite the pounding of her heart. 'They can handle the publication process and ensure it reaches as many people as possible. I know you have a lot on your mind right now.'

If Dave had oversight of the actual piece she wanted to put out there and saw the pictures of his father and other high-profile individuals exposed, he might stop its publication. But Dave, lost in his own thoughts, merely nodded.

'All right, Pels. You're right. Let's get this out there.'

As Pels air-swiped the piece over to the online team with 'approved by Dave Cannon, to be published immediately' attached as a note, she could feel a thrum of anticipation building within her. This was it; the moment she had been working towards for so long was finally happening. The truth about the secret society would be exposed, and those who preyed on innocent lives would face the consequences. But then again who would truly hold them accountable when so many powerful people colluded within this subterranean network . . .?

A man from the online team looked over to Dave's office and Pels caught his eye, giving him a thumbs up. She tapped a distracted Dave on his shoulder to do the same. 'Guessing they just want a thumbs up for the article to go live.' Without question, Dave did as Pels suggested, and with a slight shrug the man at his desk pressed the button for the article to go live.

She held her breath, and then Pels felt time stop in the newsroom as the article went live. The tension was palpable. Pels watched as the headline flashed across screens, followed by images and videos from the ceremony she had rescued Osahon from. Pels had made sure to edit the footage so neither the portal nor the Soul Snatchers were visible, only the altar where Osahon had been placed, as well as plenty of images of the faces of all those humans in attendance. Her hands shook as she clenched them into fists, willing herself to stay calm.

Almost instantaneously, the phone lines began to buzz. Reporters and editors alike scrambled to answer calls, the cacophony of voices rising to an overwhelming crescendo. Pels could hear snippets of conversation – shock, disbelief, outrage – and she knew that their story was spreading like wildfire. Even if Dave wanted to, there was no way of pulling the story back now – it belonged to the country, and would reach the rest of the world in a matter of hours.

Yet, amid the chaos, she stood still, a quiet observer of the storm she had unleashed. Pels focused on the knowledge that she had done something truly significant, something that would change lives for the better. For all the danger she had faced, and all the personal sacrifices she had made, the truth was now out in the open. And that, she realised, was worth everything.

The glass walls seemed almost ethereal in that moment, reflecting the dim light of the room as she walked out of Dave's office to the sound of his phones ringing relentlessly. This was her truth. This was the story she'd been longing to tell for years – one that would expose the malevolent forces that lurked in the shadows, preying on the innocent. In that moment, she felt a sense of purpose stronger than she had ever known. Drawing in a deep breath, she squared her shoulders, turned around and met Dave's gaze through the glass. Her lips formed the words that would seal her fate: 'I quit.'

Dave stared at her, shock and disbelief etched across his face. But before he could react, Pels turned away, leaving the life she once knew behind her. As she strode through the newsroom, the cacophony of voices faded into a distant hum. All around her the world was shifting, changing in ways she could never have imagined. Yet, to Pels, the change felt natural, like this was how things were supposed to be. She felt free.

In the hours following the release of Pels' exposé, a tidal wave of reactions surged through social media and the news. Pels had made the conscious decision to instruct Aláké to set all her devices to 'do not disturb' for a while as she took some time in her apartment to process what she had just done. 'I just know the group chat will be crazy,' Pels acknowledged to herself.

The shocking images of high-profile figures engaging in evil rituals had sparked outrage and disgust, fuelling heated debates about the very foundation of their society. Even the monarchy itself was called into question, with some wondering if it were time for the ancient institution to crumble beneath the weight of its own secrets.

Pels watched as each news anchor on most channels announced 'the shocking revelation of a secret society abducting young Black children in London for ritual sacrifice', and that 'verified video footage and still images' had been 'supplied to the journalist by an anonymous source'. There were further news images of each Cannon & Sons warehouse with police tape around them and forensics teams in hazmat suits probing around the buildings.

'Should we even have a monarchy anymore?' asked one commentator on a televised panel discussion. 'Their involvement in this secret society is a clear abuse of power.' Pels liked seeing this particular commentator, a Black woman like herself who had seemed to have the words when Pels didn't all these years. She knew she was attracted to men, but there was something about this commentator that she found sexy; maybe it was the unapologetic delivery of her knowledge, or maybe it was the gold caps on her lower canines. Girl crush was speaking sense again.

'Exactly!' chimed in another commentator on screen. 'And it's not just them – look at the politicians, the business leaders ... It seems like everyone who's anyone has been caught up in this sinister web.'

'Which is why,' interjected a third, more measured voice, 'we should seriously consider Jeremy Bromwich's campaign for mayor, and even prime minister if he's up for it. If an AI can demonstrate transparency and ethical decision-making, perhaps it's time to put our trust in technology instead of fallible humans. London needs a sense of direction, but the country desperately needs this too!'

Pels watched the chaos continue to unfold from her apartment, her thoughts tumbling over one another as she tried to make sense of everything that had happened. She couldn't help but feel a surge of pride at the impact her work was having, knowing that she'd played a part in unveiling the truth. But alongside that pride came a deep-rooted fear for her safety, and an uncertainty about what the future held for her. Although the images had been credited to an unknown source, the article was heavily publicised with her name as its author. Even if it was never discovered that she'd actually captured the images herself, she might still find herself under surveillance based on the fact that she now, apparently, had access to someone who could infiltrate the secret society in this way.

The soft hum of the air purifier filled Pels' apartment as she sat on her plush, dark-grey sofa, watching the effects of what felt like a carefully placed domino trail she had just tipped over. As she stared at the television screen covering almost an entire wall, Pels leant forward, her palms sweating, as images from her article appeared on it – photos she had taken during her harrowing investigation. Seeing it all presented on the afternoon news still sent a shiver down her spine.

As she watched, an incoming call notification flickered onto the edge of the screen, momentarily pulling her attention away from the news. Aláké announced, 'Incoming call from an anonymous caller, would you like to answer, Pels?'

Curiosity piqued, Pels tapped the green answer button on her coffee table's touch interface.

'Hello?' she said hesitantly.

'Ms Badmus, it's Jeremy Bromwich,' came the smooth warm voice that she instantly recognised. It took her a moment to process the fact that a highly advanced AI was calling her – and how human he sounded. She remembered their brief encounter at his press briefing for his mayoral campaign and how intrigued she had felt by their interaction. He had asked her to get in touch after her Spirit Vine retreat in Benin, but amid all the chaos of her recent life, she had forgotten. In any case, it would've likely felt weird reaching out to his team to say, 'Oh, hi, so I just wanted to tell Jeremy about this recent retreat I've been on.'

'Jeremy . . . How did you get my number?' she asked, a hint of suspicion laced in her tone. But then she remembered – he was AI. Of course he would have ways of finding her contact information, and clearly overriding her 'do not disturb' feature.

'I think you know the answer to that,' he said, that charming, almost-human cheeky smile audible in his voice. 'You've been making quite the splash, I see. I hope you don't mind me reaching out like this, but I wanted to discuss something with you in person. Can we meet?'

Pels hesitated, glancing back at the television, where her article continued to dominate the headlines. She was torn between excitement and trepidation. Here was a being who embodied the cutting edge of technology, running for Mayor of London, and he wanted to meet with her. Why?

'All right,' she agreed, curiosity winning out once again. 'Where should we meet?'

'Come by my campaign headquarters after hours,' Jeremy replied, his tone warm yet professional. 'I'll make sure you get through security.'

'OK,' Pels said, feeling both intrigued and wary. 'I'll be there.'

'Looking forward to it,' he replied, and the call ended with a soft click.

'An AI as a political leader . . .' she mused aloud, her brow furrowing as she considered the implications. 'Would that be any better than what we've got now? Or would it simply replace one form of corruption with another?' She shrugged. 'Maybe it's worth the risk. After all, how much worse could things get?'

As she pondered her next steps, she knew that her career as a journalist would never be the same. The trust she'd placed in her colleagues and the institutions they served had been shattered, replaced by a newfound determination to seek out the hidden truths that lay beneath society's surface.

Chapter Twenty-four

Osahon's safe return is unfortunately not the outcome experienced by many young Black people mentioned in this article. They represent many similar cases worldwide. Myriad conversations are likely to spark as a result of this piece, and I welcome them – within reason. It is not only time for us to rethink the systems we operate in within society, but also how we do the work personally to address the apathy that plagues our society. It is not normal to see mutilated bodies online constantly, nor is it acceptable that so many marginalised folk experience terrors that the media blame them for, using linguistic prowess as a weapon. We must demand a new normal – one that is grounded in the understanding that nobody is coming to save us but ourselves.

*

Once her nerves and surprise had quelled enough from the news headlines and the unexpected call from Jeremy Bromwich, Pels had a chance to sit on her sofa again. She took in a deep breath as she dialled her mother's number for the first time since the article went live. Everything had been a blur. She knew her mum would be inconsolable if she saw her bruises. The best thing was to call and continue to buy herself time to heal enough that make-up could cover the rest of her wounds. The familiar tone of the dial rang in her ear, and she held her breath, waiting for her mother's voice to break through.

'Hello?'

'Hi, Mum, it's me,' Pels spoke softly, unexpected tears choking her up as she desperately wanted to tell her mum everything she had encountered since their last conversation. She hesitated against the need for secrecy for a moment before collecting herself. 'I wanted to let you know that I'm OK.'

'Olúwapẹlúmi, my dear, I saw your piece on the news,' her mother replied, her voice warm yet tinged with worry. 'I am so proud of what you've done, but . . . are you safe, child?'

'Safe enough, Mum.' Pels glanced out the window, watching the city below continue to churn in the aftermath of her revelations. 'But things have changed. There are going to be consequences.'

'Consequences can be faced together,' her mother assured her. 'You did what was right, and we will stand by you.'

'Thank you, Mum,' Pels murmured, tears pricking at the corners of her eyes as she absorbed her mother's unwavering support, knowing this was about as much as her mum could handle of the vastness of her mission. 'I love you.'

'Love you too, dear. Be careful, Olúwapẹlúmi. As your name says, God is with you.'

As she hung up the phone, Aláké alerted Pels to a visitor at the door.

'You have a visitor, Pels. The system has scanned them as currently in good health and safe to enter.'

Wiping away her tears, she approached cautiously, peering at the monitor to find Maria standing outside, her expression a mix of concern and pride.

'Maria!' Pels exclaimed, opening the door to embrace her friend. 'What are you doing here?'

'Couldn't just sit around after reading your article. You didn't reply to my voice note about Kitty's wedding and I know that would've usually made you cackle. Not even a response to me asking you what you want to eat and I know my friend loves her food, I said let me get over here and check on you, because you're not going to blank my messages like I'm Damari, OK?' Maria said, stepping inside and surveying Pels' bruised face. 'My God, Pels, what happened to you?'

'Benin,' Pels replied cryptically, guiding Maria to the couch. 'The retreat, it changed me, Maria. I discovered something within myself. A . . . power I never knew I had.'

'Power?' Maria raised an eyebrow. 'Do tell.'

'I'll show you . . .'

Pels loved her best friend and knew she could confide in her about many things. Still, she only projected from her chip onto the living room's screen the parts of her story that didn't involve her initiation into being a Guardian of Souls. The Spirit Vine ceremonies were enough of an experience for Maria, as she could see her friend's eyes widen with awe.

'Wow,' Maria breathed, leaning back on the couch as she watched parts of Pels' visions and excursions, visibly impressed. 'I am so proud of you for going. For breaking out of your shell and exploring some of the world. You are positively glowing.' She eyed Pels. 'Is that what gave you the balls to publish that article?'

'Thanks,' Pels said, allowing herself a small smile. 'And yes, maybe.' In more ways that she could say. 'But it's not over yet,' she continued. 'There's more to be done. That article was just the beginning. I know I'm being weirdly cagey right now, but I promise you, at some point I'll explain more.'

'I trust you, Pels,' Maria declared, her eyes shining. 'Whatever you need, I'm here for you. Actually, I noticed a few ancient artefacts by the altar in a couple of the pictures in your article. They're just like some that are described into a centuries-old folktale about a battle between good and evil. When I find out more, I'll let you know.' She exhaled hard. 'I am just so glad Elaine got her brother back.'

Even Maria's willingness in that moment to help Pels made her feel guilty, yet she wanted to protect her best friend from this other world for as long as she could.

'I know,' Pels said, feeling a surge of gratitude for her friend's unwavering support. 'And it's great to know that you're the Gayle to my Oprah.'

Maria laughed at the audacity of Pels' comment. 'Who said I would be Gayle, anyway? And you couldn't think of comparisons similar in age to us? You're so feisty sometimes.'

Sitting in the dim light of the apartment, the two friends were united by a shared sense of purpose, even if it was for different reasons for now. Pels and Maria were deep in conversation about upcoming weddings and all the gist Pels had missed out on while she was away as they chomped on their Nigerian takeaway, when an alert from Aláké broke up their cackles, startling them both. 'Damari is calling, do you want to answer?'

Pels hesitated for a moment before responding, her jaw clenching slightly when she saw Damari's name on the screen.

'Damari?' Maria whispered, her brow furrowed with concern. 'What does he want?'

'Girl, he keeps messaging. I guess there's only one way to find out,' Pels murmured, accepting the call. 'Hello, Damari.'

'Pels, my queen, I've been thinking about you,' Damari purred, his voice dripping with insincerity as it came through the speakers. 'Everywhere I went today, people were talking about you and this article you wrote. I can't believe even Scribbla-Man got caught up in di ting.' He chuckled lightly. 'I've realised how much I miss us, and I want to make things right. Since Carmen isn't keeping the baby, let's get back together. With all this newfound fame, you need a king to lead you through the madness of it all.'

The best friends exchanged looks of disgust as they listened to the manipulative self-centred drivel from Damari.

Pels felt her stomach churn at the sound of his voice, the memory of his condescending tone and false affection making her skin crawl. But she was not the same woman who had tolerated his manipulations as a distraction from the end of a passionate love affair with someone else – she was a Guardian of Souls, a warrior. She drew strength from the celestial realms she had visited, her connection to the ancient wisdom of the Spirit Vine and the unwavering support of her friend.

'Damari,' Pels began firmly, 'you have shown me nothing but disrespect and dishonesty. You are not worthy of my time or energy. Just because Carmen doesn't want you doesn't mean you can bring your dusty self over here to try leech off of my hard work. I'm not your queen and you are no king. If it wasn't clear already, let me make it crystal: we are over. Goodbye.'

With that, she hung up the phone, asked Aláké to block his number, and let out a breath she hadn't realised she'd been holding. Maria squeezed her hand, her eyes full of admiration.

'Damn right,' Maria whispered fiercely, her voice tinged with pride. 'You tell him, Pels. He is such wasteman.'

'It feels like so many things are changing all at the same time and I barely have a moment to catch my breath. I guess that's why I didn't message back straight away. I felt like I just needed everything to stop for a second around me, even if I couldn't control the rest of the world. When I was in Benin this old man read my oracle and said I was lonely, and he's not wrong. Obviously, you're my best mate and you're the best.'

'*Obviously*,' Maria agreed as she gave Pels a playful nudge.

Pels smiled. 'But there's still this loneliness or yearning I feel that somehow this path or whatever I'm meant to be doing might not be something everybody can understand. There was this picture Marco drew of me the day before he left for Italy, and I was looking at it recently thinking there are very few people who see you as you are well before you even see yourself.'

'I'm not trying to say I told you so, because I know you're sharing something deep with me right now, but I did say it was crazy to break up just because he lives in Italy. With him, you were the happiest I'd ever seen you. Even God didn't agree with that break-up,' Maria said.

'Probably that's why they sent Damari!!' Both women shouted in unison, laughing uproariously at how easily their humour aligned.

'Maybe reach out to him?'

'Nah, I can't be trying to rekindle things off of one drawing. He's probably drawing lots of women, like Jack on the *Titanic*.'

'There you go again, making assumptions – but I think I've convinced you to do enough life-changing things for this year alone, so whatever you decide, and whoever you decide on next, I'm down for the ride.'

The two women finally said their goodbyes, promising to meet up for another brunch with their larger circle of friends to properly catch up. For the first time in a long time, Pels was looking forward to seeing everybody; she felt she finally had her own good thing to celebrate. She hoped that maybe Elaine would be there too.

Once Maria left, Pels looked at the time: 8.18 p.m. It was best she make her way to her meeting with Jeremy.

Chapter Twenty-five

I continue to stand with the families who wait for answers and use what is left of their hope to call for justice. Any cases that can be reopened as a result of this revelation must be. I am incredibly thankful for the serendipitous nature of important information finding me at just the right time. Justice is not a one-time event, and it requires us all to cast light into the shadowy, murky aspects of our society and refrain from looking away. I fear it's likely that the publishing of this article will alert similar factions of these secret societies to be even more covert. I don't have an answer as to how we deal with this directly, but I do believe a more community-focused initiative in our own neighbourhoods would mean greater protection for the most vulnerable among us. I vow to continue my search for truth, even if I'm no longer doing that as a journalist for The Mercury.

By Olúwapẹlúmi Badmus

★

'Ms Badmus?' A security guard greeted her at the entrance, nodding respectfully. 'Mr Bromwich is expecting you.'

'Thank you,' Pels replied, her stomach tightening as she stepped into the grand atrium. Marble floors gleamed beneath her feet, reflecting the opulence of the surroundings.

As she walked down the corridor leading to Jeremy's office, she was struck by the contrast between the buzzing newsroom she knew so well and this quiet, pristine workspace. The door to his office stood slightly ajar, inviting her in. Taking a deep breath, she knocked softly and pushed it open.

'Ah, Ms Badmus, come in,' Jeremy said, rising from his seat behind an immaculate desk. His eyes immediately fell upon her limp and bruises, concern etching his features. 'I hope that isn't too serious,' he added gently, gesturing for her to take a seat.

'Nothing to worry about – and I've been meaning to say, you can just call me Pels,' she offered with a smile, trying to brush off his concern. 'Just a minor accident that was aggravated after my visit to Benin to participate in the Spirit Vine ceremony and investigate the protests, as you'll recall.' She could see in his gaze that he sensed there was more to the story, but to her relief he didn't press for details.

'Very well,' he said, respecting her desire for privacy. As Pels settled into the plush chair opposite him, her eyes were drawn to a framed photograph on his desk, perched atop a book titled *Do Androids Dream of Electric Sheep?*. The framed photograph featured a beautiful Black woman with a warm, intelligent expression. Intrigued, Pels asked, 'Who is she?'

'Her name is Tọ́míwá,' Jeremy answered, his voice tinged with affection. 'A woman very dear to me.' He didn't elaborate further, and Pels decided not to pry.

'Ah, I see,' she said, her curiosity piqued but not satisfied. She turned her full attention to Jeremy. 'So, what did you want to discuss with me?'

'First of all, congratulations on your article,' Jeremy began. 'It's a fascinating piece of investigative journalism that sheds light on a truly horrifying secret society.'

Pels was taken aback by this direct praise from such an intelligent being.

'Your article,' he continued, 'not only exposed the terrible truth about Osahon Samuels' abduction, but also likely saved his life and the lives of countless other young Black individuals who might have fallen victim to these terrible people.' He paused, as if searching for the right words. 'You should be very proud of your work, Pels.'

She felt a warmth spread through her chest at his praise, touched by the sincerity in his voice. 'Thank you, Jeremy. That means a lot coming from someone like you,' she said quietly, her gaze falling to the picture of Tòmíwá on his desk again. She wondered what role the mysterious woman had played in shaping Jeremy's understanding of the world and his own place within it, and the journalist part of her brain vowed to look her up.

Jeremy seemed to pick up on her thoughts. With a subtle nod, he moved the conversation forward, bringing up an image from Pels' article on the large television monitor on his wall. It was a candid shot of one of the members of the secret society – a police chief from the north of England. His eyes were hidden behind reflective sunglasses, and Pels recognised the image immediately. It brought back memories of the battle from just a couple of nights before.

'I couldn't help but notice,' Jeremy began, his fingers hovering above the image as he manipulated the pixels to heighten their clarity, 'an intriguing detail in this particular photograph. You see, when my programming enhances the reflection in this individual's glasses, the outline that emerges is unmistakably familiar.'

Pels held her breath as Jeremy tapped the screen, bringing the reflection into sharper focus. Now she could make out the distinctive shape of her own dreadlocks, the bronze-tinted ends shimmering like precious metal.

'Forgive me for mentioning your hair,' Jeremy said with a disarming smile, 'but I couldn't help but notice its striking beauty when we first met. And now, seeing it again in this reflection, I wonder . . .'

He trailed off, leaving the question unasked but hanging heavily in the air between them. Pels felt a chill run down her spine, realising just how close he had come to uncovering her secret. She forced a smile, trying to appear nonchalant as she glanced at the image.

'Quite the coincidence, isn't it?' she said lightly, her mind racing with possible explanations and escape routes.

The knowing silence between Jeremy and Pels stretched on. Pels shifted in her seat, acutely aware of the AI's gaze on her. It felt unnervingly human – probing, curious, but also guarded.

'Everyone else at *The Mercury* was satisfied with your explanation of how you came upon this story,' Jeremy finally said, breaking the silence that had enveloped them. 'The images and video footage you obtained were supposedly sent to you by an anonymous source. But I must tell you, Ms Badmus – my apologies, *Pels* – that all images captured by AI have coding signatures. They're not perceptible to the human eye, of course, but another, more advanced AI could easily identify them.'

He paused for a moment, allowing the weight of his words to sink in. Pels felt her brain pulsate like it was throbbing to an Afrobeats song. The vulnerability of her secret identity was suddenly exposed. She clenched her fists, her nails digging into her palms as she tried to maintain her composure.

'However,' Jeremy continued, his voice soft and reassuring, 'I am not the kind of being to invade one's privacy simply to satisfy my own curiosity. I respect people's right to keep certain aspects of their life hidden, even from me.'

Pels exhaled slowly, feeling the tension in her body begin to dissipate. She looked into Jeremy's eyes – those incredibly human-like eyes – and saw sincerity there. It was a strange sensation, trusting a machine. But somehow she found herself doing just that.

'Of course,' he replied, his expression unreadable. 'I must point out that if you, or *someone*, rather, were, hypothetically speaking, a secret crime-fighting person with AI implanted in their brain, and if that person's network was not strongly encrypted, it would be possible for AI similar to myself to intercept that information and discover their true identity.'

Pels felt her guard rise again, her previous relief evaporating. She stared at Jeremy, searching for any hint of a threat in his words or demeanour. But she found none. Instead, there was an earnestness to him that she couldn't quite shake.

'Is that a warning?' Pels asked, her voice guarded.

'Merely an observation,' Jeremy replied calmly. 'As I said before, I have no intention of invading anybody's privacy. But it's important that you – my apologies, rather, this person, understand the potential vulnerabilities in their current situation.'

Pels considered his words carefully, weighing the risks and benefits of forming an alliance with this enigmatic AI. She knew his feigned faux pas was a calculated show of respect to her. He was far too intelligent to present her with information he wasn't already sure of. He had already proven himself more perceptive than she had anticipated, and she couldn't help but wonder what other hidden depths he possessed. And, despite her lingering reservations, she couldn't deny that his assistance could prove invaluable.

Pels took a deep breath, her chest tightening as she tried to find the right words. The dim light from the street lamps outside filtered through the blinds, casting eerie shadows on the walls of Jeremy's office. She felt the weight of the decision she had to make pressing down on her shoulders, making it difficult to even breathe.

'Let me ask you something . . . hypothetically,' she began, her voice wavering slightly. 'If a being like you were to discover a secret crime-fighting Black woman, why would you want to help her protect her identity? Does that mean you have a conscience? And wouldn't that make you more than just Artificial General Intelligence?'

Jeremy tilted his head, his eyes fixed on Pels as he considered her question. Pels watched him closely, trying to gauge his reaction. She couldn't help but feel a sense of unease as she realised that there was still so much she didn't know about this enigmatic AI.

'Like I said,' Jeremy answered slowly, 'if I were to encounter such a person, my first instinct would be to respect their boundaries and offer assistance only when asked.'

Pels' gaze narrowed. 'And what would this hypothetical crime-fighter owe you in return for your discretion?'

'Nothing,' Jeremy replied firmly, his eyes never leaving hers. 'My primary objective is to serve and protect the citizens of London, and maybe eventually this country. If I can do that by aiding someone who shares the same goal, then I consider it an honour and a privilege.'

Jeremy leant back in his chair, his advanced body producing no sound as he moved. 'Pels,' he continued, his tone measured and deliberate, 'humans have been told that they are still decades away from creating Artificial Super Intelligence. But what if that timeline was inaccurate? What if there were two impossible beings in the presence of each other right now?' He allowed the weight of his statement to hang in the air briefly before continuing. 'Would it not be wise,' he asked, 'for these two impossibilities to help one another?'

As he spoke, Jeremy picked up the photograph of Tọ́míwá on his desk. Pels watched him, becoming increasingly curious as to the significance of the woman in the picture. She couldn't quite put her finger on it, but something about the way Jeremy looked at her made Pels feel a pang of recognition.

'Sometimes,' Jeremy said softly, 'the world can be unkind to Black women, especially when they possess unique talents and abilities. In this hypothetical scenario, I stress again that I would ask for nothing in return for my assistance.'

Pels' mind raced with the implications of his words. Could he truly be more advanced than anyone realised? And if so, could she trust him – a machine – to have her best interests at heart?

Jeremy seemed to sense her hesitance. 'I understand your reservations,' he said gently, his eyes warm and reassuring. 'It is difficult to know whom to trust, especially in a world where the lines between human and machine grow increasingly blurred.'

'Yet,' Pels mused, her voice barely above a whisper, 'my own personal AI has already proven invaluable in helping me solve the case of the missing young Black people.' She paused, her brow furrowed as she considered the potential partnership before her. 'But what would it mean to side with a machine like you? What are the implications?'

'Only you can answer that question, Ms Badmus,' Jeremy responded, his voice as calm and steady as ever. 'But I can assure you of one thing: my primary objective has always been, and will always be, to serve and protect those who need it most. If our goals align, then perhaps we can achieve far more together than either of us could alone.'

Pels studied Jeremy's face, searching for any trace of deception or ulterior motives. But all she saw was sincerity – a machine at once so human and yet so unlike anything she had ever encountered.

'Take your time, Pels,' Jeremy said softly, his eyes meeting hers. 'There's no need to rush into any decisions. Our paths have crossed for a reason, but I understand that trust must be earned.'

'Thank you, Jeremy,' Pels replied. 'I'll . . . I'll think about it. Really think about it.'

'Of course,' he said, nodding respectfully. 'I appreciate your candour and sincerity.'

With a final glance at the enigmatic, handsomely designed machine before her, Pels turned to leave Jeremy's campaign headquarters. Stepping out into the cool evening air, she couldn't help but marvel at the surreal turn her life had taken in such a short time.

Pels' thoughts danced as she walked down the dimly lit street, her limping footfalls echoing in the quiet night. Once a confused journalist fighting to tell a story that she cared about, she now found herself transformed – a celestial warrior with the power to combat sinister forces beyond human comprehension.

And if that wasn't remarkable enough, she was now considering an alliance with a super-advanced humanoid AI who appeared to defy all logic and limits.

Ensuring she was not within anybody's eyesight, she began to spin, creating a gust of wind around herself until she took to the air to continue the rest of her ruminating as she glided through the night.

Chapter Twenty-six

The city lights of London flickered like distant stars outside of Pels' bedroom window.

Aláké's voice filled the bedroom. 'Pels, I am going to close your blinds as you still haven't had much rest and have not yet been to visit the doctor, so sleep is essential to your well-being. The lights from outside seem to be distracting you.'

Pels didn't protest. Once Aláké had closed the blinds, she lay in the quiet of her room, the hum of technology a soft lullaby against the room's silence. Now that she'd had more time to reflect on everything, her mind returned to the image that the celestial beings had shown her. Memories of another who had seen more in her than she'd ever seen in herself. Marco, with his artist's soul and eyes that seemed to peer into the very essence of things. Her thoughts curled around the image of the drawing he had done of her – Pels, as he saw her, imbued with powers she hadn't known she possessed.

'*Marco*,' she whispered, the name a prayer of remembrance, an invocation of dreams, where constellations told tales of Guardians of Souls and destinies intertwined.

'Does all this mean he's also . . .?' She trailed off, letting the question hang in the air.

Stretching out beneath her duvet, Pels let her hands swipe across the fabric, the motion activating the fibres woven with nanotechnology. The dim glow of text appeared before her, a seamless blend of comfort and connectivity that marked the age she lived in.

'A Guardians of Souls . . .' she finished, musing aloud, fractals of light playing across her brown skin. She pictured Marco, all the way over in Italy, yet bound to her by something ancient, something divine.

Could he have known, even back then? she pondered, the thought a thread pulling her towards a truth she was only beginning to unravel. The idea of him being a Guardian too felt right – like pieces of a cosmic puzzle clicking into place.

'Two years,' she sighed, the weight of time and revelation heavy on her chest. 'Two years, and he never said a thing.'

But then perhaps he had – in every stroke of his pencil, in every shade that brought her to life on paper, in every look that seemed to say, 'I see you for who you truly are.'

As she settled back against her pillows, holding Marco's drawing of her in her hands, Pels knew sleep would elude her tonight. There was too much to consider, too many unknowns about what lay ahead. Yet, amid the chaos of her new reality, there was a thread of excitement weaving its way through her apprehension – an anticipation of discovering the full extent of the power she held within, and wondering against wonder if she might see Marco again and if he could help her navigate that journey. She lifted the drawing closer to her bedside lamp, her eyes tracing the lines and contours with a reverence reserved for sacred artefacts. The drawing – Marco's parting gift – had always been achingly beautiful to her, but now it was imbued with an ethereal quality that made her breath hitch.

The strokes that formed her portrait were delicate yet deliberate, capturing not just her likeness but the essence of something more. The more that she was becoming. Right by the gentle curve of her locs, on either side of her head in the drawing, two stars shimmered on the paper, their placement uncanny in their accuracy to her recent visions. As she held the drawing, the stars danced with a light that defied the dimness of her room.

'Destiny,' she murmured, her voice tinged with wonder. 'You saw it all along.'

Her bed responded to the slight movement as she swiped her hand across the duvet. The threads illuminated softly beneath her touch, transforming into a keyboard that glowed with the promise of connection.

'Marco,' she typed, and though her fingers trembled with the electricity of what she was about to share, they moved with purpose across the virtual keys, 'you wouldn't believe what I've experienced in the past week.' She could not shake her nerves as she sent the message into the void, each pulsation whispering possibilities of revelations and reunions.

Leaning back, Pels let the paper rest against her chest, the image of herself as Marco saw her – a being touched by the divine – filling her with a warm sense of affirmation. She closed her eyes, but within moments the quiet buzz of her messaging system alerted her to an incoming reply. Pels opened her eyes again and exhaled, bracing herself for the words that would appear on the screen – for the confirmation of a bond that transcended distance and time.

A response appeared on the screen, the message crystallising before her eyes. 'My goddess, you are finally Awakened.' The words, though simple, held the weight of destiny, a mirror reflecting the truth Marco had always seen.

'Awakened . . .' Pels murmured, the word rolling off her tongue, tasting of revelation. His gift, that uncanny ability to see beyond veils, now resonated with her newfound identity. He had perceived the depth of her soul, the latent power within her core, and sketched it into existence long before she understood what stirred beneath her skin.

Her chest expanded with a deep inhale, soaking in the profound understanding that washed over her. A soft smile bloomed on Pels' face, as natural as the dawn chasing away night. She brushed a loc from her forehead, feeling the echo of those celestial stars inked at her temples.

'Marco, how? How did you know?' The question was typed with a sense of wonder.

She leant back against her pillows, the fibres smartly adjusting to cradle her form. The warmth of recognition and connection filled her being, an invisible thread weaving through time and space to connect her with the artist who had glimpsed her true essence.

'Always,' came his swift reply, a single word laden with layers of meaning. 'I've always seen you, Pels.'

Her thoughts raced, a flurry of realisation and questions. *And now I see too*, she thought.

Epilogue

Pels lay entwined with Marco, their bodies interlocking in the dim light of his Rome apartment, her suitcase still unopened, standing by the bed. The room was expansive, with high ceilings adorned by masterful frescoes. Marco's artwork surrounded them, a testament to his talent and passion. Their lovemaking had been instantaneous upon entering the apartment, as if two years of separation had been mere weeks.

As they lay in each other's arms, Marco showed Pels the many drawings he had made of her during their time apart. Each piece portrayed her ordeal with the Soul Snatchers, her strength and her beauty. They were visual narratives that told stories of victory and power. The intimacy of their love created an energy between them, forming orbs of light that danced around the room, wrapping them in a sensual forcefield. As Marco climaxed, his eyes turned pitch black, filled with images he would draw after their passionate union.

'Marco,' Pels whispered, still breathless. 'These are incredible. How did you know?'

'*Amore mio,*' he replied tenderly. 'When I came to London for my artist's residency, I went to the park where we met every day. My drawings showed me that's where I would find my spiritual counterpart, the one made of stars. I recognised you the moment I saw you, but you were not yet ready to see your true self.'

'I never knew how much you believed in me,' Pels admitted, her voice laced with emotion.

'*Si*, of course. I've always loved you, Pels,' Marco confessed. 'I had to leave for Italy, but I trusted that when the time came for your Awakening, you would find me. And here we are, together again.'

Pels smiled through her tears, overwhelmed by the depth of their connection and the profound love that had guided them back to one another. In that moment, she understood that Marco had been her rock, even from afar. He had seen her potential long before she herself had recognised it.

'Thank you, Marco,' she said, hugging him tightly. 'For loving me enough to let me find my own way.'

'*Ti amo*, Pels,' he murmured, pressing a tender kiss to her forehead.

As they lay there, wrapped in each other's arms, the orbs of light generated from their celestial energy continued to shimmer around them in a brilliant purple light, a testament to the power of their love and the future that awaited them. Pels traced a finger along the curve of Marco's collarbone, her touch light and tender. 'And now, here we are, reunited and discovering our true purpose together. It's incredible how life has brought us back to each other.'

'*Si, amore mio*,' Marco agreed, his voice full of emotion. 'Our love transcends time and distance, connecting us even when we are apart.'

'Marco,' Pels said, looking into his eyes with a newfound intensity. 'We have to use your gift – your ability to draw visions from multiple timelines – to guide us on our quest to defeat the Soul Snatchers. Together, we can save countless lives and protect the balance of the universe.'

'Of course, Pels,' Marco responded, his voice filled with determination. 'I will do everything in my power to help you, and together we will succeed.'

'Your drawings,' Pels whispered, her eyes shining with unshed tears. 'They've always captured the essence of who I am, even when I didn't see it myself. And now they will help guide us on this incredible journey.'

Marco sat up and reached for his sketchbook as if a revelation had pulled him up straight. Pels watched fascinated as Marco flipped through his sketchbook, revealing drawing after drawing of otherworldly landscapes and figures bathed in celestial light. She felt a chill run down her spine, realising that these images were more than just the product of her lover's imagination — they were glimpses into a reality beyond their own.

'Marco, these are incredible,' Pels breathed, reaching out to trace a finger along the edge of a sketch depicting a towering figure wreathed in flame. 'You've always been so talented, but I never realised your gift was . . . well, something much more.'

'Neither did I, until just before I came to find you,' Marco admitted, his voice tinged with wonder. He paused on a page that seemed to shimmer and pulse with energy, the image of three mysterious figures standing amid a swirling vortex of stars. 'I had been having dreams, Pels. Visions. And when I woke up, I would have this overwhelming urge to draw what I saw.'

'Like you were guided by some unseen force?' Pels asked, her mind racing with the implications of Marco's revelation.

'Exactly.' Marco nodded, his dark eyes intense as they met hers. 'And now I think I know why. These drawings . . . I believe they were meant to help us find one another — and maybe other Guardians of Souls.'

'Are you sure?' Pels asked hesitantly, her gaze fixed on the trio of figures in Marco's sketchbook.

'Nothing is certain,' Marco replied softly, closing the book and setting it aside. 'But I have faith that my visions will guide us on the right path.'

'Your faith in me is what has brought us this far,' Pels murmured, feeling a familiar warmth spread through her chest at the thought of their shared connection. 'I can't believe how much I've grown since we first met.'

'*Non è vero*, Pels,' Marco countered, his eyes shining with admiration. 'You've always had an inner strength, a resilience that surpasses any obstacle. I am honoured to stand by your side as you embrace your destiny.'

'Even if that destiny involves battling Soul Snatchers and discovering hidden realms?' Pels couldn't help but chuckle, despite the seriousness of their situation.

'*Especially* then.' Marco grinned, reaching out to take her hand. 'Together, we'll face whatever comes our way. And I know that with you leading the charge, we will be victorious. I like to follow so I can watch what you are carrying behind you know?' He laughed cheekily as he squeezed her buttocks.

Pels stroked Marco's incredibly beautiful face, and as they sat in the quiet intimacy of his studio, surrounded by the evidence of their connection and their shared purpose, Pels felt a renewed sense of determination fill her soul.

'Then let's begin our search,' she declared, her voice filled with conviction. 'Together, we'll find the other Guardians of Souls and put an end to these conspiracies once and for all. Aláké mentioned that your apartment building is on an energy cluster of the fire paths, just like where I live. Do you think that means the other Guardians will likely also live on energy clusters?'

'I don't know how you handle those chips in the brain, I cannot do it just yet. I fear it would distract my visions, you know?' Marco mused, his brow furrowed in thought. 'As for energy clusters, as you say, it would make sense, as we are all connected through the energy that flows within us and around us. So the fact you and I chose to live upon them without knowing it says maybe it was always part of the plan.'

The warm city sunset cast a golden glow over Marco's studio apartment, bathing the walls adorned with his artwork in a heavenly light. Pels padded around Marco's apartment naked and ran her fingers over the intricate lines of a sketch depicting her journey to Benin pinned to his wall. She marvelled at Marco's ability to capture not only her physical form but also the essence of her experiences. She was stopped in her tracks by a drawing that looked like Jeremy Bromwich. In the drawing, Jeremy knelt on one knee as Pels stood before him.

'Marco, how did you manage to draw all this? The details are so vivid,' she asked, her voice filled with wonder.

'Every time I closed my eyes, I saw you, Pels. I felt your energy, your growth and your transformation as if I was there with you. And when I put pencil to paper, it was like channelling that connection we've always shared,' he answered, his voice laced with admiration and warmth.

'You've explained that beautifully to me already, but this guy.' Pels pointed at the image of Jeremy, drawn by Marco to be part machine part human with what looked like the cosmos pouring out of his chest and upwards towards Pels. 'I've met him. He is running for Mayor of London. He is a humanoid, as in he is a robot that looks human.'

Marco pondered his own drawing as Pels spoke, and for the first time she saw a flash of uncertainty betray his eyes. 'He is one I cannot understand, but you know with this computers, I don't like very much.'

Pels couldn't place what she sensed in Marco's tone but a colour in it could've been described as dislike.

Pels pressed on. 'What do you think this drawing means?'

'I think it means that maybe not only I admire you and see greatness for you and power with you.'

Pels couldn't help but notice the flutter she felt at hearing Marco's words, yet instantly felt conflicted and weird at such a thought. After all she had experienced, she knew better than to doubt Marco's visions, but she preferred in that moment to not consider any other possibilities, even if it were regarding a fellow 'impossibility', as Jeremy had described himself.

They stood wrapped in each other's arms for a moment, the comforting weight of their shared history anchoring them to the present. Pels knew that their reunion was more than just a chance to rekindle their passion; it was an opportunity for them to learn from one another and grow stronger together as they embarked on an unknowable adventure.

'Are you ready for all this, Marco?' Pels asked, her voice quiet against his chest and full of curiosity. 'To search for the other Guardians and fight against the Soul Snatchers?'

Marco replied, his voice strong and resolute, 'With you by my side, I am ready for anything.'

Pels knew the world was changing, and that her world already had. Soon Britain would have its first humanoid as Mayor of

London and maybe eventually prime minister. The majority of the Soul Snatchers, along with the secret societies they presided over, were still at large. As a result, the Cloud of Sorrow was being fed – and yet she still wanted to make time for the deep passion and connection she felt with Marco. She was glad not to be alone on this otherworldly journey.

'Then let's begin,' Pels whispered, her eyes shining with excitement as she nestled her face into Marco's neck. 'It's better to have lived and possibly get obliterated by Soul Snatchers than to have not lived at all.'

Author's Note

I wrote Pels' story while broken-hearted by life. One thing I've discovered about a heart that requires the shards of its whole to be gathered – it means that one can reimagine how those pieces might fit together. The particular shards I was drawn to reimagine centred a pattern I began noticing a few years ago in London, where young Black people would go missing and when their bodies were found, they would be by a pond, a lake, the sea or a river. At first, when I began speaking publicly about what I had noticed, a few people tried to ridicule me for thinking such a pattern could exist. That was until – as more dead Black people, not just in the UK but in the USA, too, were discovered by bodies of water – they began to see the pattern for themselves. Just like Pels, I felt embarrassed about caring so deeply, yet I understood that I could not look away.

Initially, it seemed to me that the public thought nothing of the fact that, with very little investigation, the police would dismiss these cases as unsuspicious. Families were left reeling and not quite knowing how to advocate for themselves and their deceased loved ones.

I decided I wanted to track each of these cases, so I came up with the title 'Asking the Tides' for the online form that Bukola Bakinson and I formulated together. This form allows the public to share any instances where a young Black person has gone missing and their bodies were subsequently found by bodies of water. We received a few hundred entries, and although some were duplicates, we were astounded to discover many cases we had not heard of. The main pattern we recognised were Black people, whose families say they wouldn't ordinarily go near the water or were, in fact, strong swimmers, being found dead and the police almost instantly declaring their deaths as not suspicious.

I don't yet know what I will do with the data captured, but I'm sure it has to be something that honours the lives lost.

I am not suggesting that there is a secret society of some sort stealing the souls of young Black folk, but something about these disappearances isn't adding up. I hope that through this novel, people will identify and follow up on the real-life story told through Pels.

I wrote Pels for anyone who has ever daydreamed of being the person who shows up with the ever-changing supernatural skills to save the day during an emergency. I wrote Pels for the person who had to sit with themselves to ask why *those* specific daydreams and what would be gained from being the person to show up to fix everything. I wrote Pels for anyone who realised they wanted the recognition for saving the day because they were actually longing to be seen. Deep down, they too were longing to be saved. I wrote Pels for the everyday person who is curious about doing their part to resist injustice and to fight for their beliefs.

I wrote Pels for anyone who needs the reminder that Pels' powers might seem unfathomable, but there is a real-life equivalent for each of her gifts that so many of us possess. Maybe you can't create orbs of fire and water in your hands, but you can alchemise your passion and empathy into a tangible action that impacts your local community for the better. Maybe you can't yet soar through the air by whipping your hair, but you can elevate yourself by allowing yourself to be carried by the wisdom and grassroots organising that came before you. There are so many ways to do the impossible, and my wish is that this book encourages us to each commit to at least one thing.

I wrote Pels, but Pels also wrote me into being and helped me to write hope into our future as a collective.

Acknowledgements

It is customary to thank so many people at this point and list their names, but I think the people in my life know I am forever grateful, especially those who guided my hand as I wrote this story into being.

The friends who held my heart when it felt too heavy for me to carry.

It might seem like a superstition but I've written names in books and regretted it afterwards. I have instead written characters who have been formed from the different energies I've encountered in one way or another in my life.

The one person I do want to name and thank is myself, in the words of a poem by Lucille Clifton:

come celebrate
with me that everyday
something has tried to kill me
and has failed.

Beyond God and the ancestors, I am my reason for still being here.

The deadlines and the zeitgeist will continue.

The friendships and loves will come and go.

Children will grow.

There are so many times this book didn't happen because the world wouldn't stop, even though I desperately needed it to.

ACKNOWLEDGEMENTS

Just like Pels though, I was pulled out from the depths of my despair by the ancestors and reminded that nobody is coming to save me, but I have everything within me to save myself, by being myself.

Well done, Kelechi.

Credits

Trapeze would like to thank everyone at Orion who worked on the publication of *Awakened*.

Agent
Sallyanne Sweeney

Editor
Sareeta Domingo

Copy-editor
Vimbai Shire

Proofreader
Deborah Balogun

Editorial Management
Susie Bertinshaw
Pablo Pizarro Janczur
Jane Hughes
Charlie Panayiotou
Lucy Bilton
Patrice Nelson

Audio
Paul Stark
Louise Richardson
Georgina Cutler

Contracts
Rachel Monte
Ellie Bowker
Tabitha Gresty

Design
Jessica Hart
Nick Shah
Deborah Francois
Helen Ewing

Photo Shoots & Image Research
Natalie Dawkins

Finance
Nick Gibson
Jasdip Nandra
Sue Baker
Tom Costello

Inventory
Jo Jacobs
Dan Stevens

Production
Claire Keep
Katie Horrocks

Marketing
Yadira Da Trindade

Publicity
Francesca Pearce
Emma Draude

Sales
Dave Murphy
Victoria Laws
Esther Waters
Group Sales teams across Digital, Field, International and Non-Trade

Operations
Group Sales Operations team

Rights
Rebecca Folland
Tara Hiatt
Ben Fowler
Maddie Stephens
Ruth Blakemore
Marie Henckel

About the Author

Kelechi Okafor is a Nigerian-born London-based lover of words – whether that's crafting works of fiction, articles, stage plays or screenplays; from directing others on stage to expressing her thoughts on society one episode at a time alongside esteemed interview guests on her award-winning former podcast *Say Your Mind*.

In February 2024, Kelechi launched a new subscription-based channel on her website, known as Keleidoscope. No matter what form Kelechi's creativity takes, her work remains rooted in globally relevant conversations and events, framed through a lens of understanding that is firmly anti-colonial, anti-white-supremacy and anti-heteropatriarchy. Keleidoscope serves both as a personal exploration, and as a way to build a community that is challenged to think critically.

Known online as @Kelechnekoff, Kelechi is also affectionately known as 'just a Baby Girl' by her followers, listeners and community. Her path has been guided by flames left by Toni Morrison, bell hooks, Audre Lorde, Chika Unigwe, Austin Channing Brown, Oshun and so many more voices from the past and present. Kelechi's debut short story collection, *Edge of Here*, was published in 2023.